MISFIT PACK

CURSED WORLD BOOK 1

STEPHANIE FOXE

STEEL FOX MEDIA LLC

The Foxey Betas

A big thank you to my ART (Advanced Reader Team). Their advice cleaned up the book and helped me to be more confident launching a new series.

Amber Searcy, Janice Day, Jen Plumstead, Laura Rogers, Natasha O'Brien, Stephanie Johnson, Tami Cowles, Thomas Ryan

To my proofreader Ranting Raven. You provided me with a clean draft to send to the ART team, thanks for the hard work.

To Alida with Word Essential, thank you for your help with the outline. The story *did* need tension and danger, and that bit of advice helped me take the book to the next level.

Lastly, I want to thank Sarah Burton at An Avid Reader Editing. Writing in third person, especially with multiple points of view, was new to me. Your advice made a huge difference in the finished product. Thank you so much for sharing your knowledge!

what is stronger
than the human heart
which shatters over and over
and still lives
- rupi kaur

The Sun and Her Flowers

To the strong-willed, the resilient, and the misfits. To the families we choose. To the ones who love us unconditionally.

CONTENTS

Chapter 1	1
Chapter 2	11
Chapter 3	17
Chapter 4	21
Chapter 5	29
Chapter 6	45
Chapter 7	51
Chapter 8	55
Chapter 9	61
Chapter 10	67
Chapter 11	71
Chapter 12	75
Chapter 13	81
Chapter 14	85
Chapter 15	89
Chapter 16	95
Chapter 17	101
Chapter 18	105
Chapter 19	109
Chapter 20	117
Chapter 21	123
Chapter 22	131
Chapter 23	139
Chapter 24	143
Chapter 25	149
Chapter 26	153
Chapter 27	159
Chapter 28	163
Chapter 29	169
Chapter 30	173
Chapter 31	177
Chapter 32	183

Chapter 33 187

Chapter 34 193

Chapter 35 199

Chapter 36 203

Chapter 37 207

Chapter 38 211

Chapter 39 215

Chapter 40 219

Chapter 41 225

Chapter 42 229

Chapter 43 235

Chapter 44 241

Chapter 45 245

Chapter 46 247

Chapter 47 255

Chapter 48 261

Chapter 49 263

Chapter 50 267

Chapter 51 271

Chapter 52 279

Make a Difference 285

Follow me 287

More by Stephanie Foxe 289

CHAPTER 1

AMBER

"There are reports that yet another area has been discovered where magic simply does not work. Jan Compton is on the ground with the most recent update. Over to you, Jan," the reporter said, her face a serious picture of concern.

Amber tied off her braid and snorted. "Unable to use magic? What a tragedy," she muttered as she snatched up the remote and shut off the television.

Witches and Elves and all the rest of them were so dependent on magic. As a human, she had no problem getting by without it. She didn't hate it or anything, but the panic over three little spots where magic didn't work had gotten old real fast. They had probably always been there, and it just so happened that someone had finally stumbled across them.

She grabbed her leather jacket and pulled it on, running her fingers over the material that was soft from regular use. When the weather was cool enough, she wore it every day. And in Portland, it was almost always cool enough in the evenings to want a light jacket.

Amber patted her pockets. Keys. Wallet. Mace. With a nod,

she slipped out of her studio apartment and locked the door behind her.

Her neighbor, Mrs. Huntington, was just coming in. She narrowed her eyes at Amber, then hurried into her own apartment. That woman was nosy as hell and a pain in the ass. Last week she had reported Amber for "coming back too late" and "slamming her door." The woman had *As the Witch Burns* blaring out of her television twenty-four seven. There's no way she heard anyone doing anything.

Amber was tempted to kick her door as she walked past, but she shook off the pettiness. Tonight wasn't about crappy neighbors. It was supposed to be fun…whatever that was.

There was a free concert in the park with some new local bands, and a few older ones whose popularity had fizzled as their fan base had grown up. The Troll Bangs was going to be on stage around eleven that night. Since that was the only band she was interested in seeing, she had skipped the first few hours of the concert.

Her twin, Dylan, had loved The Troll Bangs to an almost embarrassing extent. He had dragged her to three of their concerts in high school one summer. Amber hadn't hated them, but Dylan had taken his fanboying to a whole new level. She pulled out her keys to unlock the ugly, old red truck she drove, shaking her head at the memory. Watching the band without him would be bittersweet.

The truck didn't have keyless entry or elf-spelled air conditioning like a new model would. She had rebuilt it with her dad as a graduation gift, one of the few things she ever did with him one-on-one. It still ran, but only thanks to her constant maintenance. Maybe in a year or two she'd be able to afford something new.

In order to avoid the traffic of downtown Portland, she took the long way to the concert. The Market had appeared there a couple of weeks ago, and for the next two weeks it was going to remain a pain in her ass to get to work.

Despite her annoyance with the traffic, she was glad The Market had popped up nearby. She hadn't been in years, not since it showed up in Texas a few months before she moved away. The Market was old and made up of so much magic that no one knew how it worked anymore. It disappeared and reappeared every new moon, always in a different location, and always completely unpredictable. The only things that were sure about The Market were that it liked populated areas and that it somehow always made room for itself no matter where it landed.

The merchants who traveled with it had to sign an unbreakable contract that lasted for at least one year. Openings were hard to come by, though; merchants who got a spot never seemed to want to leave.

The narrow streets that led to the concert were lined with vehicles. She parked her truck at the first open spot. There was no point in driving around for thirty minutes, hoping for something closer, when she didn't mind the walk.

A group of elves clambered out of a car that had parked a few spaces ahead of her. They wore flower crowns that shimmered with magic. Fluorescent butterflies fluttered around their heads every few seconds. They must have been to The Market before coming there.

A pixie flew out of the bushes and chased one of the butterflies around an elven girl's head, trying to eat the magical illusion. She shrieked and batted it away, knocking her crown askew. The pixie jabbered its displeasure, then landed on a car and watched them walk away sullenly. Pixies were odd, gray little creatures with wide mouths like a frog and wings like a bat. They'd eat almost anything, but preferred metal and bugs. Amber's dad had always been chasing them out of the garage when they got into the screws.

Her phone vibrated in her pocket, and the custom ringtone,

an engine revving, rumbled loudly. She hesitated, then pulled out her phone. Her oldest brother, Derek, would just call over and over until she picked up. He was persistent like that.

"Hey, big brother. Grandma Kelly didn't kick the bucket, did she?"

Derek chuckled. "You're so morbid. And no. She does have a date tomorrow, though."

She grimaced. "I didn't need to know that."

"Neither did I," Derek said. She could hear the shudder of horror through the phone. "Anyhow, that's not why I called."

"Well, I'm waiting," she said when he didn't immediately continue.

Derek sighed. "Dad got in a wreck this afternoon."

"What?" She stopped in her tracks. "And you're just now calling me?"

"He's fine. No one got hurt," Derek said quickly. "The only reason I called is because Mom—because I just thought you should know. It's a problem with his eyesight. We've been trying to get him to go to the doctor for months, but it took this to get him to make a damn appointment."

Amber sighed. She got her stubbornness from him. They all did. But he was in a category all by himself.

"Thanks for letting me know. It's probably going to take another wreck to get him to actually do what the doctors tell him, though," she grumbled, kicking at a rock as she started walking again.

"Tell me about it. He was still trying to argue he was fine in the ambulance."

"Hard-headed idiot," she said, shaking her head. She hesitated before she asked her next question. She wanted to know...and she didn't. "How is Mom doing?"

Derek stayed silent for a beat. "You have her number, Amber. Just call her."

"She has mine, too, and you don't see her calling me. She doesn't want to talk to me, Derek."

"You don't know that—"

"Yeah, actually I do." She was tired of this old argument. Derek refused to believe her. "I know that because she told me when she kicked me out of the house."

"That was almost six years ago," Derek argued.

"We'll talk again when she invites me back," she said, her tone making it clear she was done talking about it. She took a deep breath to ease the knot of guilt in her chest. "Thanks for calling, okay? I appreciate it."

"Yeah, of course," Derek replied, his words clipped. "I'll keep you updated."

"Thanks, bro. Talk to you again soon."

"Sure. Bye," Derek said, ending the call.

She lowered the phone from her ear and shoved it in her pocket. It was never good news when family called. She used to be close with all her brothers, but so long away from home and the relationships had just…fizzled.

The sound of familiar music drifted toward her. A sense of nostalgia warmed her, and she picked up the pace. The main parking lot was packed. She wove through the cars, passing a few people that were leaving the concert already.

A growl cut through the sounds of the concert and chatter.

She frowned. That was odd. Shifters didn't normally run around shifted in public. One of them was probably messing with a friend.

She scanned the area as she walked toward the pavilion. She didn't see any wolves or bears roaming around trying to startle people, but she couldn't quite shake the unsettled feeling the growl had given her.

She stepped out from between two cars. A loud scream rattled her eardrums, and a girl with pink hair crashed into her. A growl made all the hair on her arms stand on end. It was a lot closer this time.

Amber shoved the girl behind her and faced the source of the growling. Bright yellow eyes locked onto hers, and a huge black wolf bared its teeth. Saliva dripped from fangs as long as her hand. The wolf took a step forward, and Amber reached for the mace in her pocket.

She was too slow.

∾

GENEVIEVE

*T*he woman that Genevieve ran into had an arm stretched out in front of her. Like that could stop the werewolf. Genevieve took a step back, trying to decide if she could run fast enough to get away from the crazy-ass wolf. There was something in its eyes that made it seem wild. It looked insane.

Her heel slipped on a large chunk of gravel. She gasped and tipped backward, her hand flying out to grab the woman's leather jacket, but her fingers slipped.

The wolf lunged at them with a snarl, and the woman's body slammed into Genevieve, driving them both to the ground.

Sharp claws cut into her side, and gravel dug into her bare arms. She screamed, trying to cover her head with her arms, but she couldn't move with the weight of the woman and the wolf pressing down on her. The woman was fighting back and shouting, but her words were lost among the growls. Genevieve couldn't tell if it was aimed at her or the beast.

Teeth clamped around her thigh. She screamed and slapped at whatever had her. The dull pain grew sharp as her leg was wrenched from side to side with vicious shakes. Her hands hit fur and teeth. The pain kept her from taking a full breath.

The woman had her arm wrapped around the wolf's throat as though she were trying to strangle it, but she couldn't pull it away. Genevieve lifted her other foot and drove her heel into the wolf's face in a frantic stomping motion.

A rock bounced off the side of the wolf's head, and the creature turned toward whoever had thrown it with an enraged growl. In an instant, the weight was gone, and so was the woman. Genevieve forced herself upright, frantically looking around for somewhere safe to run to.

A teenager with a shocked look on his face stood right in the path of the charging creature. He threw another rock, hitting it right in the face, but it would take a whole hell of a lot more than that to stop two-hundred pounds of muscles and rage.

The wolf barreled into him, latching onto his shoulder, and he went down with a yell. The red-headed woman that had tried to help Genevieve jumped on the back of the wolf with a crazed shout. It turned, locked its jaws around her arm, and shook her like a rag doll. The woman slammed into the ground, still trying to fight back.

Before she had time to regret it, Genevieve jumped to her feet. Her leg almost gave out on her, and pain shot all the way up to her hip, but she gritted her teeth against it. Her foot hit the same stupid rock she had tripped over. If she could distract the creature for just a moment...maybe they could get away.

She picked the rock up and flung it at the wolf.

It hit the wolf's neck. The creature paused in its attack, dropping the woman's arm, and turned its freaky, yellow gaze on her. The red-headed woman grabbed something from her pocket with her uninjured arm, and a stream of liquid hit the wolf in the eyes.

It yelped and flinched back, shaking its head back and forth, pawing at its face. The woman jumped up and kicked it square in the chin. The wolf turned and ran, snaking through the cars until it disappeared.

Genevieve looked down. Her dress was ripped, and blood dripped from a deep bite on her thigh.

"Well, fuck."

~

TOMMY

*N*o. No no no.

Tommy lay in the dirt with his hand clutched to the ragged bite on his shoulder. He choked back tears of pain and struggled to sit up. He should have just run. He shouldn't have gotten involved.

A woman in a leather jacket stood over him with a can of mace in her hand, panting. Everyone else that had been in the parking lot had fled. He doubted anyone had even bothered to call the police.

"Shit, kid, are you okay?" she asked, extending her uninjured arm to help him up. Her other arm was smeared with blood that dripped down from the bite.

He took it and let her pull him to his feet. "I just—shit. I've been bit." The implications of what had happened sunk in.

"I've been bit," he repeated uselessly. This couldn't be happening. He took a step back and looked up to the sky. It was a full moon.

The woman followed his gaze. "Yeah, this is not great," she said.

The girl with the pink hair she had been protecting walked up behind her. Blood was streaming down her leg. "Did we all get bit?" she asked, her voice shaking.

"Unfortunately," the woman said, looking back at her. "What's your name?"

"Genevieve," she replied.

"I'm Amber," the woman in the leather jacket replied with a nod. Amber turned back to him. "What's your name, kid?"

"Don't call me that," Tommy snapped. His whole body shook, but not just with adrenaline. He could already feel some freaky magic shit starting inside of him. This couldn't be happening. His life was already hell. He couldn't deal with this on top of it.

He took a step away from the women. Amber watched him, worried. She held out a hand like she might try to grab him.

"Look, calm down, okay?" she said, stepping closer.

"I just got bit by a werewolf on the *full moon* and you want me to calm down?" he shouted at her, taking another step back. "Are you kidding me?"

She grit her teeth. "I get it. I'm freaking out too. Just don't—"

Tommy turned and fled. He had to get away. He couldn't stay around people and let someone trap him. He had to *run*.

CHAPTER 2

AMBER

"Shit," Amber said as the nameless kid took off at a run. He could hurt somebody. Hell, so could she.

"Are we going to change?" Genevieve asked.

She turned to face her. "Yeah. Assuming we don't die."

Her hands shook and her insides churned with guilt and fear as memories she desperately wanted to forget rose to the surface. Dylan screaming. His body twisted in pain as his bones broke, but couldn't reform. His eyes as the magic tortured him and stole his life.

A thump of something *other* beat inside Amber's chest. "We need to get to the woods," she said, her voice edged with a growl.

She grabbed Genevieve's arm and dragged her toward the dark line of trees. It looked like safety. She had to get Genevieve there, and she had to find the boy. The drive to do so overwhelmed the fear and guilt.

Genevieve struggled against her grip. "What are you doing?"

Amber stopped in her tracks. "Can't you feel it?" she asked, looking straight at Genevieve. "Do you want to be standing next to some stranger when the change happens?"

Genevieve shook her head and she dropped her arm.

"Just follow me. Please."

Genevieve nodded, biting her lip uncertainly, and Amber turned back to the tree line. She would follow or she wouldn't.

Footsteps crunched in the gravel behind her, and Amber breathed a sigh of relief.

"How long do we have?" Genevieve asked, jogging a little to catch up and walk beside her.

"I don't know exactly," she said. "It varies from person to person. Not long, though."

Genevieve was silent for a moment, then asked, "How bad is it going to hurt?"

"It won't hurt if your body can take the magic," she said, closing her eyes against the memory of the alternative.

"And if it doesn't?" Genevieve pressed.

Amber stopped and whipped around to face her. "Then you die a painful and bloody death."

Genevieve stared at her with wide eyes. "Shit."

"That about sums it up," she agreed, continuing into the forest. Something inside her relaxed as they passed under the cover of the trees.

"Do you know a shifter or something?" Genevieve asked.

"No," she said tersely. "I knew someone that didn't survive the change."

"Oh," Genevieve replied, her voice much quieter.

A strange warmth curled through her limbs. She stopped and looked up at the sky, her breaths coming a little faster. Something woke up inside of her, opening its eyes for the first time. They stared up through the leaves as her muscles twitched.

The shift rippled along Amber's skin. She watched as claws extended from her fingertips and fur prickled down her arm. Grief warred with the foreign elation inside of her. Why? Dylan had been the one they chose. Why did this kill him and not her? Why did she have to be the one to survive?

TOMMY

ommy fell to the ground as a panic attack stole his breath and blurred his vision. His muscles trembled, and he wheezed as claws pushed painlessly from his fingertips, digging into the soft dirt. It didn't hurt. He thought it would.

Barely able to process what was happening, he forced himself upright and pulled off his shirt. It felt like it was suffocating him. He tried to pull off his jeans, but they got hung up on his shoes.

He fell backward and blinked up at the sky. The moon peeked through the trees, and he couldn't tear his eyes away from its bright face. It was brighter than he had ever seen before. It sang to him, and something inside of him sang back.

With a sickening snap, his bones began to shift. Fur rolled over his skin and his feet fell out of his shoes as they narrowed into paws. His face lengthened into a snout, and his teeth morphed into sharp fangs. Light his human eyes couldn't process now illuminated the dark forest. He could see every branch and every leaf perfectly.

He lifted his hand toward the moon, but a paw attached to a long leg was what moved instead. With a yelp, he twisted and tried to stand. Four wobbly legs scrambled against the dirt underneath him. He stood, panting and shaking.

Tommy was afraid, but there was something else in his mind, and it was not scared at all. It was exultant. The wolf yipped in excitement, turning in a circle and sniffing at the clothes that lay in a pile where he had changed. He picked them up gently and stuck them by a tree, nosing leaves over the top of them. They were poorly hidden, but the wolf seemed pleased.

With an approving huff, the wolf turned and sprinted deeper

into the forest. Human feelings warred with the wolf's instincts, but Tommy's worry couldn't overcome the joy of the wolf. It was a full moon. It was a night for running and hunting, not thinking. The wolf lifted its head and howled as it ran.

The forest was silent for a moment, then an answering howl echoed through the trees. He slid to a halt. Another howl joined it.

Pack. Family. Home. He turned and ran toward the other wolves.

~

GENEVIEVE

Genevieve stared at the ruddy wolf across from her. She shifted on her paws, muscles tensed and ready to flee. The wolf watched her with yellow eyes that glinted in the bright moonlight, then took a step forward.

Genevieve hunched down. Something about this other wolf made her want to show her belly. She didn't like the feeling. It was unnatural. To her at least. The wolf inside of her was practically purring; it *wanted* to submit.

Amber made a rumbling noise in the back of her throat, then turned away. She looked back over her shoulder as though she was asking her to follow.

Genevieve took a careful step forward, and Amber took off at a run. A thrill ran through her and she raced after the larger wolf.

Her new body sang with emotions she didn't recognize. Curiosity at every scent. Delight at her speed. A fierce desire to win the race. Genevieve hated competition of any kind, but the new presence inside of her loved it. She dug in and pushed her strange new legs to go faster. Though she was smaller than the reddish wolf, she was gaining on her.

A howl cut through the night. Amber stopped short and Genevieve slid in the leaves, bouncing off the other wolf's flank. She shook her head to clear it and waited, tense, to make sure she hadn't pissed Amber off.

Amber was looking through the trees, ears standing straight up. She tilted her head back and howled in return. The sound did something to Genevieve. To the wolf inside of her. It coursed through her with a mixture of longing and a desire to prove herself.

She lifted her snout toward the moon and joined her howl with Amber's. After a moment, Amber stopped and waited for a response, but the forest was silent. She took off in the direction it had originally come from.

Genevieve raced after her, determined to beat her this time. She had to show the other wolf she was fast and strong. The creature inside of her knew she wasn't just some submissive puppy. Her muscles strained against their limits, and slowly, Genevieve gained on Amber. She willed her legs to go faster and she began to pass the larger wolf.

A bitter scent distracted her. The wolf inside of her growled in anger. Human. Intruders. This was her pack's territory now.

Trespasser.

She snarled in anger and veered away from Amber, racing toward the smell of unwashed human. Fury coursed through Genevieve's body. It wasn't her emotion, it was pouring out of the creature that now shared her mind. She couldn't think. Instinct took over, driving her forward. Protect. *Kill.*

Genevieve could see the human now. He was laying under a tree in an old sleeping bag. She lunged toward him, but teeth closed around her leg and jerked her to the ground. She yelped and turned on whatever stopped her, teeth snapping as she growled her displeasure.

The ruddy wolf growled right back and leaped toward her, wrapping her jaws around the back of Genevieve's neck. Amber's teeth didn't break the skin, but Genevieve knew they could. Her body went limp. She twisted, showing her vulnerable belly to her alpha.

Alpha. The word felt right to her and the wolf inside of her.

But Amber wasn't letting go. Her teeth tightened on Genevieve's neck, and a growl vibrated in her mouth. Genevieve twisted farther and whimpered. Her alpha was rejecting her.

A branch cracked behind them, and Amber whipped around, dragging Genevieve with her. A gray wolf stood a few feet away, watching them anxiously. He shifted from paw to paw, then lowered down to his belly.

He slunk forward, staying low to the ground, his eyes never leaving Amber. He slid up beside Genevieve and lay his snout over her neck. Tommy looked up into Amber's eyes and whined, the sound pleading.

Amber huffed around her mouthful of skin and fur. Something changed. Amber's teeth broke through her skin but it didn't hurt. A new magic flooded through Genevieve. Warm. Bright. Comforting.

Amber dropped her and gently wrapped her jaws around the back of Tommy's neck. Genevieve felt the moment Tommy accepted Amber as alpha.

For a brief moment, golden threads shimmered between them, connecting them all. Amber's eyes flared bright red. The golden threads disappeared, but the new bond did not. They were a pack.

CHAPTER 3

AMBER

*W*hat the hell had she done? Amber stared at her now-human hands. The pack bond was a steady presence at the back of her mind, along with the wolf. It was curious and intelligent.

Her hands shook. She was a werewolf. A shifter. Amber felt strange new instincts she didn't completely understand. She wanted to claim the forest around her, protect it and her pack.

Amber put her face in her hands. God help her, she had a pack.

"Amber?" Genevieve asked tentatively.

She curled her fingers into a fist and took a deep breath to calm herself down before looking over her shoulder at the other woman. "Yeah?"

"I don't suppose you remember where we left our clothes, do you?" Genevieve asked, standing with one arm crossed over her chest, and the other hand hiding her crotch. The pink hair that had perched on top of her head in matching buns last night was a mess of tangles around her face.

They had slept in a pile after running through the forest most of the night. Unfortunately, they had woken up this morning human and very nude.

"Vaguely." Amber shrugged. She looked at the boy and sighed. "You don't want me to call you kid, right?" she prompted.

The boy looked back at her, then covered his eyes and turned his head away again. "My name is Tommy," he said, a blush creeping up his neck.

"Alright, Tommy," Amber said with a nod. "Nice to meet you. Genevieve and me are going to go retrieve our clothes. Hopefully. Did you manage to get yours off before you changed?"

"Um, yeah, I think so," he said.

"Well, why don't you go get yours too, and we can meet back up in the parking lot?" Amber asked.

"Sounds great," Tommy said as he scrambled to his feet. He hurried into the trees without a backward glance.

Genevieve covered her mouth to stifle a laugh. "I thought he was going to die of embarrassment," she whispered.

Amber grinned. "He's probably never seen a boob before in real life."

Genevieve snorted, losing her battle to keep from laughing. "He was blushing so bad."

"Better that than gawking at us," Amber said, feeling fond of Tommy already.

"Agreed," Genevieve said with a smile.

Amber turned in a circle and sniffed the air. Then felt stupid for trying to sniff her way back to their clothes. The wolf was peering out of her eyes, and its instincts were getting mixed up with her own.

"This way, I think," Amber pointed in the opposite direction from where Tommy had headed.

Genevieve nodded and fell into step beside Amber. They walked silently. Genevieve stared at the ground, and Amber looked straight ahead. Being naked was awkward even though they were both girls. No one wants to go hiking in the nude. Especially with a stranger.

"Thanks for...you know," Genevieve said, making a biting motion with her hand. "The homeless guy."

Amber nodded. "No problem. I'm just glad neither of us were alone. I think it made it easier."

"You can feel the thing, right? The bond or whatever?" Genevieve asked.

"Yes." Amber rubbed her hand against her sternum. She could feel how far away Tommy was and had a vague sense of both of her new pack member's emotions. She thought she might be able to tell more if she focused on it, but it seemed intrusive. She certainly hoped they couldn't feel hers.

After a few more minutes, they found their clothes strewn in the small area where they had shifted the night before. Amber pulled on her underwear and jeans first, then picked up her jacket. The sleeve had a jagged hole where she had been bitten. She stared at it and tried to decide if she would be able to patch it or stitch it back up.

"That thing has seen better days," Genevieve said with a laugh.

"I'm going to fix it, "Amber snarled at her before she could stop her overreaction.

Genevieve lifted her hands in apology. "Sorry," she said. "I didn't realize it was important to you."

Her shoulders slumped and she turned away. "It was my brother's."

She wanted to tell Genevieve it was okay, but her emotions were all over the place. She didn't want to be a werewolf. Not after what had happened to her brother. Her family would never accept it, not that they wanted her around now anyhow.

Genevieve didn't ask any more questions after that. Amber pulled on her shirt and draped the ruined jacket over her arm.

They headed back towards the parking lot. She could feel the tension in Genevieve and had an urge to try to mend it. Her wolf was frustrated and irritated with her for hurting Genevieve. It was protective of its pack members. Amber was irritated with it for existing, much less having an opinion.

CHAPTER 4

AMBER

The first thing Amber heard was a snarl, then she felt Tommy's fear. She broke into a run, and Genevieve followed her.

Some big, bald guy had Tommy backed up against a car. His hands were fisted in the collar of Tommy's shirt. Fury ripped through Amber. Neither she, nor the wolf inside her, would stand for someone threatening her pack.

With a speed not her own, she sprinted toward them, hitting the other werewolf from the side. Tommy's shirt ripped as the guy's claws were torn out of the fabric.

"Don't touch him," Amber growled, shoving the other wolf back again. She made sure she was between him and Tommy.

The werewolf snarled, but didn't move toward her. The scent of other shifters drifted toward them. Amber looked up and saw three bulky men headed their way through the mostly empty parking lot.

The man in front wore a blazer over a plain shirt. He walked a few steps ahead of the other two, and Amber immediately identified him as the leader of this little group. Whether he was the alpha of the pack or just the highest-ranking werewolf present, he was definitely in charge.

Amber put herself between him and her pack.

He stopped next to the man that had been threatening Tommy and looked her up and down. "I guess we just discovered what that omega got up to last night," the man said. "Did you idiots kill anyone?"

"Touch my pack again and I might," Amber said. The wolf inside her wanted to charge this man and tear him down in front of the others. The desire to challenge him was almost overwhelming, but Amber resisted. No matter what instincts she had now, she wasn't going to be stupid. They were outnumbered, and challenging him would put the two wolves she was responsible for in danger.

The man gave a disbelieving snort. "I'm sorry, your what?"

Amber bit the inside of her cheek, uncertain. She had intended to keep the whole alpha thing under wraps before she had blurted out that Tommy was hers. She wasn't sure what it meant to be an alpha, or if she even wanted the responsibility.

"You heard me," Amber said. Now that it was out there, she'd be damned if she'd let this douchebag laugh at her for it.

The guy shook his head. "Bitten wolves can't be alphas," he said, looking at her like she was stupid. "You don't have what it takes."

Amber straightened. This guy was a bully and a bigot. Something in his tone told her he wasn't an alpha himself. She curled her lip in disdain. The wolf peered out of her eyes, and red tinted her vision as she felt alpha power rise in her. The wolf's instincts told her that the other werewolf had to back down, or challenge her.

An angry blush crept up his neck and he took a step back, lowering his eyes. "How the fuck did you do that?"

"How about you tell me why a werewolf that you seem to know was running around a concert last night attacking people?"

She took another step toward the other werewolves and was satisfied to see the wolves move back again to keep distance between them.

"That would be because Samuel didn't do his job," a deep voice said from Amber's left.

Amber turned, startled. She hadn't heard the guy coming at all.

The man walked toward them; he was different from the others. There was a weight to him that was unnatural. This was their alpha.

The werewolf that had been taunting her stared hard at the ground. If he had a tail, it would be tucked tightly between his legs. She was surprised Samuel didn't drop to his stomach in human form.

"We're close to finding Peter—" Samuel began.

The alpha looked at Samuel, who snapped his mouth shut. Turning back to Amber, he put on a more pleasant face. "My name is Donovan Lockhart. I'm sorry for the way my *gamma* embarrassed himself today, Samuel is correct that it is unusual to see a bitten wolf take up the mantle of alpha. It is, of course, also not legally permitted. However, I can help you with that if you would like to join my pack."

Amber racked her brain for where gammas fit into the pack. It had been a long time since she had studied the pack hierarchy. All she could remember was that they were below the beta, but somewhere above a regular pack member.

Even more confusing, this had taken a turn in a direction she had not seen coming. "Join your pack? There's normally an application process that takes a year," Amber said, skeptical of the offer. The way this alpha was speaking to her was all wrong; and her wolf hated him. "I don't want to be in a pack with a douchebag like Samuel either," she said, pointing at the idiot who was still staring at the ground.

Donovan bristled slightly, but kept his expression calm. "You would be of a higher rank than Samuel. I'm sure you could cope."

"Why would you want us?" she asked, gesturing to Tommy and Genevieve behind her. More than anything, she was suspicious of his offer. It was too good to be true. "You don't know anything about the three of us."

"Us? The offer is for you, and you alone. There is a limit to how many wolves I can add to my pack each year. Going over the quota would force me to pay some very hefty fines. Besides," he said, eyeing Tommy and Genevieve distastefully, "I'm not interested in weak wolves."

"Then what would happen to us without an alpha?" Tommy blurted out. He immediately shrunk back when all eyes turned to him.

"The other two would be put into the system," Donovan said, speaking directly to Amber and ignoring Tommy. "They would find a pack, eventually."

Tommy's panic ripped through Amber like an alarm. Her heart beat like a drum in her chest and the wolf in her head snarled angrily. She had to protect him, but what could she do? She wouldn't be able to stay his alpha if it was illegal. Hell, she didn't even *want* to be a werewolf. Being an alpha came with responsibilities she knew nothing about.

"This is your fault," Amber snapped, stepping forward. "Whether Samuel was supposed to be watching that omega or not, this is still on you, *Alpha*."

Donovan's expression grew dark, and his eyes flashed red. "You are in no position to chastise me, little girl," he said, his voice edging toward a growl. "I offered you a chance. Take it or leave it. If you want to go in the system with the others, who am I to stop you?"

"I am not leaving them behind," Amber insisted. "And how many more people did Peter attack last night? How can you be so callous?"

GENEVIEVE

*G*enevieve watched the exchange grow more heated by the moment. Amber was refusing his offer, which was insane. The *system*, as the other alpha put it, was terrible. Bitten werewolves went in for a year, but they never came out with a pack. After their stay was up, they'd be dumped back in a city and told not to make trouble. Most ended up homeless.

Tommy edged closer to her. He was trembling. Putting a comforting hand on his shoulder, she shut her eyes and took a deep breath. She didn't get involved with shit like this normally. There was a reason that she hadn't used her degree, despite having passed the bar exam almost two years ago. She didn't want anyone depending on her; she always ended up letting them down.

Amber yelled at the other alpha again and Genevieve stepped up to her side, putting a hand on her elbow.

"This whole conversation is stupid." Her voice came out quieter than she had intended. Clearing her throat self-consciously, she continued, "Amber can remain our alpha. She doesn't have to join anyone's pack," she said, louder this time.

Donovan turned his creepy red gaze on her. "You have no idea what you're talking about," he said, dismissing her.

"Actually, I do," she said, stepping past Amber. "A bitten werewolf may become an alpha the same way a born wolf can. The Alpha Trials are open to anyone that can find a sponsor."

Donovan curled his hand into a fist and glared at her, losing the final remnants of his friendly pretense. "And who would sponsor her?" he asked, spreading his arms wide as if he expected her to have someone volunteer right then. "No pack around here would do something that stupid."

"It doesn't have to be a werewolf," she said, jutting out her chin stubbornly. Her heart was racing in her chest and she thought she might vomit, but there was no backing down now. "It can be any paranormal that can fund the pledge. Amber has until the next full moon to prepare."

The alpha snorted. "She will never pass the Trials."

"Yes, I will," Amber said, stepping up next to Genevieve. Her expression was one hundred percent determined.

She had no idea how Amber could be so fearless, but it bolstered her own confidence. "She has the right to try. You can't stop her."

"We'll see about that," the other alpha said. He turned away, snapping his fingers at the other three werewolves. They followed him to an SUV on the other side of the parking lot and climbed inside.

Genevieve couldn't see them through the darkly tinted windows, but as they sped off, gravel flying from under their tires, she got the impression she was being flicked off. She slumped in relief. She never did that kind of thing. Part of her wanted to take it all back and just let whatever happened...happen.

"A sponsor?" Amber asked quietly, glancing at her.

"Yeah," she said, feeling awkward for volunteering Amber for something she barely understood. Finding a sponsor wasn't going to be easy either. "We'll have to find one soon. At least a week before the Trials."

"What exactly are the Alpha Trials? I've never heard of them," Amber said.

"Um, that's because they're kind of shrouded in secrecy." She twisted her fingers in the hem of her shirt, feeling like an idiot. She had volunteered Amber for something crazy and Amber had just backed her up without question, giving up her chance at getting a pack. "I actually don't know much about them, other than that they exist, and any wolf is eligible to take them with a sponsor."

Amber stared at her blank-faced for a moment before speaking again. "What is the sponsor for?"

"From what I remember, they have to cover any fines should the alpha or pack do something stupid," Genevieve explained, trying to remember the details she learned in her magical law classes. "The month between the time the werewolf claims alpha status and the Alpha Trials are a test of sorts. If they can't keep control of their pack during that first month, there's no point in them completing the Trials. The sponsor is also somehow responsible for whatever the pack does. I don't remember the details, though."

"I'm surprised it doesn't have to be a werewolf." Amber running her fingers through her tangled hair.

Genevieve shrugged. "A technical loophole. A werewolf sponsor is expected, but not legally required."

Amber looked back at Tommy, who, now that Genevieve thought about it, was being weirdly quiet. Tommy stood with his arms wrapped around himself, staring at his bare feet.

"Tommy," Amber said, "I'm not going to let them put you in the system."

He looked up and laughed once, a despairing sound. "You're going to *try*, but you don't know anything about being a were-wolf. None of us do."

"Hey," Amber said, marching up to him and grabbing his shoulders. "If I became an alpha, there has to be a reason. I'll jump through these assholes' legal hoops, and then we'll all be fine."

"Well, technically the only reason you became alpha is because you happen to be naturally more dominant than either of us. It doesn't really mean..." Genevieve trailed off at the irritation on Amber's face. Oh. She was trying to calm him down. "But you seem to be a natural, so I'm sure it'll all be fine," she said, plastering a fake smile on her face.

Tommy jerked out of Amber's grip and scuffed his bare toes on the pavement. "I couldn't find my shoes," he muttered.

"I can take you back home to get some more," Amber said gently.

Tommy scowled at her. "I don't have a home," he snapped.

Looking at him more closely, it was obvious. His clothes were dirty and threadbare like he wore them every day. His shaggy hair hung almost to his shoulders and was knotted pretty badly. He couldn't have been more than sixteen.

"Then you can come and stay with me," Amber responded without hesitation. "I'll get you shoes and some clothes too. And a haircut if you want one."

Genevieve thought about going back to her friend's apartment, but the wolf inside of her really didn't like that idea.

"Can...I come too?" Genevieve asked, feeling like an idiot.

"Of course," Amber said with a frown, rubbing her hand against her stomach. "The idea of being separated makes me feel all wrong inside."

Amber fished her keys out of her pocket. "Come on," she said, waving at them to follow. "Food, shoes, and then sleep. In that order."

Tommy looked at Genevieve, waiting for her to follow Amber before he did as well. They walked silently behind her, each of them lost in their own thoughts.

CHAPTER 5

AMBER

*E*arly morning sunlight streamed into the small apartment, muted by smoke drifting past the window. Amber hurriedly flipped the bacon out of the pan. Half of it landed on the floor, the rest on the counter. The bitter smell of burned food filled the kitchen.

"I think I have some ramen in the pantry," Amber said, eyeing the bacon with distaste. She could rebuild an engine, and stick an IV, but cooking just wasn't her thing. They had gone through everything easy to make in the refrigerator the evening before, which, to be fair, wasn't much for three people.

Tommy's stomach growled loudly behind her. She threw down the spatula and turned to face him and Genevieve, hands on her hips. "You know what, let's just go to The Market. They have food stalls. My treat."

"The Market?" Tommy asked tearing his eyes away from the ruined food and perking up. His face cracked into the first smile Amber had seen. "I've never been."

"If you've never been, then we have to go. It'd be stupid to miss it while it's in town," Amber said. The wolf inside her watched eagerly as excitement shivered through the pack bond. Providing for them felt right.

"Anything to get food," Genevieve agreed. "I've never been this hungry in my life."

"Is that a werewolf thing?" Tommy asked as he carefully pulled on his new shoes. He treated them like they were made of glass. Amber was surprised he was willing to walk in them.

Amber wiped sweat from her brow and nodded. "We haven't had a proper meal since we shifted. It takes a lot of energy and makes you super hungry. We need protein more than anything else right now."

Before she could sweep it all into the trashcan, Genevieve swiped the least burnt piece of bacon from the counter. Amber raised a brow.

"I'm really hungry," Genevieve said, shoving the blackened pork into her mouth. She grimaced, but swallowed resolutely.

"How do you know so much about werewolves?" Tommy asked, his voice was carefully neutral, casual almost, but Amber could feel his suspicion like an alarm bell through the pack bond.

She swept the last of the bacon that had fallen on the floor into the dustpan before answering. "I applied to join a pack when I turned eighteen," she explained carefully. The last thing she wanted was to get into the details of what had actually happened. "Didn't get accepted, but I spent close to a year learning about basic werewolf stuff. Unfortunately, nothing about being an alpha, since I didn't think it mattered."

"You'd have had a hard time finding any information on it anyhow," Genevieve piped up. "The werewolves don't like all their rules being public knowledge."

"Speaking of," Amber said, eager to turn the attention away from her history. "How do *you* know all this stuff that isn't supposed to be public knowledge?"

Genevieve shrugged and looked at the floor. "I studied magical law in college."

Amber narrowed her eyes. Genevieve didn't look old enough to have gotten through college, but she decided not to push it. She didn't want to talk about her past, either.

She grabbed her keys and reached for her jacket, then remembered it was shredded.

"Do you want me to try to patch it?" Tommy asked hesitantly.

Amber looked at him. "You could do that?" She knew she had said it too harshly as soon as the words came out of her mouth. Her desperation to have it fixed had come off like she was angry, which was far from the truth.

Tommy shrank back. "Yeah, it wouldn't be perfect or anything, but it would hold together."

Amber forced herself to relax and stop freaking Tommy out. "Anything you could do would be great. Thank you," she said softly. "We'll get whatever you need to patch it while we're out, if that's okay?"

Tommy straightened a little and nodded. "Yeah, that's fine."

"Let's go," Genevieve said, waiting by the door impatiently.

They headed downstairs and piled in the truck. Genevieve sat in the middle of the bench seat while Tommy scooted as close to the door as he could get.

"How old is this thing?" Genevieve asked, eyeing the dials on the dash skeptically.

"Old on the outside, but the engine was replaced six years ago," Amber said, patting the steering wheel. "She's built like a tank."

She cranked the engine and it sputtered ominously. Genevieve raised a brow and turned to say something, but Amber raised a hand in warning.

"Speak ill of her and you'll be walking to The Market," she threatened.

Genevieve snapped her mouth shut and turned back to the front. On the second try the engine turned over and rumbled to life. Amber threw it into gear and glared at her passengers one last time before pulling out of her parking spot.

∼

TOMMY

hey'd had to park almost a mile away from the Market. Tommy's stomach growled impatiently. A few food trucks were parked along the street, and the smell of cooking food made him ravenous. His new shoes pinched at the sides of his feet, but Tommy was relieved to have something without holes to wear. Something *clean*. He hadn't appreciated how nice it was to be able to wash his clothes regularly until he couldn't anymore.

"There it is," Amber said, pointing in the opposite direction he had been looking.

The Market was…magical. He stopped in his tracks as people surged around him and stared at the archway that led inside. It had planted itself between two one-hundred story office buildings in the center of downtown. The sight hurt his eyes; it shouldn't have fit, but there it was.

The archway itself shone like a beacon even in the bright sunlight. The word MARKET hovered overhead, spelled out in green fire that twisted in on itself, making each letter appear to writhe. The concrete sidewalk gave way to opalescent cobblestone that shimmered every time a step landed on it. With so many people walking on it, the path seemed to wobble.

"Come on," Genevieve said with a grin, grabbing his sleeve. "It gets better."

Even Amber was smiling softly. She was less intimidating when she wasn't scowling at everything that moved. Tommy followed Genevieve. She'd put her hair up in those buns again; they made her look like she was eighteen or nineteen, but he got the impression she was actually in her mid-twenties. She slipped sometimes, shifting from teenager to adult when she wasn't thinking about it.

Amber never slipped. She was wary, and angry. They were all upset about being turned, but he knew there was something worse going on with Amber. He just had no clue what it was. She'd practically bitten his head off this morning when he'd mentioned he could patch her jacket, but she hadn't been angry. She was just desperate, which was even weirder.

They passed under the archway, and all thoughts of why Amber was acting weird fled from Tommy's mind. Music and chatter pounded against his newly sensitive hearing, but he didn't care. This place was *magic*. Not just magical. Every part of it seemed to be created from pure magic itself.

The first stall was formed out of a flowering tree. The workers stood inside the trunk, leaning over a counter created by a low hanging branch that curved at a ninety-degree angle. Purple and pink blooms unfurled as people approached, releasing a sweet scent. A pretty elvish girl harvested a few flowers and wove them into a hairband that was then sold to the next customer.

Ahead of them a man dressed in colorful silk was juggling fire. Actual fire, not flaming batons or chainsaws, but large balls of fire. Every few rounds he tossed one high in the air and it exploded with a shower of blue sparks, then snapped back into shape before he caught it again.

A weird scraping noise overhead caused Tommy to look up, and where the sky should have been, there was water. Strange shapes flitted through the darkness. A face appeared, and Tommy startled. Webbed hands pressed against the surface of the water, and the slitted, green eyes of a mermaid stared down at him. Her tail swished behind her. It was a brilliant rainbow of colors, but the fins were lined with serrated spikes. She smiled, her teeth razor sharp, then disappeared from view.

"Don't worry, they can't get you," Amber whispered with a grin right next to his shoulder.

"I'm not—it's just cool. I've never met a mermaid before," Tommy stuttered out.

Amber grinned. "You can trade with them farther down, I think."

"I don't have anything to trade." Tommy shrugged.

"You might be surprised," Amber said cryptically before walking further down the path.

He moved to follow, but a familiar scent stopped him short. Curious, he turned back toward the entrance, but couldn't see anything. He wasn't sure what he was smelling, anyhow.

A bony hand wrapped around his arm, and claw-like fingers bit into his flesh. He spun around and found an old woman draped in shawls leaning out of her stall. Her arm was stretched taut between them. If he took another step forward, he'd drag her right out of the opening. Her foggy eyes looked past him, unfocused.

"Care to hear your fortune?" she asked, her voice strangely distant. It beckoned him...it...

"No thanks," Amber said.

Her voice cut through the haze in Tommy's mind. He shook his head to clear it and jerked out of the crone's grip.

"She's not even a real fortune teller," Amber muttered, dragging Tommy further down the road.

"Aww, you should have let her read him. I bet he would have freaked out when she predicted death and dismemberment," Genevieve said, licking a glittery ice cream cone.

"Death and dismemberment?" Tommy asked, looking back at the old woman. She flipped them off, then disappeared in a puff of green smoke.

"She's a witch," Amber explained. "They use spells to put on a convincing show, but they have no way of telling the future. And they always predict you're going to die for some reason."

"I mean, they're not wrong," Genevieve said with a shrug. "We all die eventually."

Amber rolled her eyes. "Come on, I smell barbecue."

They wove through the crowd following the smell of meat. The stalls got larger as they went. In the distance, a tower loomed. It was at least fifteen stories high and wrapped in glittering balconies. The golden exterior shone in the sun.

The smell of perfectly cooked steak pulled Tommy's attention away from the tower. The source of the scent was a massive barbecue pit, with *Devil May Grill* emblazoned on the side. It was manned by the biggest troll he had ever seen. The pyrotechnic pit erupted with fire, and the flames morphed into a horned demon that cackled loudly.

Genevieve took off for the outdoor restaurant at a jog, followed closely by him and Amber. They got in line, and Tommy's stomach growled loudly. Even though they were at least ten people back, the line moved quickly.

They reached the front of the line and the troll loomed over them, his bulging muscles glistening with a sheen of sweat from the heat of the grill. His tusks jutted sharply up toward his upper lip. The ivory bones were pierced three times on each side. He had no idea how they managed to pierce something like that.

Most trolls were nerds. Buff nerds, but they liked to read and collect knowledge way more than they liked to fight. This troll looked like he ate nerds for breakfast.

"What'll you have?" the troll asked in a deep, rough voice. His purple eyes scanned their faces expectantly.

"I'll take the Fresh Kill Special and whatever they want," Amber said, gesturing at him and Genevieve.

"Same, that looks amazing," Genevieve said, standing on her toes to look at the piles of meat to the troll's right.

"I'll take the Roadkill Roast," Tommy said, mouth watering as he eyed the hunk of meat.

"Aye, and you'll all take it rare, won't you?" the troll asked with a laugh.

Amber grinned, all teeth. "Aye," she mocked.

The troll winked and slapped their meat down on the grill. It sizzled, the juices igniting the flames beneath it. Everything cooked in fast motion, sped along by magic. The troll tossed their orders on plates the size of platters, then waved them down the counter to pay.

Amber handed over the money and they hurried to a table. Tommy picked his slab of beef up with his hands and took the biggest bite he could. Juices dripped down his chin as he closed his eyes in pleasure. There was nothing like a good, hot meal when you were starving. He hadn't had that in longer than he could remember.

They didn't speak as they ate; their mouths were too busy being stuffed with amazing barbecue. He could feel his body relaxing as the hunger was finally sated.

That scent drifted toward him again and he looked up sharply. The wolf, previously sated by the food, awoke in his mind. Shit, he knew who that scent was. It was the werewolf that slammed him up against the car the day before.

He hunched over his plate and took another bite, scanning the crowds carefully. The wind shifted and the scent grew stronger. A bald head glinted in the sunlight. Tommy looked away, keeping track of the werewolf in his peripheral vision. He was watching them.

"What's wrong?" Amber asked, plastic fork clenched in her hand like a weapon. Her eyes flicked between him and the people around them.

"One of the werewolves from yesterday is here." Anger boiled in his gut. He was used to being scared when he was threatened, not angry. He had an urge to confront the guy, which he shoved down. "He's looking at us right now. I thought I smelled him when we first came in, too."

"It's possible one of them is just at The Market today," Genevieve suggested.

Amber shook her head. "I don't like coincidences," she said, anger clear in her voice as she stared at the remnants of food on her plate. She wasn't going to let this go. He almost regretted saying something, but the idea that they were being followed filled him with dread.

Amber wiped her face off and threw down her napkin. "Let's keep walking around. If they're following us, I want to catch them in the act."

"And then do what, exactly?" Genevieve asked, raising an eyebrow. "Are you going to pick a fight in the middle of The Market? It'll chew you up and spit you out."

"I know that," Amber retorted. "That's why this is the perfect place. If they try to attack, The Market will kick their asses for us. It's our best chance."

Tommy hadn't been here before, but everyone knew The Market was a neutral zone. It would dump whoever threw the first punch outside and never let them back in. A few idiots still started fights, but they were over in the blink of an eye.

"We should probably split up if we want to catch them following us," he said. "If I go off on my own, they'll probably follow me since I'm alone. The two of you can get behind them, then we can corner them."

Amber cocked her head to the side and gave him an odd look. "That's...a great idea. Do you get stalked often?"

Tommy shrugged and looked down at his feet. "No, it just seems logical."

The real answer was that he had been obsessed with *Werespy* when he'd still had access to a TV. It was a ridiculous show, with loads of action and hot women. The main character had used this technique before. That didn't make the plan stupid, but he still wasn't going to admit any of that.

"Alright, let's walk around for a little bit together. When you smell him again, break off from the group. I'll give you a few minutes to lead them away, then we'll corner them under the tower," Amber said.

He nodded in agreement. Genevieve shook her head and tossed her napkin down on the table, but didn't object further.

This area of The Market was mostly food stalls and small cafes. It was three solid minutes of walking before they made it to more shopping. The closer they got to the center, the larger and more ornate everything became. Instead of stalls there were buildings, some a couple of stories high. The luminescent cobblestone gave way to large, inky black stones. The smells changed too; everything here was old.

Tommy paused in front of a building, turning just far enough to see that Baldy and some douchebag werewolf in a fedora were still following them. Amber glanced back, and he nodded at her. She looked hesitant for a moment, but kept walking.

Slowing his pace, he fell behind the others, then took a right down one of the narrow paths that led away from the main street. A vendor shoved a sample in his face that smelled like old fish. He dodged the foul snack and hurried through the crush of people. When he glanced back, the werewolves were gone. They hadn't followed him.

He froze for a moment, then decided it didn't matter. The plan would still work, just in reverse. He jogged ahead, then cut across another side street, and came back out onto the main street, catching glimpse of Baldy as he turned a corner. Genevieve's bright pink hair was easy to spot in the crowds. Amber was still with her. The werewolves were keeping a decent distance between them.

He slipped back onto the main street and stalked after them, barely seeing anything around him; he was completely focused on the threat to his pack. Slowly, the distance closed between him and the werewolves. The thrill of the chase pounded in his chest.

The wind shifted again, blowing past Tommy toward the wolves. Baldy stopped and turned his head to the right, his nose twitching. Tommy ducked down and pretended to look in the window to his left. They started walking again, but faster.

Unease filled him as he trailed behind them. They had probably made him. What if there were more of them? He glanced over his shoulder, but he couldn't make out a threat in the crowd. His muscles tensed with the urge to shift.

The wolf urgently drew his attention back to the men following his pack. Baldy had split off from Fedora and was disappearing down a side street. With only a split second to make a decision, he let the wolf's instincts guide him. He followed Baldy.

This street was much narrower, and less crowded. The scents were sharper and the shadows seemed longer, like this was a place you went if you needed to hide what you were doing. The wolf urged him forward; it wanted to corner its prey. It wanted a fight.

He had to step around a small group of witches whispering about a hard to find ingredient when he noticed that the other werewolf had followed him. And he was closing in.

Resisting the urge to panic, he tried to think logically. If they were following him, then he just needed to get to the tower. He picked up his pace, but realized he had lost sight of Baldy completely.

A large, burly man with a beard down to his chest bumped his shoulder and scowled down at him. "Watch where yer goin', *puppy*," he grumbled.

Curling his hands into fists, he hurried around the man, or whatever he was. He smelled like magic and blood, which wasn't exactly a friendly combination. He had to get out of here. The wolf wanted to stay, to fight, but that wasn't what he did.

With a quick glance behind him, he took off at a run, darting down an alley, then behind a stall and down another street. Every turn he took the tower grew closer. He just needed to get back to Amber. If the werewolves were following him, then they could confront them that way. He wasn't going to risk getting trapped alone with them.

After two more turns, he paused to catch his breath. He couldn't see either of them, and this place was eerie. The fake sky dipped down in pillars of greenish water, casting an unearthly glow over the whole area. This must have been the place Amber was talking about where you could trade with the mermaids.

He pressed his back against what he thought was a glass tank, but cold water seeped through his shirt and trickled down his back, and a hand pressed against his shoulder. Jerking away, he bit down on a yelp.

A mermaid hovered directly behind him. Her vibrant, luminescent hair waved around her head in the gentle currents. She wasn't beautiful exactly, at least not by human standards, but Tommy couldn't tear his eyes away. She swam closer and pushed her face out of the water. Her green skin was dull in the direct sunlight.

"I'll offer you a trade," she whispered. Her silky voice echoed around Tommy, and he wasn't exactly sure if she was speaking out loud or in his mind.

"I don't have anything to trade," he said, taking a step back.

She grinned. "I want what's in your pocket."

"My pocket? Look, I'm sorry, but I'm in a rush," he said, catching sight of Baldy headed toward the tower, he was scanning the crowds looking for either him or Amber. Tommy took another step back.

"I'll tell you what they've been whispering if you trade," the mermaid said, stretching her webbed fingers toward him eagerly.

Tommy stopped and looked back at her, surprised. How could she hear them? They were getting farther and farther away, but if she knew what they wanted, he had to try to find out.

He pulled out the contents of his pocket. A paperclip, a two inch bit of copper wire he had stripped from a power cord, and a dime. The mermaid wiggled her fingers, eager and demanding. He dropped the items in her hand, confused how she knew he had them, much less why she wanted any of it. She closed her fingers around it and held the payment tightly to her chest.

"Please, I have to hurry," Tommy begged. The wolf inside of him wanted to chase after the men following his pack.

"They whisper about the red one. She's the only one they care about," the mermaid said before she sunk back into the brackish water and vanished.

Tommy ran in the direction Baldy had been heading, but skidded to a halt when the werewolf stepped out from between two stalls, blocking his path.

"You seem like you're in a hurry," Baldy commented, stalking forward with even steps.

He didn't have to turn around to know that the other were-wolf was right behind him. "Not really, just stretching my legs."

Fedora huffed behind him. "I can smell your fear."

Tommy looked over his shoulder. "Stop sniffing me, weirdo," he said, narrowing his eyes. Splitting up with Amber had been a bad idea. He made a vow to never volunteer to be bait again. "Why are you following us, anyhow?" he asked, deciding he might as well be blunt.

Baldy chuckled. "Just making sure the dangerous new were-wolves don't cause any trouble. It's a public service, really."

He snorted. "I don't have to be a werewolf to know that's a lie."

"You're not kidding," Genevieve said, walking up from his left. He had been focusing on the other two wolves so hard that he hadn't noticed her approach at all.

Amber stalked up behind Baldy, her expression furious. She stopped right behind him and leaned in to whisper in his ear. Baldy stiffened and jerked around to the side so that she wasn't standing at his back.

Fedora stepped around Tommy and walked toward Amber, a growl rumbling in his chest. Genevieve jumped in front of their alpha and bared her teeth at him. Her eyes glinted yellow as her fingers curled into claws.

"Gen," Tommy said carefully, "it's not worth it."

"Don't worry, it's not like she could land a blow on me anyhow," Fedora taunted.

"Why did Donovan put you up to this?" Amber demanded, walking toward Genevieve, whom she was eyeing warily. Tommy was too. Genevieve was way too close to shifting and losing control.

"Genevieve," he whispered, trying to draw her attention away from their stalkers. His wolf was restless. It wanted to protect his packmate, it wanted to attack, but he knew that would be a huge mistake.

"Donovan is responsible for the safety of everyone in this city. If a werewolf were to embarrass us by losing control, it would reflect poorly on him," Baldy said in a condescending tone. "This is for your safety and the safety of everyone around you."

"Everyone knows bitten bitches can't be trusted," Fedora taunted, leaning in close to Genevieve.

Genevieve's low growl turned into a roar and she took a step toward the asshole werewolf.

"Genevieve, don't!" Amber shouted as she lunged toward her. Tommy managed to grab her arm, but it was too late. She swung at the werewolf with a growl. A moment before her hand connected with his face, she disappeared in a flash of light.

Tommy stumbled forward, his hand abruptly empty. Amber caught him and shoved him behind her.

Fedora burst into laughter. "The way she lost it was almost poetic," he taunted, a self-satisfied grin plastered on his face.

"When I find you outside of this place, I'm going to make you pay for that," Amber said. The power in her voice made Tommy want to drop to his belly.

Even Fedora flinched, though he jutted out his chin like it hadn't affected him.

"Let's go." She pushed Tommy forward and took a few steps backward before turning and walking beside him.

He looked over his shoulder at them. The other werewolves watched them walk away with a hungry expression on their faces. They wanted to chase after them.

"Is Gen okay?" he asked quietly.

"Getting cast out doesn't hurt anything but your pride. I don't think she completely lost control, but she's probably not happy," Amber replied, her brows pinched tightly together like she was listening for something really far away.

He was almost sure at this point that she could feel them somehow, but didn't want to ask about it. "It's weird," he said, a sense of foreboding settling in his chest. "They haven't reported us to the police, but they're still following us. Why does Donovan want you so badly?"

Amber looked at him, confused. "You think he wants me?"

"Even when I split off from the group, they kept following you at first," he said. "And you were the one he made the offer to. Even then, it just seemed like..." he let the thought trail off, uncomfortable with speaking so plainly.

"Seemed like what?" Amber asked, nudging him with her elbow.

"It seemed like he was lying. About letting you in the pack. He was almost desperate for it, which doesn't make any sense. I don't know, it's stupid."

"No, it's not." She shook her head firmly. "The way he showed up the next morning and wasn't surprised to see people had been bitten is odd. Werewolves, bitten or not, don't lose control every day. Donovan wanted us to be changed, and he knew we would be. They found us, but they acted like they had no idea where or who the omega that attacked was."

"There's easier ways to get new pack members," he said.

"Yeah, but I wonder how many ways there are for someone to become an alpha?" Amber asked, her face tight with anger as she looked over her shoulder to make sure the two werewolves weren't still sniffing around for them.

"One of the mermaids overheard them talking," he said, shoving his hands in his pockets. "She said they only cared about you."

"A mermaid? How'd you manage to get that out of one of them?" Amber asked, raising both eyebrows in surprise.

"I made a trade, just like you suggested," he said with a sly grin. It was nice to be the one with a secret for once.

Amber snorted in amusement and smiled at him. "You're resourceful, I'll give you that."

He was almost embarrassed by the way he swelled with pride, but it was the first time in a long time that he'd been given a compliment like that.

CHAPTER 6

AMBER

*A*mber went through the motions of brushing her teeth while staring into the mirror with a blank expression. Her eyes used to be hazel; now they leaned more toward brown with a hint of red. She leaned over and spit in the sink then rinsed her mouth with water.

Dylan would have loved it. He would have wanted to catalogue every change and post pictures on social media. Her fingers clenched tightly on the edge of the sink. Claws crept out of the tips. The porcelain cracked under her hands and her breath came in short pants. Angry that she was in this situation and having to relive these memories all over again pushed her eyes all the way to red.

A hesitant knock on the door startled Amber. She stepped away and the claws slipped back into her fingers. With a deep breath, her eyes returned to normal.

"Are you...okay?" Tommy asked hesitantly. "I thought I heard something break?"

Through the pack bond, she was flooded with concern, and a little fear. It was brave of Tommy to approach her when he thought she was freaking out. She had to get it together. They deserved better than an unstable alpha who might bite their heads off.

She plastered a smile on her face and opened the bathroom door. "I'm fine, just had a…" she sighed, then finished lamely. "I dropped something in the sink. Did you find the extra blankets?"

It was apparent from Tommy's expression that he knew she was lying, but he didn't call her on it; he just nodded and walked back to the living room. Amber followed. She didn't want to be by herself right now. All that did was give her time to think about things she didn't want to think about.

Tommy seemed to want to intrude in her apartment as little as possible, but Genevieve did not have that problem. She was sprawled on the couch with a bag of chips and a beer from the fridge.

"Why is your reception so crappy?" Genevieve asked as she flipped to another grainy channel on the television. She had been grumpy and embarrassed the entire drive back to the apartment, but once she had settled on the couch with more food, she had calmed down. Any attempts to talk about what had happened had been met with stubborn silence, so Amber had given up for now and decided they'd had enough arguments for one day.

"I don't pay for the enchanted signal," Amber shrugged. "I don't really have time to watch TV."

Genevieve looked at her like she was an alien, then flinched away from the window. "There's someone—"

A knock at the door interrupted her warning.

Amber waved Tommy behind her and approached the door as quietly as she could. She was nervous, and the wolf prowled inside of her, ready to face any threat to her territory. The peephole showed Donovan standing in front of the door, a pleasant expression on his face.

Donovan, she mouthed to the other two, motioning for them to stay back. She unlocked the door, but left the chain, and cracked the door open.

Donovan raised a brow. "Amber," he greeted with a nod. "I'd like to talk."

"How do you know where I live?" she asked.

Something flickered across Donovan's face. "I simply asked arou—"

"So you didn't have two of your pack members following us all day?" She was fed up with the bullshitting.

Donovan took a deep breath like he was trying to remain patient. "May I come in? I wanted this to be a friendly conversation."

She yanked the chain out of the latch and opened the door wide. It wouldn't have stopped him if he'd really wanted to get in anyhow; keeping it closed was just petty.

He walked in, eyeing the other two before taking a seat at the small table. Tommy crossed his arms and stood in the middle of the living room while Genevieve stayed on the couch and shoved a chip into her mouth. Her chewing was the only sound for a moment before he cleared his throat and turned his attention to Amber.

"I have been thinking over the offer I gave you yesterday morning, and have decided it was unfair to not extend the invitation to all three of you," he said, looking around the room at the pack. "Your new instincts won't allow you to split your pack up like that, and honestly, if you had accepted, it wouldn't have reflected well on either of us."

Amber crossed her arms and looked at him closely. This reeked of desperation. "If we were to even consider this offer, I'm going to need some honesty first. How did the wolf that attacked us lose control? What happened to him?"

"Loss of control is an issue for bitten wolves," Donovan said, leaning back in his chair in a display of nonchalance. He traced his thumb along a groove in the table. "And he has been punished appropriately for his actions, but the nature of that punishment isn't something I can share with you."

"Why not?" Genevieve asked, licking chip dust from her fingers.

Donovan's jaw clenched. "Despite your education, there are still some things you don't know about werewolf laws. Things you will not know until you are part of a *proper* pack."

"It's amazing to me that even while you're here practically begging us to join your pack, you still talk down to us, like we're less than you because we've been bitten," Amber snapped.

Donovan bristled immediately and rose to his feet. He seemed to grow in size as his eyes bled red. "I am offering you something no other pack would ever consider, but if you are going to throw my generosity back in my face with insults, then you can consider my offer withdrawn," he bit out.

Genevieve dropped the bag of chips and stood, advancing on Donovan. "You can't call it generosity when you told your wolf to turn us."

"Careful what you accuse me of, little girl," Donovan growled.

Amber dropped her arms, claws pricking at her fingertips. "Get out of my apartment, and don't come back."

Tommy and Genevieve stepped closer, and she was relieved to feel their determination through the pack bond. Donovan didn't intimidate them.

The last of the facade fell away and he snarled at them. "I will make you regret this," he threatened before turning and yanking the door open. He slammed it shut behind him, and Mrs. Huntington banged on the wall they shared, shouting demands for quiet.

Amber walked over to the wall and banged right back. "Kiss my ass, Mrs. Huntington."

The woman huffed and shuffled away. Amber let her head drop against the sheetrock. She was drained, and while she knew turning Donovan away had been the only option, that didn't mean she was confident everything would be okay.

"He needs you for some reason," Tommy said, echoing his comments at The Market.

"It's because she's an alpha," Genevieve said, crossing her arms. "I'm just not sure how that helps him."

"We keep coming up with more questions and no answers," Amber said, laughing humorlessly. She ran a hand down her face and squared her shoulders. "We'll figure it out tomorrow. We have a little time."

CHAPTER 7

AMBER

*T*he smells of the hospital were almost overwhelming. Amber tried breathing through her mouth, then grimaced. That made it worse. She had gotten used to the smell of antiseptic when she first started working as a nurse, but now, she could easily smell the rot of infection and the feces from someone a nurse hadn't gotten to help yet.

Pressing her hand over her mouth and nose, she grabbed a file to distract herself. She'd get used to this, too. Eventually.

Burning through her time off wasn't an option, especially with the money she had spent getting Tommy a new wardrobe. Since he needed a place to stay, she was already thinking about seeing if she could upgrade to a two bedroom apartment without breaking her lease. She'd be able to afford it; she just wouldn't be able to put money in savings like she had intended.

It had been cramped with all three of them in the studio apartment, but she was glad they both agreed to stay with her for now. Having to come to work today made her uneasy. The wolf inside her was practically pacing, constantly tugging at the pack bond to make sure it was still there.

"Amber, can I speak with you?" her boss Cory asked.

They got along fairly well, though Cory did have a reputation for playing favorites. But now, the elf's voice was off. The tips of her pointed ears were pink, and she was staring at the floor intently.

"Sure," Amber said, setting the patient's chart down on the nurse's station. An ominous feeling crept up her spine. She thought of every patient she had worked with for the past month. She hadn't screwed anything up, at least nothing too bad. Everyone made mistakes. If she had really messed up, surely she would remember what she'd done.

Cory led her away from the ICU and into a little office. A man from HR, the one that none of the nurses liked, was waiting for them.

"What's going on?" Amber demanded, stopping just inside the doorway.

Cory had a hand on the door, but couldn't shut it without hitting her.

"Please stay calm, ma'am," the HR representative said, lifting his hands and moving them in an overly deliberate manner. "Neither of us will attempt to harm you. You are safe here. You are not trapped in this room."

Amber looked at him like he was crazy, then at her boss. "Cory, is there something wrong with him?" she asked.

Cory shifted on her feet. "Look, it was reported this morning that you are an unregistered, bitten werewolf. It's against hospital policy. No one would insure us if we let someone who had been a werewolf for less than a year work here. I'm sorry."

The HR representative pushed some paperwork toward Amber. "This is your final write up for nondisclosure of a condition that makes you ineligible to work here. Please sign it, and we can give you your final paycheck," the HR representative said, tapping an envelope next to the paperwork.

A series of thoughts tore through her mind. Who reported it?

It had to have been Donovan. He had found out where she lived, and apparently where she worked.

She bit her tongue to keep from shouting at the two people tensely watching her. They expected her to attack them. That was the stereotype after all. Bitten werewolves were out of control when they were new, while born wolves were zen masters of control. It was all bullshit.

Still, the rage she felt was amplified by the rage of the wolf inside her. She wanted to find the other alpha and rip him apart.

Forcing her arm to move, she grabbed the pen and scratched her signature onto the paper.

"This isn't right," she said, looking up into the eyes of the HR representative. "And you know it."

"Legally, the hospital is obligated to—"

She grabbed her final paycheck and walked away. Her claws dug into her palm as the howling in her head drowned out everything else.

CHAPTER 8

AMBER

*A*mber sat in her truck staring at the contact list on her phone. She could call her dad; he would give her whatever she needed. Tightening her grip on the phone she dropped her hands in her lap. No. She refused to slink back home a failure. She had lost her nursing job, but she could do something else. Fix cars maybe, or work as a waitress.

She flung her phone into the passenger seat and started her truck. It grumbled and clanked, then turned on. Genevieve and Tommy weren't expecting her back at the apartment until tonight. She was supposed to be working a twelve hour shift. That gave her almost eleven hours to try to find something else. Anything.

With her tires screeching against the pavement, she sped out of the parking lot, leaving the hospital in the rearview mirror. She cranked up the radio and tried to drown out the whirlwind of negative thoughts racing through her mind.

The wolf was restless, and angry. It was ready to fight, but there was no one to fight. She couldn't growl at the insurance company or at a policy that wasn't even written by the asshole who fired her.

She gripped the steering wheel tightly. Donovan was responsible for all of this. For the attack and for taking away the job she had studied four years to get.

The light turned red just before she was able to get through. She slammed on the brakes and skidded to a stop halfway onto the crosswalk. A guy walked past and smacked the hood of her truck then gestured rudely.

She snarled and had the door halfway open, intending to beat his ass, before she realized what she was doing. Yanking the door shut, she counted down from ten with deep breaths. This wasn't what she wanted, at all, but she wasn't going to let it ruin her life. Somehow, she was going to make it through the Trials and become an alpha. She was going to prove everyone wrong.

~

*A*mber parked in front of a small cafe with a woodsy theme and a "Help Wanted" sign in the window. The restaurant was built into a massive tree that was obviously grown by elven magic. No tree grew that wide naturally.

The outside seating was covered by a canopy of heavy, flowery branches. As she walked up the pathway cool air skated across her skin. They had likely charmed the area to be a perfect seventy degrees year-round.

Pixies were fighting with birds over dropped food, trying to grab little morsels and hide under the bushes that fenced in the property. She ducked under one that flew straight across the path in front of her.

The door opened ahead of her as a couple walked out of the cafe. The scent of coffee and fried food drifted toward her, making her stomach growl. She hadn't even thought about lunch after she'd been fired, but her new appetite was more than happy to remind her.

She stepped inside and looked for the hostess, but the post was empty. The place was nice but not too fancy. Elves tended to go for the *be one with nature* vibe. She'd always liked it, and their food was great. Nobody could grow a vegetable quite as well as an elf.

She was startled by a loud squeal and then a shout. "No, you can't have him!"

The angry shout brought the wolf to the surface as Amber whipped around to see what was going on. A witch with curly, blonde hair floating around her head like she just stuck her finger in a light socket had grabbed a pixie around the middle. Another witch with black hair had the small creature by the wings.

"It's a stupid, little pest," the dark-haired witch snapped. "I can take it if I want. You don't own it!"

"I won't let you—"

The other witch yanked back and the pixie's wings were ripped from its body. It let out a piercing squeal of pain.

"You bitch!" the blonde witch yelled, lifting her hand to cast a spell.

The other witch's friend moved faster and Blondie was thrown back, the pixie flopping out of her hands onto the floor. The witch that ripped off its wings jumped forward, foot poised to crush the pixie.

Amber stepped in her path and shoved her from the side just in time for her foot to come down on the tile floor instead.

"What the hell is wrong with you?" she shouted, forcing herself between the witch and the pixie. "Leave it alone." Nobody really liked pixies, but that was just cruel. There was no reason to torture the damn thing.

The witch lifted her hand, turning her hateful gaze on Amber. Amber grabbed it, squeezing the witch's wrist tightly.

"Try it and see what happens," she growled, her eyes flashing red. She had just ruined her chance to get a job here, but she'd be damned if she just stood by and watch those witches pick on a defenseless little animal. She couldn't fix everything that had gone wrong today, but she could stop this.

The witch smirked and a flash of green hit Amber in the face. She doubled over and vomited, lumpy slime pouring from her mouth. She shoved the witch with a growl, then vomited again.

Light flashed through the cafe, blinding her and everyone else. A hand wrapped around her arm and someone dragged her toward the back.

"We need to run," the blonde girl whispered.

At least she hoped it was her. She smelled right. The cool air of the patio swept over them as she let the woman drag her outside. She stopped and vomited, the putrid slime making her gag all over again.

"Come on," the blonde said impatiently. "Vomit and run."

Amber tried to glare at her, but she still couldn't see right. Spots danced in her vision, and everything was blurry.

"What did you do to me?" she asked the woman leading her farther away from the restaurant.

"Just a blinding light spell," the witch said. "Sorry, I couldn't warn you without tipping them off, and we really needed to get out of there."

They slipped behind a building and her vision finally cleared. The witch clutched the bleeding pixie to her chest, but it looked like it was dead.

"I'm Ceri, by the way," the witch said, smiling at her. "Thanks for trying to help back there. Most people don't give a crap about pixies."

"It's messed up to hurt them like that," she said, shaking her head. "And I'm Amber."

Another wave of nausea hit and she doubled over, vomit splattering on her shoes.

"Witch on a stick, she really hit you hard with that spell," Ceri exclaimed. "If you come back to my house I can make you something to counteract that. It'll last for hours if I don't."

Amber burped loudly, and unpleasantly. "Please. This is fucking awful."

Ceri peered around the corner, to make sure it was safe. "Come on, my car is parked down the street."

CHAPTER 9

CERI

*C*eri ran two tires up on the curb in her haste to get the car parked. Amber flung her door open and hit her knees in the grass, vomiting for a third time on their drive here.

The witch grimaced and jumped out of the car. The sooner she got a remedy down this girl's throat the better. The pixie, still in her hand, was worrying as well.

"Just come inside when you can," she shouted back over her shoulder while unlocking the door. She left it open behind her and jogged toward the family spell room. Even though she wasn't part of her family's coven, she still used the spell room when she needed to. Well…she did when her mother wasn't pissed at her.

Carefully, she laid the pixie on a small towel on the table. Its gray body was limp. There was a little stub of a wing left on one side, but on the other side the wing was broken off at the joint and a strip of skin had been torn away.

She grabbed a wound-mending elixir off the shelf and doused the pixie's back. It was a lot of magic for such a little thing, but she had to try. It would take at least twenty minutes for it to work, so she turned her focus to the other urgent issue.

Her mind whirled through the possibilities for a remedy. The slime-vomiting hex was a childish spell mostly used by bullies in school. It was obvious the witch that used it on Amber intended it as an insult, *you're as threatening as a child.* She felt a little guilty for thinking it, but the way Amber had tried to help had been a little...stupid. You didn't just grab a witch. Every werewolf knew that; especially an alpha.

She grabbed a lighter and a half-burned bundle of sage, then stuck it in its holder. Smoke curled from the tightly bound herbs as soon as the flames of the lighter touched it. She blew lightly across the top to encourage it, and the sharp, cool scent cleared the stench of the slime from her nose.

"Ceri?" Amber said from the front of the house.

"Back here!" she shouted back. "Just follow your nose!"

Amber muttered something but appeared in the doorway a few moments later. She closed her eyes in relief as she stepped into the room. "That smells so much better."

Ceri grinned. "Just vomit in the trashcan if you get nauseous again," she said, pointing at it in the corner.

Amber nodded, but she was distracted, looking around the room.

"Never been in a spell room before?" she asked as she picked the ingredients she needed off the shelves.

"No," Amber said. "I've known a few witches, but they never let anyone but coven inside."

"My mother probably wouldn't be thrilled if she knew," she admitted. That was closer to a lie than an understatement. Her mother would be furious, but she didn't have to know. "I've always thought that was kind of silly if your clan wasn't in the running for a position with the conclave or something. No one is trying to steal our family magic."

"Y'all have one of those family covens?" Amber asked.

Ceri looked up with a laugh. "Y'aaall," she said, exaggerating the drawl. "Are you from Texas or something? I didn't think anyone actually said that."

Amber gave her an unimpressed look. "Yes, I'm from Texas."

"Sorry," she held up her hands in apology, "I wasn't trying to mock you. Anyhow, my family does have a coven, but I'm not part of it." her smile faltered, eyes straying to the pixie. She'd have to get the pixie out of here, or her mother would chop it up for parts.

"Sorry," Amber said quietly. "Didn't mean to bring up..." She let her thought trail off and waved her hand at Ceri's expression.

"Perfectly normal assumption," she said, forcing a smile back on her face. Flipping open her old spellbook, she scanned through the list of remedies, then flipped to the recipe. She froze when she saw the ingredients, pressing her lips into a thin, white line. So, the insult wasn't directed toward Amber after all. It was meant for her. The remedy required pixie wings.

She slammed the spellbook shut. She'd just have to come up with something else. Really, what the magic wanted was a sacrifice. Ritual, ingredients, and the spoken phrase were all part of the trade. She could come up with her own remedy.

The reason most witches wouldn't let anyone into their spell room was to make sure their coven's spells weren't stolen. There were standardized spells, but every coven, and every witch, had their own. Ceri had always enjoyed inventing new spells, but as she grew older, it had changed from passion to necessity.

She took a deep breath to steady herself and immediately regretted it as Amber vomited into the trashcan.

"I'm going to kill that witch," Amber croaked from the corner of the room.

"I'll help," she said, forcing herself to reopen the spellbook. If she wanted to modify the remedy, she needed to understand it first.

Poring over the smudgy text, she studied each step. It had three parts. The potion, the purge, and the spell. The potion pulled the spell from the body into itself, the purge expelled them both, and the spell restored. She straightened as a thought raced through her mind. The potion was there to make the purge easier, but it wasn't absolutely necessary if she knew another way to pull the spell from the body. Luckily for Amber, she did.

"Alright," she announced, turning to face her unhappy patient. "I know how to fix this, but it's going to be a little uncomfortable."

"I don't care as long as it stops," Amber groaned, and she immediately vomited again.

Ceri cringed. It was getting worse. She grabbed and lit another bundle of sage, then dragged Amber and the trashcan to the center of the room.

"The remedy involves more vomiting," she explained. "But then it'll all be over."

Amber looked unhappy about the news, but nodded resolutely and braced her hands on the rim of the trashcan.

All spells, especially hexes, were limited and temporary. Even this one would wear off on its own eventually. Ceri's grandmother had always told her that if she was lousy enough to get hit with a hex, she should at least know how to get back on her feet quickly. Grandma Gallagher had then proceeded to hex her. She had then made Ceri learn the counter-hex she had invented while she was under the painful effects of the nasty spell.

She could still hear Grandma Gallagher's gruff voice in her head. *"If yer stupid enough ta get hexed, then ya ought ta pay the price, lassie."* Ceri grabbed the boning knife from the counter and jabbed her finger, then grabbed Amber's and repeated the process.

"What the hell—"

Ceri slapped her hand against Amber's chest and chanted the counter-hex under her breath. Amber's face turned green and she bent over the trashcan as the slime and the magic were purged from her body violently.

She grabbed the sage and continued with the rest of the remedy. Hands together, clockwise twice, the Chant of the Sun for restoration, then finally, the cast. She spread her hands an inch apart, then turned her palms outward. The magic flowed from her hands into Amber in a bright stream of light.

Amber straightened slowly. The color returned to her cheeks as the magic poured into her body. Her eyes bled red and her hands shook at her side.

Ceri completed the spell and opened her mouth to ask Amber how she felt, but she was still shaking. "Uhh, Amber, are you okay?" she asked, trying not to freak out.

Amber shut her eyes and clenched her hands tightly. "The magic made me feel weird and…like I needed to shift."

"Of course, it's restorative. Pretty much any helpful spell will do that to you, especially as an alpha. How do you not know that?" she asked, trying not to sound too critical. She wanted to like Amber, but first she had grabbed a witch, and now this?

"Because I was bit two days ago," Amber said, clenching her jaw tightly.

Ceri took a step back. "Two days ago? There's no way you can be an alpha!"

"So I've heard," Amber snapped. "But here I am. I didn't ask to get bitten. Some crazed werewolf just ran through a parking lot and attacked me and my…pack."

"You were changed against your will?" she asked, horrified.

Amber nodded. "Three of us were, and since I was the most dominant of the three, I ended up the alpha." She crossed her arms, practically daring Ceri to challenge her on it again.

"That explains a lot," she said instead.

"I should go," Amber sighed, turning toward the door. "I need to find a job and somehow get a sponsor so I can go through some kind of alpha trial."

"You're going through the Alpha Trials?" Ceri asked, eyes going wide. Amber had been human, and she obviously didn't know what she was getting into. "Do you have any idea how dangerous they are?"

Amber paused at the door. "No, I don't. I know the basics of pack life, but it's not like information on werewolves is freely available to the general public. So I don't know what I'm getting myself into, but I have no choice. I can't let my pack end up in the system. They'll be omegas for the rest of their lives," Amber said, getting angrier and angrier as she spoke.

Ceri crossed her arms. She had an idea that may or may not work. Part of her didn't want to use the favor that creepy, old elf owed her like this, but she knew it was a selfish thought. Amber had jumped in to help her with nothing to gain. Helping her in return was the right thing to do, but more importantly, she just wanted to. Goddess knew she had little enough chance to actually make a difference in the world. "I might be able to help you get a sponsor."

"What?" Amber asked, the anger switching to hope.

"There's someone that owes me a favor, and he's more than capable of sponsoring someone," she explained.

"Why would you help me like that?"

"You jumped in to help me save a pixie. It was kind of crazy, and kind of dumb, but you did it anyway because you thought it was the right thing to do," Ceri said, squaring her shoulders. "I'm helping you for the same reason. I know what happens to shifters who get put in the system. Besides, you saved my ass, and now I can save yours."

Amber looked like she might reject the offer for a moment, then nodded and held out her hand. "It's a deal."

Ceri took her hand and shook it. A subtle twist of magic shivered between them, but Amber didn't seem to notice. Ceri flexed her fingers. She'd have to figure out what that was later.

CHAPTER 10

TOMMY

*T*ommy jerked awake, swiping at the dark figure leaning over him with a growl. They jumped back with a curse.

"Tommy! It's me!" Genevieve shouted.

His heart raced in his chest, and the urge to shift and fight pounded along his skin. He blinked up at Genevieve, his eyes adjusting to the light streaming in the apartment window. Her hair was tied back in a neat bun, and she was wearing a pant suit. She looked like a completely different person.

"Sorry," he said quietly. "I'm not used to being woken up by anyone friendly."

"Right," Genevieve said awkwardly. "I didn't think about that, sorry."

"You can just throw something at me next time." He didn't want her to feel bad. It wasn't her fault. He'd been living on the streets for the past year, and after being jumped while asleep, he'd learned to wake up swinging.

She smirked at that. "I have to go to work. Just didn't want you to wake up to an empty apartment. Amber left super early and said she'd be back around six this evening."

"Alright, thanks." He could barely believe his good fortune. He'd have the whole apartment to himself all day.

Genevieve waved goodbye and hurried out the front door. He listened intently as her footsteps led away from the apartment, then started down the stairs. He lost her after that, but it was good enough, she was definitely gone.

He leapt off the air mattress. The clock on the microwave said it was just past noon. He couldn't believe he had slept so late, but the apartment did feel safe. He couldn't remember the last time he had felt safe in the place he was sleeping. Not even before he got kicked out.

He put his new clothes in a pile first, then started looking around the apartment for anything valuable. Guilt gnawed in his gut, but he had to make a run for it before things got any worse. Amber meant well, but she had no clue what she was doing. There was no way she was going to pass some weird trial to become an alpha. Especially not with another alpha having it out for her.

The wolf in his mind fought his every step. It hated what he was doing, but he ignored the feeling. He was good at ignoring things. Hunger. Fear. Exhaustion. None of it mattered more than just surviving.

There was no cash in the apartment other than a small jar full of coins. He grabbed it. There was probably twenty or thirty bucks in there. There was no medicine in the cabinet in the bathroom. He yanked open the drawers and found a small box. Inside was some jewelry. Most of it was fake, but there was one necklace with a diamond that might be real. It looked old, like some kind of family heirloom.

He picked it up, but froze. His hand shook a little. He looked at the open drawers, the pile of things on the bed, and he wanted to throw up. He hadn't meant to become like *her*.

The memories overwhelmed him, and for a moment he was

standing in that little two bedroom house that reeked of cigarettes and old beer.

"*W*here is it?" *Tommy demanded, shoving the empty ring box in his stepmother's face. "What did you do?"*

She slapped his hand away and surged up off the couch. "Show a little fucking respect to your mother," she snapped, her voice slurred from the alcohol and who knew what else.

"You're not my mother!" he shouted.

She snorted. "Your mother is dead, kid. I'm all you got, and it's not like she needed it anymore."

Rage and anguish rushed through him at her callous words. He barely realized he was moving before he shoved her back as hard as he could. "What the fuck did you do with it?"

She slapped him across the face, her nails scratching his skin. He stumbled back. Tears stung at his eyes, but he refused to let them fall. He wouldn't ever let her see him cry.

She yanked a crumpled dollar bill from her pocket and threw it at his face. "Here's what's left," she sneered.

He grabbed the money, staring at it in horror. "You sold it?"

"The pawn shop gave me like two-fifty," she said, swaying unsteadily.

He lunged at her with a shout. Pain lanced through his fist as it connected with her bony face.

*T*ommy dropped the necklace and slammed the box shut. He'd only gotten one hit in before his dad had dragged him off her. He had managed to escape before his dad could beat the hell out of him, but he had never dared to go back.

He wanted to throw up. He couldn't do this. He *wouldn't* do this. He'd survived this long without stealing from people that didn't deserve it, and he could keep going. He'd take the clothes, because she had given them to him, but that was it. He put everything back exactly as it had been in the bathroom, then hurried out to fix the rest of the apartment.

CHAPTER 11

AMBER

They had intended to go straight to the elf's house, but Amber had felt Tommy practically panicking through the pack bond. She had decided to go back and see if he'd come with them. Her wolf would feel better being able to keep an eye on him.

Ceri followed her up to the apartment, looking around curiously. She'd poked at all the truck dials on the way here too. She reminded her a little of a pixie, especially with her wide blue eyes.

She unlocked the door and walked into the apartment. Tommy was sitting on the couch looking particularly guilty, which wasn't what Amber had expected, but the expression was replaced with surprise when Ceri followed her inside.

"Tommy, this is Ceri. Ceri, Tommy." He kept glancing at Ceri like she was a threat, so she added, "She's a new friend, and she thinks she can help us get a sponsor."

"I thought you were at work until really late." He shuffled slightly to move in front of his bag on the ground. It was packed.

Self consciously, she smoothed her hair back. She didn't want to tell him what had happened, especially if he had already been trying to run away, but she had a feeling he'd know if she lied. "I got fired this morning. They don't allow newly bitten were-wolves to work as nurses, apparently."

"Oh," Tommy said quietly. He tugged his beanie down on his head and crossed his arms. "Sorry, that sucks."

For an awkward moment they were all silent. Ceri's face lit up with a grin and she beamed at Tommy, who, in return, looked alarmed.

"Do you have a job?" she asked out of nowhere.

"Me?" he asked, pinching his brows together. When Ceri nodded he replied, "No, I mostly just fix computers for people when I can. Resell stuff."

"The shop I work at needs a temporary, part-time stocker. It'd be about twenty hours a week, and you could start tomorrow. If you're interested."

Amber felt a tangle of emotions run through the pack bond. Surprise, hope, frustration, worry, and more guilt. This kid was more of a mess than she was.

"Ok, I guess I could try, but I've never had a job like that," Tommy said.

"It's just putting stuff on shelves," Ceri said.

The box in her hand let out a squeak and Tommy flinched at the noise. "What…is that?"

Ceri cracked the lid open then pulled a small vial out of her pocket. She poured a little liquid in the box and closed it again. "A pixie," she explained, putting the vial back in her pocket. "Some witches ripped his wings off earlier. That's actually how I met Amber. She came to our rescue."

Tommy snorted. "She does that a lot."

Ceri grinned, then turned to Amber. "Mind if I leave the pixie here? He's gonna be out cold for a while."

"That's fine," she said, ready to get this sponsor thing over with. "Tommy, want to come with us to meet this potential sponsor?" She really needed him to say yes. She had a feeling that if he didn't come with them, he might not be here when they got back.

Tommy hesitated for a moment, glancing at Ceri before seeming to make a decision. "Sure, I guess."

CHAPTER 12

AMBER

*T*he potential sponsor's estate was outside of Portland, away from the bustle of the city and past the sprawling suburbs. The property was wedged between the Multnomah Channel, just north of where it split off the Willamette River, and one of the small lakes that dotted the area.

Based on the location, which was prime real estate for elves and other races that were fond of the outdoors, she had expected something nice. She stopped the truck at the entrance to the property and turned to look at Ceri.

"Are you sure someone lives here?" she asked. The rusted gate was overgrown with vines, and the driveway had more ruts than gravel. Elves were usually meticulous about maintaining their yards and gardens. They were called the flower children for a reason.

"Yeah," Ceri said. "He's a little...eccentric. I'm not really sure what his deal is, but he doesn't go outside much, and the place is falling apart. Obviously."

"How do we get in?" she asked, still skeptical.

"Just pull forward," Ceri said, waving her on. "The gate will open."

Amber inched the truck forward and, sure enough, the gate creaked open. As she drove through the gate a shiver of magic rolled over her skin. Runes glowed on the stone pillars that held the gate. The vines shivered, and a few reached toward the truck like they wanted to grab it.

"The property is falling apart, but he still keeps active wards on the gate?" Amber asked, incredulous. Those kinds of spells were *expensive*, not to mention hard to get. Enchanting was a difficult branch of magic that not many practiced; most chose to study witchcraft like Ceri.

"Eccentric, like I said." Ceri shrugged.

"This place gives me the creeps," Tommy said. His discomfort crackled through the pack bond like a warning.

Amber silently agreed. The truck bounced down the driveway in the shadow of towering maple trees. It was late October and the branches were heavy with brilliantly colored leaves. It should have been beautiful, but her skin crawled with the sensation of being watched. She wanted to trust Ceri, but she was starting to wonder if the witch actually had any idea what she was getting them into.

The driveway and the lane of trees framed what must have once been a beautiful mansion. The grey stone exterior was hidden behind creeping vines, but what was visible was dirty and worn. The front of the mansion had three sharply angled sides, with towers standing guard on the front corners. The spire on the left one had broken off, and it looked like it had taken half the wooden shingles with it. A tarp covering the hole flapped in the light breeze. A balcony with a crumbling balustrade stretched between the two towers, sheltering the entryway.

Bay windows protruded from the house every few feet, but no light came from any of them. The driveway ended abruptly in front of the house. Amber parked the truck and squinted up at the windows. They were all boarded up from the inside.

"Okay," Ceri said, appearing to brace herself. "Don't let him intimidate you. He's all bark and no bite."

Amber glanced back at Tommy, already regretting bringing him. He was flighty enough when he wasn't scared.

"Let's get this over with," she sighed, pushing the truck door open. Ceri climbed out on the other side after Tommy.

To the left of the house, set back in the trees, was a cottage. It wasn't as ornate as the mansion, but it looked cozy with a chimney and a wraparound porch. It must have been the groundskeeper's house back in the day.

Grass and weeds grew over the cobblestone that was once intended as pathway up to the main house. They picked their way over it, then walked up a short flight of steps. A wide walkway covered in leaves and other debris led all the way around the house.

Ceri walked ahead of the group and approached a dark green door set back in a stone archway. A brass knocker hung askew, pulled sideways by a delicate green vine. She tugged the knocker out of its grasp and rapped firmly on the door three times.

Amber listened intently, but the old mansion remained silent. Ceri waited with hands on her hips, then knocked again, louder this time. The sound echoed through the house.

"You're sure he still lives here?" Amber asked as the silence continued.

Ceri nodded firmly. "I was here just a few weeks ago."

"What did you do for him that he owes you a favor now?" Amber asked. She hadn't wanted to pry before, but she was starting to realize she needed to have a better idea of what she was getting into.

"It's kind of complicated," Ceri deflected. She grabbed the knocker and slammed it against the door as hard as she could. "This is stupid," she muttered. "I know Thallan's just hiding out in his study being a damn hermit."

"Then let's go find him." Amber walked up to the door and

tried the handle. It was unlocked. "Seems like an invitation to me," she said as she pushed the door open with a creak.

"Wait, don't—" Ceri said, reaching for Amber's arm.

She shrugged out of her grip and walked inside. The entryway was dimly lit. It would have been completely dark if it wasn't for the sunlight streaming in through the french doors tucked behind the staircase.

"This is a bad idea," Ceri muttered as she and Tommy followed her inside.

The house extended in two directions. To their left, the hallway led into darkness, and the floor itself was dusty. To their right, a single light bulb illuminated the hallway. It still looked barely used, but it was moderately clean.

"His study is this way," Ceri said, pointing to the right.

Amber started down the hallway. She desperately needed a sponsor, but everything about this elf was off. The house seemed abandoned, the grounds were falling apart, and anyone that ignored someone banging on their front door for five minutes obviously didn't want visitors. She hated needing help like this. She glanced at Tommy and grit her teeth. If it weren't for her pack, there'd be no way she would stoop to begging a stranger for a handout like this.

Ceri jogged to catch up and walk beside her. "I'm sorry this is so weird, but I really think he'll help."

"You didn't have to try to help me with this. Whether it works out or not, I really appreciate you trying at all," she said, forcing a smile onto her face.

They passed a few rooms as they walked down the gently curving hallway. The furniture inside was draped with sheets that were covered in a layer of dust. As Amber had seen from the outside, even the windows on the first floor were boarded up. Whoever had done it had simply slapped plywood over the windows without caring what they damaged. The antique wood paneling was split in places from the nails.

Ceri slowed and pointed at the room at the end of the hallway. The door to the study stood open, Amber's nose twitched as the cloying scent of cigars—or something equally smelly—drifted out of the room. Ceri squared her shoulders, took a deep breath, and marched inside.

The study was the cleanest room Amber had seen so far. A tall window overlooking an unruly garden illuminated the space. To her left were bookshelves that extended to the ceiling. A desk covered in stacks of unopened mail sat in front of the shelves.

"Has old age finally gotten to you and made you go deaf?" Ceri demanded. "I knocked for almost five minutes."

A chuckle emanated from a wingback chair set in front of the tall window. A curl of smoke drifted up from a slender hand that lay on the plush velvet armrest. Thallan tapped a long finger rhythmically against a worn spot on the velvet. "Hearing a knock at the door and caring about it are two different things, little witch," Thallan said. His voice was smooth, but he sounded strangely tired. "There's no need to sound so offended. I unlocked the door for you."

Amber looked at Ceri, wondering if that was possible. Ceri just shrugged.

"I have a couple of friends with me that I'd like to introduce to you," Ceri said, gesturing at them.

"What do you want?" Thallan asked. "Skip the pleasantries. I know you didn't come here to chat."

Amber stepped forward. "I was bitten a few nights ago, on the full moon along with two others. Since we changed together, I ended up the alpha. No pack will take us, and if I want to be able to stay an alpha, there are these trials I have to go through."

Thallan's finger stilled. "And you need a sponsor."

"Yes," she said, her fingers curling into a tight fist.

"No," Thallan said. He didn't sound angry, or even annoyed, simply uninterested.

"I'm calling in my favor," Ceri interjected. "You owe me."

Thallan stood from the chair. White-blond hair extended halfway down his back, the sides neatly plaited. He turned to Ceri. His face must have been handsome once, but a twisted, red scar cut through his patrician features.

"The favor you ask is not equal to the favor owed," Thallan said sharply. "In fact, the favor I owe you is worth so much less than what you are asking that I find the demand insulting." The calm tone he had held at the beginning of the conversation was gone. He stubbed out his slender cigar in an ashtray and stalked toward Ceri. "Take your little band of misfits and get out of my house. As a *favor*, I'll refrain from calling the police to report you for trespassing."

Ceri's pale face went red in anger and embarrassment. "All you'd have to do is put down a bond and show up to the Trials, I don't see how that's—"

"I'm not risking that money and what's left of my reputation on a newly bitten werewolf I don't even know," Thallan snapped. "Get out of my house."

Amber had to turn to face Tommy to keep from lunging at the elf. It had been stupid to think there was a chance he would help. Her hands shook with anger. Tommy watched her with a worried expression. He looked like he was ready to bolt.

"Let's go," she said, glancing back at Ceri. Thallan stood in front of the fireplace, disdain apparent on his scarred face. He looked at her briefly before turning back to his window.

Ceri threw one last glare at Thallan, then followed her out the door.

CHAPTER 13

GENEVIEVE

*G*enevieve was tired, angry, and hungry. She wasn't sure why she had bothered to come here. There was no way she'd be able to talk him into helping, but for some reason, she wanted to try.

"Steven, just open the door!" She pounded her fist against the stained dorm room door. She could hear him in there, typing away and ignoring her. Either that or the music blasting out of his headphones was drowning her out. He always listened to it way too loud. He was stupid, and thoughtless, and always so busy with his precious thesis.

Irritation turned to anger, and she took a step back from the door, then slammed her foot into it. The door flew open, splinters of wood flying from where the latch used to be. Steven, who was leaning back in his chair, flailed and toppled out of it.

"What the fuck?" he demanded, ripping his noise-canceling headphones off of his ears.

She stood in the doorway, panting, and asked herself the same question. The door was busted, and it had dented the sheetrock. She hadn't paused to think before she had kicked the door open, she had been so mad—just like in The Market.

"I—" she hesitated. "I need your help," she said finally, straightening her shoulders and trying to look reasonable.

"You broke my door down!" Steven shouted, clearly not ready for the calm part of the conversation. "How the hell did you break my door? You weigh like ninety pounds!"

"That's not important," she said, brushing a piece of door off her slacks. "The point is, I could really use your help."

He ran his hands down his face and groaned. "You are insane. Less than a month ago, you dumped me because, and this is a direct quote, 'you are too clingy, and you never have time for me,' which is a complete contradiction by the way." His voice rose into a shout. "And now you've literally kicked down my door for no reason because *you need my help?!*"

She cleared her throat uncomfortably. "I was knocking and you didn't answer." Maybe kicking down the door had been an...overreaction.

"You were..." He let the thought trail off and stared at her with wide eyes. "Oh my god, you've finally cracked. I always thought it was inevitable, but it's happened. You've lost your mind completely."

"What do you mean it was inevitable?" she demanded, anger shocking her out of her embarrassment.

"You refuse to talk about anything! You bottle everything up and...and let it fester! And now this." He threw his arms up, waving them over his head like an explosion.

"I wouldn't have come here if it wasn't important," she said through gritted teeth.

"Oh really," he said, acting like what she had just said was insulting. "Then please explain what is so important that it compelled you to come back to the one place you swore you would never return to when you dumped me."

She crossed her arms. "It's...personal."

"Get out," he pointed at the hallway behind her. "Leave now."

"Fine," she said, dropping her arms with a sigh. "If it's that big of a deal I'll explain."

"No," Steven snapped. "I don't want to hear it. You are still exactly the same, and I am *so done*. Get out."

Genevieve wanted to rake her claws across the scowl look on Steven's face. He'd be sorry then. He'd probably beg to help. He'd...

Genevieve ground her teeth together, turned on her heel, and walked away. She had to, or she knew she would kill him.

CHAPTER 14

GENEVIEVE

*G*enevieve hesitated in front of the door, but the smell of Chinese food compelled her to walk inside.

"Hey, sorry I'm..." she trailed off, staring at a woman with curly blonde hair sitting at the table next to Tommy. She was dressed like an elf in frilly dress, but she didn't have the pointed ears.

"This is Ceri. We met earlier today," Amber said, nodding toward the woman.

Ceri waved at Genevieve with her chopsticks. "Hey," she said with a smile. "Me and Amber got into it with some witches."

"Is that a pixie?" Genevieve asked. A little gray creature was stumbling around on a hand towel, squeaking.

"Yeah, some witches ripped its wings off," Amber said with a frown. "We saved you a little of everything. Weren't sure what you liked." She gestured at the half empty cartons that littered the table.

"Oh thank Merlin. I'm so hungry," Genevieve exclaimed, dumping her purse by the door. She grabbed a carton and began shoveling food in her mouth.

Ceri passed the pixie a piece of chicken with her chopsticks. It grabbed it, shoving the whole bite in its mouth at once. Its cheeks bulged as it chewed happily.

Genevieve's wolf growled, anxious and irritated. It didn't like intruders in the den.

She paused at the thought. Her wolf's instincts were getting out of hand, and she had no idea how to handle it. Magical law didn't get into how werewolves controlled their urges, just that they had to.

"Were you working late or something?" Amber asked. Her tone was even and calm, but Genevieve felt the distrust she implied like a punch to the gut. She shifted uncomfortably in her heels and shrugged.

"Yeah, and I might have to work late a few nights this week," she said before shoving a huge bite of shrimp in her mouth.

It was a lie, and Amber looked like she could tell somehow, but she wasn't ready to explain everything to her. She wasn't sure she would get Steven to help, and if she couldn't there was no reason to give Amber another reason to dislike her. So far, Genevieve knew she had been worse than useless. Getting kicked out of The Market still made her want to die of embarrassment.

The pixie squeaked loudly, then toppled off the table. Tommy's hand shot out, catching it before it hit the ground.

"Dude, you can't fly," Tommy said as he set it back on the hand towel. The pixie flailed its arms angrily, then fell over.

"It will probably take a while for it to understand," Ceri said, worry creasing her brows.

"What happened to its wings?" Genevieve asked, happy to turn the conversation to a different topic.

Ceri's face darkened with anger. "Some Blackwood witches ripped them off."

"Blackwood? Aren't they that huge coven that owns half of Portland?" she asked.

The pixie glanced at Tommy, then took a running start for the edge of the table. He caught it again and held onto it while it wriggled instead of setting it back down.

"Yeah, those Blackwoods," Ceri confirmed. "Pixie wings are used in a lot of spells. It's barbaric to rip their wings off, but they don't care because they're just *pests*." She spit out the word like a curse.

"It's mean to mutilate them like that, but they are just frogs with wings," Genevieve said with a shrug.

"They're not," Ceri said, leaning forward and bracing her arms on the table. "No one ever pays attention, but they talk to each other. I think they can understand us to a certain extent, they just can't speak our language."

"You think they're what...sentient?" Genevieve asked, glancing at Amber and Tommy to see if she was the only one that thought Ceri was crazy.

"Everyone looks at me like that," Ceri said, "and I don't care. I'll prove it one day."

The pixie made another frantic run for the edge of the table and Ceri grabbed him just in time.

"You're going to have to stick it in the bathtub tonight to keep it from jumping to its death," Amber said, amused.

Ceri's shoulders slumped. "I don't think it's safe to keep him at home actually," she said. "If my mother finds out, she'll chop him up for parts just to spite me."

Tommy looked up sharply. "Then you have to leave him here," Tommy demanded. "I'll take care of him." He paused and glanced back at Amber. "If that's okay?"

"Yeah, of course," Amber said without hesitation. "I don't mind it being in the apartment."

"What about tomorrow at work?" Tommy asked. "We can't leave him here alone, can we?"

"We can take him to work with us," Ceri said with a smile before exchanging a glance with Amber when Tommy wasn't looking.

Genevieve felt completely out of the loop. There was obviously something going on with Tommy that this stranger knew about and she didn't. She looked back down into her carton and picked out the last shrimp. There was no reason for her to feel so hurt, it was just the instincts again. She shoved the shrimp in her mouth and glared at the ugly, wingless pixie that had everyone's attention.

CHAPTER 15

TOMMY

*T*ommy looked curiously around the stockroom. It was stacked with boxes and shelves of items waiting to be placed in the store. The front of the shop was half bookstore and half supplies for witches. Aileen, Ceri's aunt, owned the shop. She'd sent them back here and told Ceri to put him to work.

He walked over to one shelf that held what looked suspiciously like pickled rabbits feet. Grimacing he turned away and poked at a dusty old jar. A weird scent tickled his nose, and he sneezed loudly.

"Blessings," Ceri said politely as she dug around through a pile of discarded boxes. She found an empty box with a lid and set the pixie, now dubbed Woggy, inside.

He squeaked in irritation, reaching his spindly arms up to her.

"Sorry, buddy." She set a small cup of water and a bowl of shredded tuna in the box next to him, which improved his mood immediately. He crouched over the tuna and stuck his face in it, chewing loudly. "Can you check on him every half hour or so and make sure he's okay?"

"Sure," Tommy said. Woggy still kept trying to fly; he would have kept an eye on him even if Ceri hadn't asked. It was stupid to get attached to Woggy since he probably wouldn't survive, but he couldn't help it. He had a soft spot for underdogs and broken things.

The door to the back room opened, and a young troll walked in.

"Deward, hi! I'd like you to come meet Tommy. He's going to be helping out for a little while," Ceri said, waving him over.

He must have been around Tommy's age, since his tusks barely extended over his lips. His bright blue mohawk lay neatly slicked back, and his biceps bulged against the sleeves of his crisp button-up shirt. Black-framed glasses were perched on his nose. He had a book tucked under one arm. Deward was a walking stereotype, unlike the troll that had served them barbecue the day before.

"Deward Tuskbreaker," the troll said, extending his moss green hand in greeting.

Tommy shook his hand, able to match the firm grip with werewolf strength. "Just Tommy."

"No last name?" Deward's thick brows drew together in confusion.

"I'm not on speaking terms with my family," he said with a shrug.

Aileen shouted for Ceri from the front of the store.

"Coming!" Ceri shouted back before turning to Deward. "Can you show him the ropes? Aileen just wanted him unloading the truck, then stocking the shelves today."

"Of course, my pleasure," Deward said politely.

"Thanks a billion," Ceri said with a grin before hurrying out of the back room.

Deward looked at Tommy nervously before clearing his throat and setting his book down next to the box. "I prefer to stay in the back and unload, so I'll show you how to stock the shelves before the store gets too busy."

"Okay," Tommy said, shoving his hands in his pockets. He was nervous about screwing up since he'd never had a real job before, but he was still excited to have this chance. He'd volunteered for various things after school, and he'd been paid for tutoring most of his junior year, but this was different. This made him want to stay.

∽

ommy sat down in the a folding chair in the stockroom and chugged half a bottle of water. He had *thought* stocking the shelves might be the easier job, but it still involved lugging around fifty pound boxes. For the first time, he was truly glad of the extra strength he'd gained. The exercise even felt good.

Taking another long drink of cold water, he leaned back in the chair. A tug at his jeans startled him. He looked down and saw Woggy climbing up his pant leg with shaky arms.

"How did you get out of your box, little guy?"

Woggy squeaked imperiously in reply.

"Ah, of course," he said as he leaned down and plucked Woggy from his jeans and set him on his shoulder. Woggy babbled excitedly and pointed around the room. He must have wanted to be up high where he could see.

"Is that some sort of pet?" Deward stood to his left holding out another stack of books for Tommy.

He hadn't heard him walk up. It was creepy how quiet he was. "Yeah, I guess," he said, standing to take the books. "Ceri rescued him, and I'm helping take care of him until he adjusts to not having wings anymore."

"The odds that the pixie will be able to be reintroduced back into its natural habitat are nonexistent," Deward said, adjusting the glasses on his nose.

He resisted the urge to knock them askew for that comment. Deward was technically right, but he hoped Ceri would find a way to beat the odds. "I figured. I don't think Ceri is going to try that, she just needs him to stop jumping off the table. He doesn't understand why he can't fly yet," he said with a shrug.

"It is incapable of rational thought," Deward said before turning and walking away.

Tommy shook his head. Trolls were odd. He adjusted the books in his arms and noticed that the top book was titled Sign Language: Magical Chants for the Deaf. He had learned Sign language in school. One of the many after-school programs he had joined to avoid going home. He'd picked it up quickly, but it had been a long time since he had signed, so he'd be rusty at best.

Woggy hopped down onto the books. Tommy adjusted to hold them with one hand and signed hello at the pixie. To his surprise, Woggy repeated the motion. Leaving the pixie perched on the books, he headed out to the store front to put up the books. Woggy signed hello over and over, though the motion was garbled after a bit, turning into more of a salute than a hello.

Ceri thought Woggy could learn to communicate, though. This might be the way he could. As soon as she had a break, he'd have to show her.

He knelt and set the books down on the floor. Woggy hopped off the books and scampered toward the end of the aisle.

"Get back here," he said trying to grab him, and missing.

The pixie crawled under a shelf and ran out the other side. Jumping to his feet, he ran around the end of the aisle just in time to see a witch viciously trying to stomp on the pixie.

"Wait!" he shouted, lunging for Woggy. He grabbed him, but the witch's heeled boot still came down on the back of his arm. Jerking his hand back, he looked up at her in alarm. His heart pounding in his ears as adrenaline rushed through him. He hadn't even seen the woman coming, and Woggy had almost been crushed.

"Why would you do that?" he snapped, rising to his feet.

The woman standing in front of him narrowed her eyes. She

had long black hair that hung down to her waist, and bright green eyes that sparked with malice. He knew that kind of look well, he'd been at the receiving end of it most of his life.

"You shouldn't let pests into stores," she said tightly. Her fingers twitched, and the sharp scent of magic filled the area. "That one looks half dead, anyhow."

Nervous, he moved the pixie behind his back. He didn't trust this witch for a second. "He's healing," he replied tersely.

The witch glanced over her shoulder, then flicked her index finger in his direction. A sharp pain stole his breath, and he stumbled, grasping his side. His vision blurred from the shock as he looked down; his hand came away bloody.

"What the hell did you do to me?" he growled.

The witch looked at him with a smirk, then screamed. She stumbled away from him and lifted her hand. Purple light flashed from her palm and fiery agony clawed at his chest. The magic shredded his shirt and the skin beneath.

"He attacked me!" the witch shrieked. "He's losing control!"

He crouched with one hand on the floor, but Woggy still safe behind his back, panting against the pain in his chest. Blood dripped steadily onto the floor. His teeth lengthened and fur grew along the edges of his face as he growled at the witch. His hands curled into claws. She had threatened Woggy, and now attacked him. He wanted to tear her apart.

He took a step forward, but Ceri jumped in front of him. "Get away from him, Selena!"

"*He* attacked *me*," Selena replied with a sneer.

He tried to shove Ceri away, but she grabbed his arms with surprising strength and forced him backward. "Tommy, you can't change here," she hissed in his ear. "They'll arrest you!" Her face was pale and fearful.

"She tried to hurt Woggy," he growled.

"I know," Ceri said, clenching her jaw tight. "But you stopped her. That's what matters."

"She's going to get away with it," he said, standing from his crouch and taking a step forward. He could see the black-haired witch just past Ceri. She was putting on her act for the store manager. She was a *liar*.

"Tommy, please," Ceri begged.

"Get that bitten piece of trash out of here! I can't believe you brought him here to work," Aileen shouted at Ceri before turning to Tommy. "You're fired if that wasn't clear," the woman bit out.

CHAPTER 16

AMBER

*A*mber had filled out applications at four different businesses, but she doubted any of them would call her back. Even if they did, it was unlikely the pay would cover her apartment and other bills. She slammed the truck door shut and jogged up the stairs. Maybe she could get Ceri to charm her boobs bigger so she could start stripping.

She paused at the top of the stairs. The hairs on her arms stood on end. Something wasn't right.

Slowly, she walked toward her apartment door, but a familiar scent made her pause again. A piece of paper taped to her apartment door fluttered in the breeze.

She approached it slowly. Her wolf pressed its claws into her mind, urging her to shift. She pushed down the instinct, but the hair on the back of her neck prickled. She was being watched, but she didn't know how or from where. There was no one behind her, and there was no one else on the walkway.

The lock on the apartment door was shiny and new. She grabbed the paper and skimmed it. An eviction notice. Her fingers dented the paper as rage tore through her. Getting her fired wasn't enough? Donovan was taking her apartment from her too? How was he even doing this?

The notice cited a report that there were multiple unauthorized people living in the apartments as grounds for eviction. The curtain next door moved and Amber jerked her gaze upward, catching Mrs. Huntington peering at her. The shift crept down her arms. Her muscles twitched as her fingers extended into claws and a growl erupted from her throat.

"Typical," a deep voice muttered behind her.

Amber whipped around. A man with shaggy brown hair and two days' worth of stubble was leaning against the banister watching her with a smirk. She hadn't heard him walk up.

"Who the hell are you?" she asked, her words slurred from the enlarged incisors crowding her mouth.

"Mark Jackson, beta of the Lockhart Pack," he said, giving her a mock bow.

Amber took a deep breath and pulled back the shift. Mark's eyes never strayed from her face as she struggled for control, but he didn't look worried, only mildly interested.

"Donovan sent you?" she demanded as soon as she could speak clearly again.

"No, of course not," he scoffed. "I was simply in the area and saw you about to lose control. I had to step in before you hurt your poor neighbor." He took a step forward. "Everyone knows newly bitten wolves can lose control at any moment."

She grit her teeth. "Stay away from me and my pack."

"Your pack?" Mark scoffed. He walked into her personal space, forcing her to take a step back. "You don't have a pack. Your eyes might glow red, but you aren't a real alpha, and you never will be."

He took another step forward and her back hit the wall. A power she hadn't felt before surged up inside of her. Donovan had fucked with her life. It was his fault she was bitten in the first place, then he had gotten her fired, and now evicted. Now he thought he could send his beta to intimidate her.

She laughed in his face and closed the distance between them until they were almost touching. "Why is Donovan so desperate to have me in his pack?" she asked, peering into Mark's eyes. He hesitated, just for a moment, but it was enough. "Oh, did he not tell you he's been trying to recruit me? Or that he promised me your position in the pack?"

He snorted in amusement. "Like hell he did."

She grinned, then shoved him back as hard as she could. Her shove lifted him off his feet and he hit the banister. The place where the iron connected with the concrete cracked loudly and the banister swayed out.

He pushed himself upright. A golden glow flickered in his eyes as a growl rumbled in his chest. "You're going to pay for that."

Red flashed at the edges of her vision and the wolf tensed in her mind. "I'm not the one that's going to pay," she snapped.

Mark lunged for her. She sidestepped and swung her leg into his stomach, snapping it back before he could grab it. Having grown up with five brothers, she knew how to brawl. The kick caught Mark off-guard and he wheezed, his breath knocked out of him.

The shift tugged at her bones and she stumbled. The wolf wanted out, but she couldn't afford to lose control now. Mark's fist connected with her cheek. The strike jarred painfully through her skull but she managed to stay on her feet.

"You hit like a pixie," she taunted, throwing a punch at his gut. He slipped out of reach and kicked her in the side as the momentum drug her forward. She hit the wall, rattling the windows.

Mark growled, his face contorting as he began shifting. Amber slid to the right and his fist slammed against the wall where her head had been. She punched twice, catching him under the jaw, then in the throat.

His half-shifted claws raked across her shoulder, ripping her shirt. Blood splattered on the concrete as she ducked under his follow-up attack. Ready to end this, she lunged forward. Catching him in the stomach with her uninjured shoulder, she lifted him off his feet and slammed him down against the concrete.

The air rushed from his lungs in a wheeze. She grabbed his arm and wrist, then stepped across his body, forcing him onto his stomach. He struggled against her grip so she drove her heel into his kidney. A low growl rumbled in her chest. He could fight all he wanted, but she had better leverage, and she was stronger.

Wild instincts rushed through her. It was time to send Donovan a message. Mark was born a werewolf, but to join a pack, there had to be a bite. A bite to change a human was always on the wrist, it was tradition. The bite to seal the pack bond was always on the back of the neck.

Her claws cut through Mark's flannel shirt easily. The white, raised scar from the bite contrasted sharply against his tanned skin. She set her claws over the pack mark. Magic pulsed under her fingertips, Donovan's magic. The pack bond. She dug her claws into his skin, cutting through the scar tissue. He shouted in agony, increasing his struggles against her.

Foreign magic flowed through her as the strength of her will fought against his. Dominance in werewolf packs was more than just who was bossier. Whatever magic enabled them to shift into wolves changed their will into something more tangible. Even though she was an alpha, there was still a chance that he was actually more dominant. This battle of wills was about proving that he was not. If Donovan wanted to challenge her, he'd have to do it himself instead of sending a lackey in his place.

The beta twitched, then shifted, ripping his clothes. His wolf form was twice the size of his human one, but she was still able to hold him down easily. He lay under her grip, his tail tucked between his legs.

"If I see you again, I will rip you apart," she whispered in his ear. She tore her claws free and stood up.

Mark drug himself forward on his stomach, keeping his head low.

"I never wanted any of this, but I won't let Donovan hurt my pack," she threatened.

Mark snarled at her, but turned and fled down the stairs. Mrs. Huntington cracked her door open and pressed her face up to the narrow opening.

"I'm calling the police," she announced in her shrill voice.

"Go ahead, you miserable old hag," she snapped.

Mrs. Huntington gasped and slammed her door shut. Amber turned to her own door. The locks had been changed, but that was not going to stop her. They could evict her, but they had no right to lock all her things up inside. She lifted her foot and kicked the door down.

CHAPTER 17

*A*mber was stuffing a fistful of clothes into her backpack when pain and fear—Tommy's—ripped through the pack bond. Her knees hit the floor, and the shift began to roll over her. She wanted to run and rip apart whoever was hurting him. Her back curved sharply, and her shirt split as the shift rushed over her. She ripped her jeans off in shreds with her teeth.

She raced out of the apartment, letting the wolf take over. For once, they were in complete agreement. The wolf drove her forward; her legs moving faster than she had even thought possible.

The parking lot blurred as she wove through the cars. Since she didn't have to stick to the road, she was halfway into town in a matter of minutes. Tommy was moving, she thought. Still in pain. Still angry. Still afraid.

Faster, she urged the wolf. Her paws pounded against hot pavement and cool grass. The scents of the city would have been fascinating in any other moment, but she ignored them as she ran.

Tommy's pull led her into a subdivision she recognized, and after another minute, she was racing up to Ceri's front door. She hit it running, but a ward flared and threw her back, singeing her fur.

Amber growled at the display of magic and prowled forward. She tensed her muscles to try again when the door was yanked open.

Ceri waved her inside. There was blood on her hands.

She raced inside, following her nose and the pack bonds straight to Tommy. His shirt hung from his shoulders, bloody and shredded. She whined and walked over, sniffing at the injuries. His chest had already healed, but she couldn't get past the scent of blood. The wolf needed something to *do*.

"Amber," Ceri said, tentatively touching her shoulder. "Please shift back. Tommy is going to be okay."

Amber huffed and nosed at Tommy's hand. He patted her head. "I healed, and the witch didn't hurt Woggy," Tommy said.

Ceri held out a dress. "Come and put on some clothes."

Giving in, she followed Ceri into what must be her bedroom, and shifted. The wolf wasn't happy about it, but seemed to agree that she could help Tommy better if she wasn't a wolf.

Ceri handed her the dress, keeping her eyes glued to Amber's face. Amber pulled the dress on over her head. It was flowy and girly and nothing like she normally wore. The material was soft, but she still felt naked with it on. She marched out of the room and headed back to Tommy.

Tommy was still in the same chair, though he had on a fresh shirt now.

"Who hurt you?" Amber demanded.

"It doesn't matter right now—"

"Tell me!" she shouted. Her voice echoed around apartment.

Tommy slipped out of the chair and fell to his knees, his shoulders hunched in pain. "Blackwood...coven..." Tommy gasped as the words were forced out of him.

Amber took a step back, panting from the strain of forcing

Tommy to submit like that. She hadn't realized it was even possible. That wasn't something they put in the werewolf literature.

"Which one? Was it the same witch that attacked Ceri?" she demanded, pointing back at her.

"Why does it matter? There's nothing you can do about it!" Tommy retorted.

Amber took a step back. The wolf was insulted, but she was overwhelmed with guilt. She hated this powerlessness. Enough was enough.

"Stay with Ceri," she snapped. "I'll come get you when I'm done."

"What are you going to do?" Ceri asked, alarm clear on her face.

"Nothing, apparently," Amber said, brushing past her. Tommy glared at her from the floor. He could hate her all he wanted, but she couldn't protect them if they tried to hide things from her.

She had let Donovan stomp all over her life, and then she had let that elf shut them down without even the courtesy of hearing them out. She was done taking no for an answer.

CHAPTER 18

AMBER

*A*mber's truck skid to a halt, the right wheel bumping up onto the first step in front of Thallan's house. She jumped out and marched toward the imposing house. He had laughed them out of the place last time, but she wouldn't allow him to do it again.

She kicked the door open and walked inside. "Thallan, where are you hiding?" Amber shouted into the dark house. Her voice echoing off the dark, wood floors was the only reply.

She turned down the hallway that led to the study. Her hand curled into a fist, the claws digging into her palm. The pain kept her focused enough to stop the shift, despite her anger. She couldn't control anything else, but she could damn well control herself. No one was going to take that from her.

The door to the study was closed, but not locked. She threw it open and walked inside. The chair Thallan had sat in last time faced the fireplace. It, and the room, were empty.

"I let you leave without considering you a trespasser once," Thallan said from behind her. "I'm not inclined to do so again."

Amber turned to face him slowly. "I came here to negotiate for you to be my sponsor."

Thallan snorted and took a drag on his long cigarette, blowing the smoke toward her. "Then you wasted your time, and mine."

"There has to be something you want," she insisted. "I need a sponsor and I'm not leaving here until you agree to be mine, or give me a damn good reason why you won't."

Thallan sneered. "I don't owe you any answers."

"Never said you did." She crossed her arms. "But I'm still not leaving until I get what I came here for."

He tapped the end of his cigarette thoughtfully. "You're desperate, and desperate people make mistakes."

"I don't care and I don't have time to worry about the consequences," Amber said. "If you've ever been desperate, then you'd understand."

Thallan laughed, a dry sound that bubbled out of his chest. He looked at her and tugged his linen shirt to the side. Over his heart lay a twisted black scar.

"I know desperation better than anyone," he said, jabbing his finger into the scar. As he pressed against the black mark, the smell of dark magic filled the room. "Do you know what this is?"

"No." She forced herself not to cringe away from Thallan, but that thing on his chest scared her.

"It's a demon mark. A favor owed that can be called due at any time," he said.

"You summoned a demon?" she asked, horrified. It was illegal, but most people weren't stupid enough to try it regardless. Summoning a demon was asking to get yourself killed.

Thallan grinned, a crazed look in his eyes as he stalked forward until he was standing toe to toe with Amber. "I was desperate to save my wife," Thallan explained. "Desperate enough to do anything."

Amber tried to keep her eyes from the mark, but she couldn't look away. She bit the inside of her cheek and forced herself to look into his eyes. "Then you should understand why I need you to be my sponsor. Tommy and Genevieve will suffer for the rest of their lives if I can't pass the Trials. They're my responsibility. I can't let that happen."

"Then take my mark," Thallan said, tapping the twisted, black scar again.

"What?" she asked, her eyes darting to the demon's mark.

"Take the mark and I will not only be your sponsor, I will also give you and your pack a place to live and hunt for as long as you need," Thallan said.

She stared at the mark. If it had been Dylan at risk, she wouldn't have even hesitated. She was out of options, and quickly running out of time.

"Fine," she said, determination settling in her gut. She would find a way to kill this demon if she had to. "How do I take it?"

Thallan pressed his hand to the mark and magic swelled between them. "That's all I needed to hear," he said. "But I can only give it to you if you are strong enough to fulfill the demon's wishes." He lifted his hand and the mark clung to his fingers like black tar.

"What happens if I'm not?"

"I remain stuck with my mistakes, and you get to walk away from all this," he said, his hand hovering between them.

She nodded. "Do it."

"A debt for a debt," he whispered as he pressed his hand to her chest, directly over her heart.

The magic burned through her shirt and into her flesh. She bit down on a scream, unwilling to show Thallan any weakness. The magic twisted into her, taking root. A dark awareness crept through her. The magic was vile.

Thallan lifted his hand and stepped backward. He stared at her for a moment before turning away. Even through the fog of pain, she could see that he looked guilty.

The wolf howled in her mind, as did every instinct she had, but it was done. She stared down at the demon mark that had buried itself in her skin. Cold radiated from it throughout her chest. She touched it hesitantly, and it twitched like it was alive.

"We're moving in tonight," she said, her voice hoarse.

Thallan nodded, then walked away.

CHAPTER 19

CERI

*C*eri drove behind Amber's truck with Tommy and Woggy in the passenger seat. Genevieve was behind them in her car. The truck bed was packed full of disorganized boxes. Amber had said they didn't need furniture, and she didn't care enough about what she had to worry about bringing it or storing it somewhere. It wasn't worth anything anyhow; it had been bought used and then banged around in moves for the past six years.

"Is it weird to you that he suddenly agreed? Thallan seemed pretty adamant when we were there last that he had no interest in helping us," Tommy said. Woggy was running rampant over the dash of the car, but Tommy grabbed him every time he got in a precarious spot or tried to climb on the steering wheel.

She tapped her fingers against the wheel. It was suspicious, but she didn't want to give Tommy any reason to doubt Amber. "Maybe they worked out a deal. I think Thallan was more insulted I was trying to use my favor for it than anything. He can be such a prick."

Tommy snorted. "Yeah, I got that impression too. He seemed a little…self-absorbed."

"That's an understatement," she muttered.

"What's his deal? He's like some kind of Jane Eyre character holed up in a dying mansion." Tommy snatched Woggy from the gear shift, tutting at him. Woggy squeaked back imperiously, smacking Tommy's fist.

She looked at Tommy out of the corner of her eye. The more he relaxed and showed his personality, the more she wondered how he had ended up homeless. He was well-educated, kind, and very perceptive. Where were his parents?

She realized she'd been silent too long and cleared her throat. "Thallan lost his wife a few years ago. After that, he drove his daughter away, let the place fall into disrepair, and became a grumpy hermit. Losing someone you love can really change a person I guess."

Tommy was quiet for a moment, then whispered, "Yeah, it can."

The truck turned down the driveway. The gate swung open, beckoning the caravan inside. She followed, despite her misgivings. She wanted to catch Amber alone and demand some answers, but she had a feeling she wasn't going to get any no matter how hard she pressed. Her mother's voice echoed in her mind, suggesting a spell that would make Amber more honest, more likely to share secrets. She shoved the thought away. She was a white witch. Dabbling in magic that took away a person's free will was black magic. Plain and simple.

Amber drove straight to the guest house they'd seen on their first visit. Ceri was curious to see inside. She'd never been able to really explore the main house, much less the grounds.

The old house had two stories with a sharply slanted roof, and the outer walls were a cheery white with deep green shutters. She could have sworn the house looked drearier last time they were here. Perhaps it was eager to have new guests. Old estates could be funny like that. The longer magic infused a place, the more… alive it seemed.

They parked in the designated spots at the end of the driveway and clambered out of the car. Woggy was eager to run. He loved being outside.

"I'm going to go let Thallan know we're here, but he said the door would be unlocked. Y'all can go ahead and pick your rooms, there's more than enough for all of us," Amber said, already walking toward the main house.

"I call dibs on the upstairs rooms," Tommy said, hurrying toward the front door.

She smiled to herself. He was as eager to be here as Woggy. That was a big change from the boy that had his bags packed and ready to go that first day.

Genevieve ran after Tommy. "I want a room with an attached bathroom."

It was cool in the house, with the faint scent of mint in the air. It was elf-spelled to stay pleasant year round, warming itself in the winter and cooling itself in the hotter months. Not that it was ever *that* hot in Oregon.

Ceri took her time walking through the space. The entryway led right into the living area, which was open to the kitchen. It was very homey, with dark wood floors, bright white cabinets, and accents of orange. A leather sectional and two stuffed chairs sat in front of the fireplace. The back door was hidden behind the staircase, which was lined with a stately, carved bannister.

Tommy and Genevieve's footsteps thundered overhead as they raced around trying to find the best room. A little twinge of jealousy settled in her gut. This weird little pack had issues, but they were starting to trust each other. They *would* trust each other eventually.

Pausing in the doorway of a small room at the end of the hall, she leaned against the door jamb and sighed. The window had a perfect view of the backyard where it sloped down into the forest. There was a window seat and a desk in the corner of the room.

She walked further in and saw a bathroom on the right, and another room on the left. The door creaked as she pushed it all the way open and peered in the attached room. There were two work benches and an empty shelf. It was a spell room.

"This one looks perfect for you," Amber said, startling her.

She whipped around. "What?"

"If you ever want to stay over, or whatever. Or if you need a place to work. There's plenty of rooms. You should consider this one yours," Amber said with a shrug.

Her heart ached a little at the kindness. It was like Amber, or the house, had read her mind. "That would be really great. I really appreciate it. This place is so cool." A grin split her face. Magic had its ways, and it never ceased to surprise her.

Genevieve appeared in the doorway. Her buns had been knocked sideways. "My room is uh-mazing," she said with a huge grin. "Is this Ceri's or yours?"

"Ceri's," Amber answered. She pointed across the hall. "I'm taking that one. It has a good view of the driveway and the side of the house so I should be able to see anyone approaching. And someone would have to pass by my room to get upstairs."

Genevieve snorted. "Okay, whatever floats your boat, *alpha*."

Amber rolled her eyes. "Go start getting boxes."

Ceri followed them back toward the cars. Amber was already thinking like their protector, but she had a feeling the inexperienced alpha would be doing that even if she wasn't a wolf. Amber had a persistent air of worry about her. It was an almost pessimistic determination, which was an odd combination.

She ran her hand along the wall as she walked. This place…it felt like home. And she would do anything to help protect that. There was little enough good in this world sometimes.

Letting her eyes slip shut, she whispered a blessing, and a prayer to the goddess of life and renewal. Magic slipped from her fingertips, seeping into the wood and binding her to the house. If anyone with ill intent ever crossed the threshold, she would know.

∽

TOMMY

*B*oxes were scattered around him and Ceri, but Tommy was focused on Woggy. Perched on a bottle of water, he was trying his best to get the cap off. He scrambled to one side then the other, back and forth. The pixie's long fingers dug into the grooves but he wasn't quite strong enough to make it move.

"Thirsty?" Tommy asked, signing as he asked the question aloud.

Woggy stopped and licked his lips, then tentatively repeated the sign. Close enough.

"I can't believe how quickly he's picking it up," Ceri said with a smile. She didn't have anything to unpack, so she had been helping him.

"We should be able to really talk to him within a couple of months, I think." Tommy picked up the bottle and nudged Woggy to the side as he opened it. The pixie wrapped his wide mouth around the opening and his tongue flicked down into the water like a frog.

"Gross. Guess that's your water now, buddy."

Thallan's voice echoed up from downstairs and Tommy froze, creeping toward his door. He listened carefully as the elf spoke. "Just keep your pack out of the main house. I don't care where else you go. The grounds are open to you."

"What is it?" Ceri asked, watching him tensely.

"Thallan is here," he replied quietly, pressing his finger to his lips and waving for Ceri to follow.

They slipped out of his room. Peeking over the bannister, he saw the elf standing by the front door facing away from him. Amber had her arms crossed, and her face was carefully blank. She looked like she resented Thallan for some reason. It made him even more curious what Amber had agreed to in order to get them this place. Surely it wasn't anything...shady.

Genevieve hissed Tommy's name, getting his attention. *Thallan?* she mouthed. He nodded, and she scurried over to his other side, crouching next to him. She looked as suspicious as he felt.

"Don't worry, we'll stay out of your hair," Amber said, her tone was half annoyance, half impatience. "Do you have any information on the Trials at all?"

"I'll look through the library. I wouldn't hold your breath though. I'm an elf, not a werewolf." He handed Amber something. "Here are the spare keys. If you actually need something, come yourself. I don't want the kid or the girl with the pink hair bothering me."

Amber rolled her eyes. "Don't worry, they don't want to talk to you either."

She was right about that. He had no intention of going in that house, or talking to that elf ever again if he could help it. *This* house, however, was awesome. There was so much room, and it felt like it wanted them there. The whole place smelled like magic, but it wasn't as weird as the stuff at The Market.

Thallan nodded and left the house. Amber's eyes immediately flicked up to their location. Panic clenched in Tommy's gut, but she just smirked at them. "Didn't anyone ever teach you not to eavesdrop?"

"We're werewolves, it's basically impossible not to hear," Genevieve said, unashamed at being caught.

The girls were starting to feel like the big sisters he'd never had. He smiled at Amber, and the irrational fear faded away.

"Get down here and help me cook dinner," Amber said, turning and walking toward the kitchen.

"Ugh, I hate cooking," Genevieve muttered.

"I don't mind," he said with a grin. Some of his best memories had been of cooking with his mother.

"Great, then I'm going to keep unpacking," she said, jumping up and heading back into her room.

He hurried down the staircase and caught up to Amber, who was putting away all the food she had bought. The kitchen was pretty big, probably built to cook for fancy parties at the now empty mansion.

"I just remembered I left something in the car, I'll be right back," Ceri said, leaving him and Amber alone in the kitchen.

His alpha shifted uncomfortably, then cleared her throat. "Sorry about...earlier. I'm not great at this, and I didn't...I just want everyone safe."

He shoved his hands in his pockets. If he was being honest, it had really freaked him out, but he could tell she was being sincere. "It's okay."

Amber's posture relaxed a little, and she gave him a half-hearted smile. "Great."

"Do you mind if I cook a family recipe? Butter chicken curry. My mom taught me when I was a kid."

Amber looked surprised, but she nodded. "Yeah, go ahead. Do we have everything for it?"

"Yeah, I...uh...dug through the spice cabinet and pantry while you were gone getting groceries. And you have chicken, and rice." He wiped sweaty palms on the legs of his pants. The wolf wanted to impress her, but he just wanted to a chance to cook in a *clean* kitchen again. Without anyone yelling at him to stop stinking up the house.

"Sounds perfect then." Amber smiled sincerely, relief clear on her face. "As you saw, I'm not exactly good at cooking, so anytime you want to take over, feel free."

He stepped into the kitchen and began gathering the ingredients. The knot of worry in his shoulders relaxed, and he forgot about everything with a knife in his hand and the warm scents filling the kitchen.

CHAPTER 20

*A*mber sat up, going from dead asleep to awake instantly. Her nose twitched as the odd scent that had woken her grew stronger. She slipped out of bed, grabbing the baseball bat she kept nearby, and pushed open her door. She had told Tommy she didn't think Donovan would try to kill them, but she was seriously regretting that statement now.

Her feet pressed into the carpet without making a sound as she crept into the hallway. Carpet gave way to the wooden floor of the living room. Pausing, she drew in a long breath to taste the air. The scent kept changing directions. Whatever it was wasn't moving normally, like it was appearing and disappearing at random.

A chuckle made her skin crawl. She whipped around, swinging the bat, but all it hit was air. Panting, she turned in a circle. She had heard it. It was here somewhere.

"I'm outside," a male voice whispered. A sulfurous scent crept toward her from the door that led out into the garden.

She swallowed and glanced back down the hall. If she was smart, she'd wake the others up. But with the way the mark on her chest was aching, she had a feeling she knew who this was. If the demon was here to collect its mark, she wouldn't put the others at risk. Cursing herself for not asking Thallan how long she had before the demon came for her, she slipped outside, leaving the door cracked open.

Goosebumps rose on her exposed skin, and she shivered at the temperature change. It was cool. Way too cool to be walking about barefoot, in shorts that barely covered her ass, and a threadbare shirt that had seen better days.

The garden was just as well-maintained as the rest of the grounds. So, it was a tangle of overgrown bushes and vines that stretched across the walkways. She followed the scent, which was still moving away from her.

"How far are you going to make me chase you?" she hissed.

"Just far enough to talk privately," the voice replied. "I'd hate for your little pack to think you'd lost it, talking to yourself like this."

She paused, the cold seeping up from the stones into her feet. "What do you mean, talking to myself?"

"No one else can hear me," the voice whispered directly behind her.

She turned and struck out with the bat again. Laughter drifted toward her on the breeze.

"I suppose this is far enough," the voice said. "You're going to freeze to death in that outfit. And what exactly are *troll bangs*, by the way?"

She resisted the urge to glance down at her shirt. Her hand tightened on the wooden bat as the air shifted. A shadowy figure topped with horns formed right in front of her. She couldn't make out a face, or even his height. The thing had no legs, only a torso, a head, and the vague shape of arms. She jabbed it with the bat, but the weapon simply slipped through the apparition.

"That tickles," it said, amusement clear in its voice.

Amber frowned. "Are you a demon?" The shadow moved in a

circle around her. She turned with it, not wanting the thing at her back.

"I am," it finally admitted, "and I was curious what sort of creature Thallan gave his mark to. It's not an easy thing to give away a debt like that." The demon surged closer, forcing her backward into a bush. "I must admit, you are not what I expected." His breath skated across her skin, hot and dry.

She cringed away from the demon's closeness. "What's your name?"

He chuckled. "Just telling you would be no fun," he said in a teasing tone. "Besides, I haven't told anyone my true name in almost fifteen years. Can't have you summoning me to the earthly planes then killing me to get rid of your mark."

"That would work?" she asked, narrowing her eyes at him.

The shadow swayed dramatically. "Already plotting my death? So callous," he said mournfully.

"What do you want from me?" She needed to get this over with. If it wanted something awful, she'd rather know now so she could figure out how to get rid of the mark or kill the demon.

"I'm not sure yet," the demon said, tapping a long finger against its chin. "I'll think of something eventually. Until then, you get to enjoy my occasional company."

"So you're basically going to haunt me?" There was a sinking feeling in the pit of her stomach.

"Haunt you? I prefer to think of myself as your guardian angel," the demon said, practically purring.

"I'm surprised you can even say the word angel without catching on fire," she muttered.

"The whole myth about us not being able to walk into churches *is* a myth. Not based in reality," the demon said with amusement.

Amber snorted and lowered the bat. "Alright, *Angel*. You really don't want anything from me right now?"

"This was more of a meet and greet, but if there's something *you* want, I can help you. For a price, of course," the demon said, drifting closer again.

The heat from his ethereal body took the chill out of her bare skin. "No," she replied quickly. "I don't need anything from you."

"You needed something," the demon said, his finger reaching out to press into the mark. She hissed as magic surged between them and tried to shove his finger away. Her hand swiped uselessly through the smoke. "What did Thallan do for you to get you to agree to take this?" the demon mused, finally removing his finger.

"None of your business."

The demon cackled. "Funny thing to say since I'm the one you owe the debt to," he drifted away. "But that's fine. It doesn't really matter except to satisfy my curiosity."

She stared at the demon for a moment then squared her shoulders and started back toward the house. "If that's all this is, then I'm going back to bed," she said as she brushed past him.

"Is that an invitation?" the demon asked.

Amber stopped and glared at him. "No, absolutely not."

A grin spread across the shadowy face, the only feature she could make out. "So grumpy, perhaps you do need to sleep."

"I thought demons were supposed to be menacing, not just annoying."

The shadowy figure tripled in size and loomed over her, flames pouring from his eyes. Long, black teeth stretched out of its gaping maw. "I can do menacing if you prefer." His voice boomed around them.

She stared back impassively. "So scary."

The demon shrunk back down. "You're no fun at all. You could have at least screamed a little. Flinched, perhaps."

"You'll have to try harder," she said, regretting the words as soon as they left her mouth.

"Challenge accepted," the demon said before disappearing with a pop.

She walked back to the mansion, gripping the bat tightly, and contemplated all of her bad life choices.

CHAPTER 21

AMBER

*A*mber tried not to scowl as Tommy trotted out from behind the house—understandably, he had refused to strip in front of the girls—fully shifted. She and Genevieve had been trying all morning and hadn't been able to.

Tommy sat down, his tongue lolling out of his mouth. If his wolf hadn't weighed two-hundred pounds and been the size of a small pony, he might have looked like a friendly dog.

She flexed her hand and tried to shift, but nothing happened. Now that she wasn't angry, she had no idea how to start it. She dropped her hand and looked back at Genevieve, whose head was bent over a book.

"Do those books say anything about how to shift when you're not about to lose control?" she asked, shoving a strand of hair out of her face. There was a nice breeze blowing through the back-yard where they were training. Sundays had been tentatively declared "pack days," since the books recommended bonding for a new pack.

Genevieve looked up and blinked owlishly. "Yeah, actually," she said, tapping the red-leather bound tome she had last read through. "You have to connect with your wolf."

"What does that even mean?" Amber asked. She hated vague crap like that. There should be an on/off switch or a magic word.

"Maybe try talking to the wolf?" she suggested, twirling a lock of bright pink hair that had escaped from her bun around her finger. She propped her head up on her hand and turned her attention back to the other book Thallan had brought them.

As part of their bargain, Thallan was now her sponsor. Apparently, that included providing training for the budding alpha. Genevieve had volunteered to read through everything, which had been a huge relief for Amber.

Connect with the wolf...what a load of crap. Amber sighed. If Dylan had been here, he would have been dragging her to meditation classes and talking about living in the woods hunting bunnies.

"I'm going for a run," she said. They had run under the full moon once, and it had been exhilarating. Maybe running now would draw the wolf out. It had been quiet ever since she had taken the demon mark. It felt a little like it was giving her the silent treatment to punish her.

Amber jogged past Tommy. He had shifted back and redressed and was now busy teaching the pixie sign language. Since the job hadn't worked out, he was the *de facto* pixie babysitter.

"Woggy, focus," Tommy chastised, but the pixie was busy chasing a bug that had flown too close. It bounded around on shaky legs, hopping and trying to grab its prey.

Amber shook her head, a smile tugging at her lips as she passed into the trees. There wasn't a clear trail through the woods. No one had been out here in years. She pushed herself into a run, weaving around trees and jumping over fallen logs.

Her breath stayed steady and her legs felt like they could go forever. Being a werewolf had changed more than just her instincts. She was stronger, faster, and her senses were heightened. While she was in human form, she couldn't hear or smell as well as she could in wolf form, but it was still ten times as well as she could when she had been fully human.

Some small creature darted across her path, and the wolf stirred for the first time. Acting on instinct, she followed it. A flash of brown fur and a white tail bobbed through the underbrush. The wolf tried to hide its eagerness to hunt but she could feel it.

"Come on, what's your problem?" she muttered, bracing one hand on a large boulder as she leapt over it.

The wolf growled, and she stumbled as the mark ached fiercely. Stopping to lean against a tree, she rubbed the black scar. The wolf had tried to do something to it.

"I had to take it," she said, irritated with the wolf. "I had to protect them."

The wolf huffed, then pressed its claws into her mind. A sharp pain shot through her skull and she grabbed her head. Her fingers lengthened into claws and her muscles twitched as the wolf forced a shift. She ripped her shirt off over her head with a grunt and rolled onto her back to kick off her shoes and shorts.

The shift was faster this time than it had been on the night of the full moon. Fur rolled over her skin as her body reformed and grew. Rolling onto her feet, she shook out her fur and took in the scents around her. The first moment after the shift was always overwhelming. She tried to take a step forward, but her legs wouldn't move. Her muscles ached as the wolf fought her for control.

What are you doing? she demanded of the silent force in her mind. She couldn't help but think of it as a separate person. It didn't seem like it could speak, but it communicated how it felt well enough with feelings and instincts.

With one last trembling push, the wolf ripped away control and ran. It was disorienting to be the passenger in her own body, especially shifted.

The trees flashed by. Anger curled in her gut, but it wasn't her own. The wolf was pissed at her. Her legs flew over the ground. It was so much easier to run in this form. Four legs moved faster than two, and her claws dug into the soft ground, propelling her forward.

Something tickled the edge of her senses. The scent of another werewolf. She slid to a halt, sniffing the air. A breeze ruffled the fur on her face, and the fading scent of the intruder grew stronger.

Nose to the ground, she followed the smell as it grew stronger and stronger. The trail led her to a fence at the edge of the property. It was broken, falling down in places, and didn't have the same feeling of magic that the front gate had. It was unprotected.

The scent wasn't fresh anymore, and Amber had no idea when it was left there. Some parts of this were instinct, but being able to tell how old something was must come from experience. The scent was familiar though. Not the beta, but another werewolf from Donovan's pack that she had been near. They could have followed her to the property the first day she visited Thallan.

She wasn't sure if it was her or the wolf that initiated it, but she tilted her head back and howled. This was *her* home now, and she would not tolerate trespassers.

GENEVIEVE

Genevieve pushed the book away and rubbed her eyes, out of practice with all this reading. Thallan's books were helpful, to an extent, but they didn't have the details about the Trials that Amber needed. She had found some information she doubted Amber would be thrilled to hear.

Honestly, she was starting to wonder if any of this was possible. Maybe they should have just taken Donovan's offer and dealt with a crappy pack. She was used to dealing with crap. It was better than uncertainty.

What made her the most upset was that Steven had the answers they needed, but he wouldn't return her calls after that disastrous attempt to talk to him at his dorm room. She stood, anger pumping through her as she kicked off her shoes and plopped down on the grass. Maybe she could figure out how to shift, since she apparently couldn't do anything else productive.

Connect with your wolf. That was what she had told Amber when she asked what the books had said, and like Amber, she thought it was a load of crap. She could feel something in the back of her mind now, but it wasn't like it had thoughts or feelings. It was just magic and instincts.

Her hand went to the scar on her thigh. She traced the jagged bite mark, remembering the pain and the terror she'd felt. Sometimes it was easy to forget she'd been changed, and then she'd feel the wolf in her head. It was so angry.

A howl erupted from the woods. Genevieve jumped to her feet. The sound cut straight through her, but instead of fear, it gave her a sense of determination. Belonging.

Tommy ran over, holding Woggy close to his chest. "Is that Amber? It...feels like her."

"Yeah, I feel it too," she whispered. "It's like she's claiming something."

They waited as the howl ended. In that place in the back of her mind, where the magic had settled after her change, she could feel Amber coming back to them.

"Should we go help her?" Tommy asked.

"She's coming back. I think we should just wait," she said, shaking her head.

The next few minutes were tense. She breathed a sigh of relief when Amber jogged out of the woods. Her bright red hair hung in tangled waves around her face. Dirt was smudged across her knees.

"Is everything okay? We heard you howl, but it just felt... annoyed? Or maybe territorial is a better word, so we thought we should stay here," she said, hardly taking a breath between words.

"One of Donovan's pack has been here, probably the same day I first visited Thallan." Her eyes still glowed with a hint of red.

"Do you think they'll come back?" Tommy eyed the forest warily.

Amber shrugged. "Maybe, maybe not. I'm going to ask Thallan why the wards aren't active in that area. He has most of this place locked down tight, it's odd that he would have missed a spot."

"Do we need to keep watch tonight?" Tommy asked. "I wouldn't mind."

Amber laughed. "I don't think we need to go that far. Donovan isn't trying to kill us, just make our lives difficult."

"Speaking of difficult," Genevieve said. She hated to bring it up at all, but she might as well get it over with. "I did find some information on the Trials."

"What did you find out?" Amber asked, her expression full of determination.

"The Trials have five parts. You have to pass at least three to become an alpha. The only part I could confirm is some kind of test of control." Genevieve walked back to the table and grabbed the book. She had stuck a leaf in between the pages to mark her place. She flipped to it and pulled the leaf out, tucking it behind her ear. "The Trials are designed to weed out the weak and the unworthy," she began reading. "It will test the potential alpha in every area in which they must excel in order to lead a pack." She lowered the book and looked up at Amber, who was grimacing.

"I guess I need to work on control some more," she said after a long pause. "My wallet is on the counter. Order something in for dinner, I'll eat anything with beef or chicken." Amber turned and walked back toward the woods, her shoulders tight.

"Do you think she can do it?" Tommy whispered.

Genevieve shut the book, but didn't respond. She didn't want to admit out loud that she didn't.

She had to talk to Steven. Amber needed more information if she was going to have any hope of passing the Trials. Tomorrow morning before everyone woke up, she was going to go back to Steven's dorm, and she wasn't leaving until he agreed to talk to her.

CHAPTER 22

AMBER

*A*mber couldn't sleep. Every time the old house creaked she thought the demon had returned to torment her for a second night. She'd given up on lying in bed about an hour ago and had been slumped in the armchair in front of the old-fashioned fireplace since then.

Her fingers idly tapped the bat resting against her knee. *Challenge accepted.* Amber wanted to slap herself. She should have just pretended to be intimidated, but of course, she had gone and taunted a demon instead.

A door creaked open in the hall, causing her heartbeat to kick into overdrive before Genevieve's scent drifted past her. She frowned. Genevieve had been disappearing a lot lately. The paranoid part of her brain wondered if she was meeting with Donovan and spying on the pack. Immediately, she felt guilty for even thinking it, but Genevieve was clearly trying to sneak out unnoticed.

She pulled her legs up into the chair to stay hidden from view and just listened. It didn't appear that Genevieve had noticed her. Her footsteps were almost too light to hear; she was still trying to sneak around. Amber wondered if her senses were stronger than

Genevieve's, or if she was just too focused on listening for movement down the hall to realize that Amber was in the living room.

The front door opened and shut with barely a sound. Amber uncurled from the armchair and crept to the window. The lights on Genevieve's car lit up the driveway. She had parked as far away from the house as possible; Amber could barely hear her car start standing at the window. It wouldn't have woken her if she'd been sleeping.

She ran to the front door and yanked it open, then walked down the driveway as Genevieve's car backed out of its spot. She couldn't see her past the glare of the headlights, but the car stopped abruptly.

The car door opened as Amber approached, and Genevieve climbed out, her face tight with irritation. "You're up early."

"Where are you going? You don't work until nine," she asked.

Genevieve rolled her eyes, but her knuckles were white she was gripping the car door so hard. "You're acting like I'm sneaking out of the house. I'm not sixteen, and you're not my mother. I don't have to fill you in every time I go somewhere."

"Until we know Donovan isn't going to do something else to try to hurt the pack, I do actually need to know," she said, resting her elbow on top of the door. "I'm not going to judge you if it's a booty call or something."

Genevieve shoved her arm off with a scowl. "You can just deal with not knowing."

"Why are you so intent on hiding this?" she snapped, the little patience she had left evaporating. She was tired, irritable, and worried all the time. The last thing she needed was a reason to doubt her own pack. "Or are you meeting with Donovan?"

Genevieve's face twisted in anger. She was close to shifting, Amber could feel it as sure as she could feel it in herself.

"You act like you aren't hiding things too!" Genevieve shouted back, balling her hands into fists as claws began pushing out of her fingertips. "You won't explain how you got Thallan to agree to be your sponsor and you haven't bothered to tell us that you can *feel our emotions*. So don't yell at me about hiding things! I have a right to a private life!" Genevieve's chest heaved with too fast breaths as she seemed to struggle for control.

Amber ground her teeth together. She had done everything she could to block out their emotions, but it had been impossible to do it completely. She hadn't mentioned it because she'd been afraid Tommy would freak out, and she hadn't anticipated how much it would upset Genevieve. "My bargain with Thallan isn't important right now. And I was going to tell you about the emotions thing when I figured it out!"

"You're a hypocrite!" Genevieve bared her teeth as a growl erupted from her throat. "And I would never betray this pack. Everything I'm doing is to help *you*."

Amidst the rage that hit her like a wall, there was also hurt. Embarrassment. Guilt. The emotions amplified what Amber was feeling. She squeezed her eyes shut and dug her claws into her palms to keep from shifting then and there.

She wanted to run away. It had been ridiculous to think she could be their alpha. She had no idea what she was doing, and she had no idea what she was supposed to be to them. Their friend? Mother? Captain?

"I'm not...good at this," she whispered. "I'm terrified the two of you will get hurt because I can't be everywhere. I can't take care of you. That witch attacked Tommy in broad daylight, in public. Donovan's men are stalking us." She forced her eyes open and looked at Genevieve. "I want to trust you, but before two weeks ago, we were strangers."

"We still are," Genevieve said, crossing her arms.

She dragged her hand down her face and took a deep breath. "I'm sorry I didn't tell you and Tommy about the emotions thing. I was worried it would freak him out especially."

Genevieve lifted her chin, but couldn't meet Amber's eyes. "Maybe I should have just told you what I was doing. I wanted to, but I was worried..." she huffed in frustration, rubbing her fingers over her eyes. "I know someone that can help us, help you, with the Trials, but he won't talk to me."

"Why not?" Amber asked, knitting her brows together.

"I kind of...dumped him a while back," Genevieve said, scuffing her shoe against the asphalt. "And then a few days ago kicked open his door and..." she sighed deeply, then continued, "and yelled at him a little."

"Okay, that's...uh..." Amber floundered before squaring her shoulders. "Well, maybe he'll talk to me. Would you mind if I came with you this time?"

"You're really asking?" Genevieve said, finally looking at Amber.

"Yes. If you want me to butt out, I will." She wouldn't like it, but she would deal with it to keep from driving her away.

Genevieve nodded as if that made the decision for her. "Sure, might as well try. He's getting his PhD in Magical Cultures and werewolves are his main focus."

"If you're still up for it, let's go convince him to help," she said confidently.

Genevieve hesitated and Amber could feel a confusing tangle of emotions warring in her, but she nodded, and a small smile crept across her face. "Let's do it."

~

Steven opened the door—and immediately tried to slam it shut when he saw Genevieve. Amber caught it with the flat of her hand and pushed it open. Steven's feet slid back on the concrete dorm-room floor.

"That's not very polite," Amber said, stepping into the room and forcing Steven to scramble backward.

Genevieve followed, trying to suppress a smile. Amber could

be scary as hell when she wanted to be. She probably shouldn't enjoy it so much, but it was fun to watch her intimidate Steven.

"Who the hell are you?" Steven demanded, tucking his trembling hands under his arms.

"Amber," she said, sticking out her hand. Steven stared at it like it might bite him. She left it extended until he gave in and tentatively shook her hand. "I hear you're getting your PhD in Magical Cultural Studies." She put her hands on her hips and looked him up and down like she might try to beat the answers out of him.

Steven looked at Genevieve worriedly, but nodded. "Yeah, why do you care?"

Amber's eyes flashed red. Genevieve had to restrain the urge to submit. The impulse pissed her off a little; she wasn't a wild animal. She wasn't going to grovel at Amber's feet.

"I need information, and apparently you can get it for us," Amber said, looking over at her.

"That's what I was trying to tell you the other day." She crossed her arms. Amber had gotten them in the room, but it was awkward doing this in front of her. "We need your help. We were bitten, unwillingly, on the last full moon."

Steven's eyes went wide. "You're...both of you...oh my god..." he trailed off, staring at her like she might shift at any moment. He shook himself out of it and hurried over to his desk, grabbing his student ID and a couple of books. "I'll help you, on the condition that I get to ask you some questions for my thesis. I'll make sure you're anonymous, but this is exactly the topic I'm researching, and the opportunity to speak to a newly bitten werewolf is... it's...I can't pass it up," he finished, breathless. His eyes darted back and forth between her and Amber.

Amber looked over at her. "I don't mind answering your questions if you help us, but I can't speak for Genevieve."

She nodded. "I'll answer your questions too, but I doubt Tommy will want to."

"There's another?" Steven asked, his excitement ratcheting up another notch.

"Yes, there are three people in my pack, myself included," Amber responded.

"What exactly do you need information on? Werewolf laws? Customs?" Steven asked, hurrying back to his desk to grab a notepad and a pen. He awkwardly laid the books over his arm and the notepad on that, pen poised over the paper to take notes.

"I need to know about the Alpha Trials," Amber said. "I have two weeks left to prepare for them."

Steven's mouth opened, then shut, then opened again before he figured out how to talk. "Two weeks? Why isn't your sponsor helping you?"

"The sponsor is an elf," Genevieve said uncomfortably. "It's a loophole in the laws, but hardly anyone takes advantage of it because there's no one to teach you when you do."

"Wow. Okay," he said, rubbing the hand with the pen over his face. "We have to go to the library. I can get you all the appropriate information there, but it won't be complete. The Trials are shrouded in secrecy, and it's nearly impossible to get an alpha to talk to you about them." He stared at Amber, gnawing on the end of his pen. "Will you answer questions about that after the Trials? If you survive them, of course."

Amber's jaw tightened briefly. "Sure, as long as you make the information readily available to other werewolves in my situation."

Steven nodded hastily. "Definitely, I can totally do that."

"Let's go then, no time to waste," Genevieve said, grabbing Steven by the elbow and dragging him to the door.

"I can't believe you didn't tell me right away," Steven said as they hurried out of the dorm. "I would have helped if I had known it was about *this*."

Genevieve looked at the ground, her irritation making the wolf restless. "I tried."

Steven opened his mouth to argue, but Amber clamped her hand on his shoulder. "Give her a break, Steven," Amber said lightly, though the warning was clear in her voice. Genevieve frowned, she hated that Amber knew she was struggling for control.

Genevieve picked up the pace. Steven had to jog to keep up.

CHAPTER 23

AMBER

*A*mber walked down the narrow aisle between stacks, scanning the rows of books for the first name on her list. Genevieve and Steven were reading the first pile of books and debating everything they found.

It had surprised her how intelligent Genevieve was. Now that she thought about it, her assumption about the other woman was based entirely on her pink hair. It was dumb to assume based on something so superficial, but that was human nature.

GLENN, E., written in swirling gold ink on the spine of a book, caught her eye. She stopped and double checked the name of the book, then grabbed it off the shelf.

Smoke rushed out of the gap and hit her in the face. Stumbling back with a strangled yelp, she hit the bookshelf behind her, rattling the entire thing.

The demon formed above her, cackling loudly. Smoke drifted up from his bright red grin.

"What is wrong with you?" she hissed, glancing down the aisle to make sure no one had heard.

The demon drifted closer, stinking up the air around her face.

"You should have seen your face." His hot breath tickled the skin of her neck. "That was priceless."

She pushed up to her feet and pinned the demon with a glare. "You are a menace."

His grin only grew wider. "Isn't that the purpose of a demon?"

With a huff, she turned and continued down the aisle. There were still three more books to find. The demon followed. "Are you stalking me now?" she asked.

"It's proving very entertaining so far. I see no reason to stop," he said, swooping through the air ahead of her. Every few feet he stuck his head in the books like he was sniffing them or peeking at the pages.

Amber bit the inside of her cheek, torn between trying to get answers and ignoring him. "Is this a normal demon thing? Harassing the people that have your mark?" she asked finally, giving in to the curiosity.

The demon shifted into a tiny red creature with a pointy tail. He was still slightly transparent, like he was made of smoke, and the edges of his form flickered. He flew over and landed on Amber's shoulder. She jerked away and tried to swipe him off, but her hand passed straight through him.

"I don't think there is a normal demon thing," he said, leaning back and settling against her hair. "What a way to stereotype."

Amber turned down the next aisle and spotted the second book immediately. She grabbed it and added it to the stack in the crook of her arm. She would have to ask Thallan about this next time she saw him. If the demon had haunted him like this too, she could absolutely understand why he had isolated himself in that mansion and gotten so grumpy.

"I don't suppose you know anything about the Alpha Trials?" she asked, deciding the demon might as well help if he was going to hang around bothering her.

He bounced off her shoulder and hovered in front of her, little red wings flapping excitedly. "Alpha Trials? Not a thing! I've had a few werewolves indebted to me before, but never an alpha. They're usually smart enough to avoid such things. Or at least too prideful to ask for help."

"Figures." She sighed and checked the name on her list again. The book should be here between Roberts and Roland, but it wasn't. Shrugging, she turned and headed back toward the others. The book must have been checked out already.

"Is that why you took Thallan's debt? Because you have to go through the Trials?"

"Go away, I have to talk to my pack." She tried to shoo him away, but the demon ignored her.

"I'm not going anywhere, this is fascinating. Best time I've had in years," he said, flying ahead of her.

With a sigh, she exited the stacks and headed back to the table. The demon zipped around Genevieve's head leaving a trail of smoke behind him. Neither she nor Steven were reacting, so they really couldn't see him. Amber ground her teeth together and steeled herself to ignore her stalker.

"I could only find two of the books," she said, setting them down between her study partners and handing Gen the slip of paper.

"That's fine for now," Steven said absently, gnawing on the end of his pen. "We can't read them all today anyhow."

"This one is very nerdy," the demon said, crossing his arms and hovering in front of Steven. He turned to Amber, thick framed glasses that matched Steven's sitting on his red face.

Amber had to press her lips together to hold in the sudden urge to laugh. He looked almost...cute. "Which one should I start with?"

Steven looked up, blinking owlishly, and pointed at the top book. "That one discusses werewolf culture fairly extensively. You need to know all of that regardless of the Trials."

"Alright." She grabbed it and sat down next to Genevieve. After nursing school, she hadn't wanted to even look at a book, much less read one for fun. This was giving her flashbacks to late night study sessions. She preferred hands on learning to reading until her eyes got blurry.

"An alpha must never show weakness to their pack," the demon read, settling by her hand. He looked up, adjusting his glasses. "I think you've already failed there."

Amber sighed. She couldn't even give the demon the retort on the tip of her tongue without looking crazy. It was going to be a long day.

CHAPTER 24

"That was not my fault!" Ceri yelled at her aunt.

The woman stood in front of her, face splotchy with rage, arms crossed. "I hired you as a courtesy to your mother, but you have been nothing but trouble! Coming in late, picking fights with customers. With the freaking *Blackwood Coven*."

"She dumped that potion on herself." She curled her hand into a fist. There were dozens of spells she could cast with a simple chant and the flick of her wrist to shut her aunt up, but none of them could fix this. She should have cursed Selena while she could.

"Enough!" her aunt screeched. "You're fired! Just get out!"

She twisted the fingers of her left hand and took a step toward her aunt. "As you have sown, so may you reap." The spell could be both a blessing, or a curse, but they both knew how it would end up. Karma was always fair.

Her aunt's face darkened. "The same to you."

She brushed past the old witch and left, slamming the door shut behind her, hands shaking with impotent rage. If she had fought back, it would look like she had attacked them unprovoked. She had hoped *family* would side with her. But, just like everyone else, her aunt loved power more than anything else. And anyone who wanted power in this city sucked up to the Blackwood Coven.

Her phone rang, the ringtone alerting her that it was her least favorite relative calling: her mother. Word traveled fast.

"Hello," she answered, voice curt.

"Enough is enough," her mother growled into the phone. "You have embarrassed us repeatedly. No matter how many chances I give you, you still manage to screw up. Your father and I are done supporting your immature decisions. Your things will be on the front lawn, and if you don't come get them within an hour, they'll be gone with the trash."

Every word felt like a knife in her gut. Of course her mother wasn't on her side. She never had been. Never would be.

"And you are not welcome in this house, or this coven. I don't want to see you–"

"Don't worry, you won't ever have to see me again." Rather than listen to any more of her mother's hateful ranting, she hung up the phone. She knew this would happen eventually, but for some reason that didn't make it hurt any less. As she walked to her car, it felt like she was floating. Like none of this was really happening. Perhaps it was all a bad dream.

She reached for the car door, but stopped short, alarm cutting through the mental fog. The beat up old car looked normal but she felt something *wrong*.

Crouching down beside it, she whispered a spell of revelation. The car lit up like a beacon. It was wrapped in dozens of curses, all nasty and meant to harm her if she touched it.

AMBER

*A*mber's phone went off, the loud jingle echoing through the library. She grabbed it and silenced it with fumbling fingers as every person in the quiet building turned to glare at her.

"Sorry, sorry," she said as she answered the call. "Ceri, what's up?"

There was silence, then a hiccoughing sound. She shot to her feet and grabbed her keys, immediately sensing something was wrong.

She covered the receiver with one hand. "Gen, I have to go. Steven, can you give her a ride back to the house?"

"What? Where—"

"Thanks," she said, hurrying toward the exit, leaving Genevieve to deal with Steven. Turning her attention back to the call, she asked, "Ceri, where are you?"

"Work, but...fired. Outside," Ceri said through her tears. "So stupid I'm crying, but they cursed my car, and I can't even get what I need to cleanse it. My mom kicked me out. I don't know what to do."

"I'll be there in just a few minutes, okay? Just stay on the line." As soon as Amber got outside, she sprinted for the truck. She knew exactly who had caused all this. Between the Lockhart pack and that stupid coven, there hadn't been a single day without someone being an asshole.

"I'm sorry. Didn't have anyone else to call," Ceri said quietly.

Amber had never heard her sound so defeated. She was usually optimistic. "You can call anytime. And you're staying with us, I won't hear any arguments about it. You already have a room, so it's a no brainer."

"But I can't stay forever—"

"Why not?" Amber demanded. She knew what it was like to have your own mother kick you out. Having the one person that was supposed to love you unconditionally push you away like that was a heartbreak not many people understood. "As far as I'm concerned, you can stay forever. You've gone out of your way to help us, and I'd like to think we're starting to become friends."

Ceri laughed, but there wasn't any real joy in it. "You're basically running a halfway house for misfits now. A wolf pack, with a witch, and a bunch of bitten werewolves."

She grinned, despite the sad truth of it. No one wanted them, but it didn't matter as long as they had each other. "Genevieve says we have to pick a pack name. Maybe we'll call ourselves the Misfit Pack."

That got a real chuckle. "I guess it's better to be a misfit than an evil dick witch."

"Dick witch?" Amber repeated with a laugh as she pulled up behind the cursed car. Ceri was sitting on the sidewalk, head resting on her knees.

"I stand by that insult," Ceri said before hanging up the phone. Standing, she walked over to the truck and climbed inside, wiping tears from her pale cheeks. Her messy blonde hair was even bushier than normal.

"It's a pretty good insult," Amber said reassuringly as she put the truck in reverse.

"What am I supposed to do now?" Ceri asked, staring at her hands.

Amber was quiet for a moment, trying to find the right words. "Tonight? Eat some ice cream. Watch TV. Tomorrow? Find a new job. We can look together."

"You make it sound so easy."

"It's not easy, but it is simple. You don't give up. When my mom kicked me out of the house I had nothing. I left the state, found a job at a mechanic shop, and went to night school, then eventually nursing school. All I could do was take it one day at a time. It sucks, but you will be okay," she said, reaching across the truck to squeeze Ceri's shoulder.

The witch gave her a wobbly smile. "This is probably for the best anyway. I was never going to be who my mother wanted. I'm not sure why I tried for so long."

"Because you love her," Amber said with a shrug. "And you always will."

CHAPTER 25

TOMMY

ommy opened the oven door and pulled out the roast chicken. He could *smell* that it was cooked all the way through now. Every spice he had used, and the rich butter he'd stuffed under the skin, filled his nose.

Woggy poked out of Tommy's shirt, smacking loudly as he reached for the chicken.

"How are you always this hungry?" Tommy asked, picking off a piece of gristle for the pixie. The pot with the potatoes began boiling over, so he quickly handed the morsel to Woggy and hurried to pull off the lid and turn down the heat.

The door opened. He heard Amber's familiar heartbeat first, but the one that followed was too fast-paced.

"Damn, that smells good," Amber said with a smile as he turned around.

"What's wrong?" he asked, taking in Ceri's puffy red eyes.

"I got fired," Ceri said, staring at her feet. "So, of course, my mother kicked me out of the house as well."

His hand tightened around the handle of the lid. "Was it that coven again?"

Ceri straightened her shoulders and brushed her curls away from her face. "Yes."

"We have to do something," he said, throwing his hands in the air. This was how it always went. Bullies got their way, and people like him and Ceri got shit on. It wasn't fair. He was strong now, he should be able to fight back. The need to *do something* was pumping through his entire body. "We can't let them get away with it."

"We are doing something. We're helping Ceri. She's going to stay with us as long as she wants," Amber said, trying to placate him.

It was insulting. He didn't need to be pacified. The muscle in his jaw twitched as he ground his teeth together.

"That's not enough. The coven isn't going to stop just because they ruined her life. Why aren't you standing up for her?" His breath was getting faster, and he could hear his heart thundering in his ears.

Ceri shifted uncomfortably. "Tommy, there's nothing she can do. I didn't—"

"No! That's what everyone says. It's not true. There has to be some way to fix this!" He threw the lid across the kitchen as anger ripped through him. This was wrong. He couldn't allow it.

A growl erupted from his throat and his vision blurred. He didn't realize he was moving until Amber slammed him against the wall.

"Enough!" she shouted, her eyes bleeding red. The authority in her voice shook him back into control. She waited until his breathing slowed, then stepped back.

He stumbled away from her, panting. Keeping his eyes on the floor, he turned and walked back to the kitchen. A soft squeak reminded him that Woggy was still hiding in his shirt. He lifted out the trembling pixie.

"Sorry, buddy," he whispered, setting Woggy on the counter

with shaky hands. He hadn't meant to lose control like that. He could have hurt Woggy, or even Ceri.

The pixie walked over to the chicken and pulled a piece free, but instead of eating it, he lifted it toward Tommy. Juices dripped down his spindly arms as he held the meat aloft.

"He wants to make sure you're okay," Ceri said, startling him. He hadn't realized she had followed him into the kitchen.

"I should be making sure you're okay," Tommy said, taking the proffered piece of chicken and eating it. Woggy looked very pleased and grabbed another piece, eating this one. Apparently food cured everything in a pixie's mind.

"I'll be fine, eventually," Ceri said. It seemed like she was being honest, but he still hated the whole situation.

He grabbed the pot of potatoes and dumped it into the strainer. They were over-cooked. Staring down at the steam rising from the uneven chunks, he felt helpless. He didn't want to feel that way anymore.

"It's almost Halloween," he said, looking up at Ceri.

"Yeah…" she said, dragging out the word curiously.

"Every Halloween the witches do those displays, showing off their power and skills, right?" he asked, his mind whirling with possibilities. "They got you fired. Maybe we can turn it around on them this time."

Ceri's eyes went wide. "That wouldn't be right—"

"Why not? It's just us finally fighting back. They're awful. Everyone should see who they really are."

Amber stood behind Ceri, her arms crossed. She looked angry and worried at the same time. "What exactly are you suggesting?"

"I don't know," he said, mirroring her posture. "Maybe we can sabotage them somehow?"

The door opened, and Genevieve walked in with some nerdy guy following closely behind her. She stopped in her tracks, taking in the tension in the room. "Hey…guys…"

The nerdy guy pulled out a notebook and started writing something down.

Amber cleared her throat. "This is Steven," she said, gesturing at the guy who waved absently. "He's helping out with research for the Trials."

"Why does Ceri look like she's been crying? More importantly, why is there a lid embedded in the wall?" Genevieve asked.

CHAPTER 26

*A*mber groaned, putting her head in her hands. Once Genevieve had been filled in on what had happened, it had turned into a revenge brainstorming session. Ceri was perking up, but every new idea had made the knot of worry in Amber's stomach grow a little tighter. She wanted to help, but with the Trials so close, it felt risky.

"Well?" Genevieve asked, annoyed.

She looked up and realized they were all looking at her waiting on an answer. Steven was surreptitiously taking notes. She wanted to smack the pen out of his hand and kick him out, but they did still need his help.

"I want to help, I do, but maybe we should wait." As she spoke, Genevieve's face darkened in anger. She could feel the disappointment from each of her pack members. Only Ceri looked somewhat content with her answer, but Amber suspected she was disappointed in her too.

"Whatever," Genevieve said, turning away. "Dinner smells great, Tommy. Is it done?"

Amber felt them closing off. Her wolf whined, equally frustrated with her. It wanted to fight. It didn't understand what was at stake, though. Clenching her teeth tightly together to keep from yelling at her pack, she slipped out the back door and left them to eat.

"That could have gone better," the demon said as he formed in front of her. His smoky body bobbed in the wind.

"Shut up," she muttered, walking faster. They could probably still hear her this close to the house. The last thing she needed was them thinking she was an asshole *and* crazy.

"I'm surprised," the demon sighed. "I thought you were more of a go-getter than this."

"You don't get an opinion. You're not even really here," she said, swiping her hand through the demon's body.

He gasped, pretending offense. "So callous! I 'm basically your only real friend right now."

"You're a parasite."

"I thought we'd established I was your guardian angel," he said swooping around in front of her. "And as your guardian angel, I am here to prevent you from making a terrible mistake."

She walked into the garden, feeling less exposed now that she was hidden behind the tall hedges. "What mistake is that?"

"Chickening out."

"I'm not chickening out!" she hissed, trying to keep from shouting. "Just because I'm not running out to pick a fight with some witches doesn't make me a coward. It makes me smart."

"Sure, just keep telling yourself that."

"Someone has to think about the good of the pack! If we get in trouble, we all pay the price. All this will have been for nothing."

The demon twisted into a new form, black wings unfurling behind him and a crooked, fiery halo settling on his head. "Cautious and prudent, the new alpha chose to retreat after an ally of the pack was attacked by witches," he said in a nasally high-pitched voice. "This was a good choice because, gosh-darnit, the odds just weren't in their favor. No one could *blame* her."

She glared at him and bit the inside of her cheek to keep from arguing. What she really needed was for him to go away so she could *think*. If only Dylan were here. He'd have known what to do. Hell, he would have been the alpha, not her. Dylan had been great with people. Everyone loved him. She had just tagged along, happy to bask in his light like everyone else.

"What would he have done?" Angel asked, his voice soft.

Her head snapped up. He couldn't read her mind...could he? "Who?"

"Your brother. He was your twin, right?"

"How the hell do you know about him? Are you reading my mind?" she demanded, advancing on the demon.

He raised his hands in surrender. "Only a little."

"Only a little?!" she shouted as she completely lost her cool. This couldn't be happening. She wanted him out of her mind. Sharing it with the wolf was plenty crowded already. "Stop it right now."

"I can't stop it. Believe me, it would be marvelous if I could, but the mark binds us together. I only get a sense of your strongest thoughts and emotions. Which you have a lot of." He changed back into the first form she'd seen him in as if he were trying to look non-threatening. "Especially when you need help. After all, I am here to serve."

"How do I get rid of the mark?" she asked, putting her hand over it and wishing that was enough to block the unwanted telepathy.

He was silent for a moment. "A time will come when you can repay the favor owed. After that, you can be rid of me."

The mark on her chest ached fiercely for a moment. This favor was going to come back to bite her in the ass, she was sure of it. But she hadn't had another choice. She hadn't had a choice about any of this.

She put her head in her hands and bit the inside of her cheek. She already knew what she needed to do, and she'd known all night. The only thing holding her back was fear. The voice in her head sounded exactly like her mother. Nagging, worrying, and fearful. Maybe she didn't deserve to be an alpha.

"This is going to be a disaster," she said, her voice muffled by her hands.

"I could make sure you succeed," the demon whispered in her ear, his voice velvety smooth.

She lifted her head. "Out of the goodness of your heart?"

He chuckled. "My heart is blackened and shriveled with pure evil, so, no. It would require a small price, just another mark."

"I'll pass," she said drily, trying to ignore how disappointed she was. He was a demon, not her friend.

"You'll pass on what?" Ceri asked, startling Amber.

She turned to the witch. "Sorry, just…talking to myself."

"Oh," Ceri said, looking around skeptically. "It sounded like you were having a whole conversation."

Shit. "Uh, sometimes it's like I can talk to the…wolf," Amber said, scrambling for a coherent excuse.

Ceri nodded, the tension in her shoulders relaxing just a fraction. "Look, I just came out here to apologize. I didn't want them to gang up on you like that. I think you're right, we should wait."

"No. I realized a couple of minutes ago that I was sounding like my mother. She worried over everything to the point that she never did anything. This is risky, but so was trying to fight off that werewolf. So are the Trials. That coven has hurt you and Tommy, and they're not going to stop just because we don't fight back."

The demon floated behind Ceri, settling with his elbow propped up on her shoulder. "She's much too nice to be your friend."

"Are you absolutely sure? Because it's okay if you're not," Ceri said, her brow still pinched with worry.

She laughed. "I don't think I'll ever be sure of anything again. Except for the fact that I'm going to do everything I can to protect my pack and my friends. And I'd like to think we're friends now."

"You were the person I called crying, so yeah, definitely friends." Ceri smiled and held out her hand. "Come on, there *might* still be some food left."

Her stomach rumbled in response. "God, I hope so."

They walked back inside. Genevieve and Tommy were sitting at the table, waiting expectantly. Steven must have left while she was outside having a mini-breakdown. Tommy's shoulders relaxed as soon as he saw them as if he could tell it had all been worked out just from a glance.

"We saved you some," Tommy said, nudging a plate toward her.

"Did y'all come up with a plan while I was out there?" she asked, pulling out a chair.

A blush colored Ceri's cheeks. "We might have."

"Good," Amber said with a grin. "Fill me in while I eat."

CHAPTER 27

AMBER

"*W*hat in the seven realms are you wearing?" the demon asked, drifting in a circle around her.

"I dressed up as Boggy Killspree," Amber explained, adjusting the tusks that now jutted out from her lips. They sparked as the charm settled into place.

She stepped back from the mirror and took in her outfit. Green skin, bright purple mohawk, shredded tank top, leather pants and bracers. It was spot on, and she was completely unrecognizable. "He's a troll. Lead singer of my favorite band."

The demon crossed his arms. "Aren't women supposed to use this holiday as an excuse to dress as slutty as possible?" he asked, sounding put out.

She rolled her eyes. "Don't be a perv."

"Just because I appreciate the confident display of a woman's body does not make me a *perv*," the demon huffed, a plume of smoke blowing from his nostrils.

"Can you even have sex?" She asked, gesturing at his lack of legs.

He chuckled, sending a chill down her spine. "Oh, I definitely can. Come to hell and I'll show you," he purred.

She grimaced. "Let's pretend I never asked that."

Grabbing her wallet, she stuffed it in her back pocket and looked around to make sure she hadn't forgotten anything. With one last admiring glance in the mirror, she went to the kitchen. This whole plan they had was a little insane, but Amber couldn't deny the sense of anticipation. The more they learned about the Trials, the more she doubted she'd survive them. This was something she could do.

She opened the refrigerator and stared at the mostly empty shelves. They went through groceries like they were starving lately. She had thought the increased appetite was only after shifts, but apparently, it was constant.

The demon's head popped out from behind a bottle of beer. She didn't flinch this time.

"I'll get you next time," he muttered, pouring out of the refrigerator. Even though he wasn't solid, she took a step back. She disliked it when he passed through her; it made the mark tingle oddly.

"What do you think?" Genevieve asked.

Amber turned around and found herself at a loss for words. Genevieve wore a bright red, spandex bodysuit. A tail waved behind her, the tip flickering with fake flames. She held a pitchfork in her left hand, and a red mask obscured her features. Her distinctive pink hair was black instead.

"Now *she* has the right idea," the demon said, a red smile appearing on his shadowy face as he circled Genevieve. She was oblivious to his presence.

Amber bit back several retorts, but only because she didn't want the others thinking she was crazier than she was.

"You look… striking," she said with a smile. Genevieve's petite frame was well-suited to the tight fabric. She didn't have an ounce of excess fat on her.

Tommy walked out, but if Amber hadn't been able to smell him she would have thought a stranger had strolled in.

"What the hell are you wearing?" she asked with a laugh as she took in the ridiculous costume. He wore a ratty gray wig topped with a pointy black hat. An old, lacy black dress was draped over his lanky frame.

"You think the witches will like it?" he asked, picking up and twirling in a circle with a smug grin that looked extra creepy behind the disguise. He paused mid-twirl and sniffed, his bulbous, warty nose twitching.

"What's wrong?" she asked.

He walked through the living room and the kitchen, still sniffing the air. "Do you smell that?" he asked, crouching down to peer under the table. "It smells weird, like smoke or sulfur. One second I get a whiff of it, the next it's gone."

She stiffened. "I haven't smelled anything weird."

Angel swooped around her, cackling. "The boy is perceptive."

She ignored the taunt and shouted toward the back of the house, "Ceri, you ready?"

"Almost!" Ceri shouted back. "I'll meet you at the truck!"

CERI

*C*eri adjusted the fur sprouting from her jaw. She'd bought a bottle of Wolf Charm for the Halloween party. No one would be able to recognize her behind this disguise, which was important considering what they had planned.

The fur sticking out of her collar itched. Scratching it absent-mindedly, she reviewed the plan in her head one last time. Amber and Genevieve were going to create a distraction, while Tommy would be her lookout. He'd make sure no one else came in until she was done with the sabotage.

That's where the hard part came in. She had no idea what they were planning for their display. Every coven guarded that knowledge like their life depended on it. No one wanted to risk being copied or shown up. Once she got in the room, she'd have to improvise.

She grabbed her phone and wallet, stuffing them in her pockets, and ran outside. They were all already in the truck. Tommy and Gen scooted over to give her some room on the bench seat, but it was going to be a tight fit. Especially with the pitchfork.

"The devil and a witch, huh?" she commented, smiling at Tommy's ridiculous costume. Snooty witches like the Blackwood coven hated ugly witch costumes. It was perfect.

Amber started the truck and backed out of the driveway. Woggy poked his head out of Tommy's wig, then squeaked in excitement. He scrambled over Gen's shoulder and launched himself at her. She caught him and helped him stand up on her palm.

"He missed you," Tommy said with a grin. "He's been signing for you all day." He leaned over and pointed at her. "Who is this?"

Woggy's long fingers formed a C that he placed over his heart. He held it there for a moment before pointing at Ceri and jumping up and down. The single remaining nub on his back wiggled as though he were trying to fly.

"That's how he says your name. He picked it out yesterday after I taught him how to say love," Tommy said.

She swallowed around the lump in her throat. "Thank you so much for teaching him," she managed, though her voice shook with emotion. She hated the witches all over again, especially Selena Blackwood, the asshole who had ripped off his wings. Tonight, she was going to pay for that. Turns out karma is a witch.

CHAPTER 28

TOMMY

*I*f they hadn't had a mission, Tommy would have been having the time of his life. This was almost better than The Market. The stately homes that filled the subdivision were lit up with magic.

They passed one house that looked like it was on fire, but the flames were cool to the touch. He wasn't sure if it was an illusion or some kind of fake flame. Kids ran in and out, shrieking in excitement.

For such a secretive bunch, he'd always found it odd how witches congregated together in these subdivisions. They must like to keep their friends close, and their enemies closer.

The busy street wound around, then dead-ended in front of the biggest house in the city. He didn't know much about witches, but *everyone* knew the Blackwood name. Blackwood meant power and money. After tonight, they'd know it for a different reason, too.

He'd already liked Ceri, but after the plan she'd come up with, he had a whole new level of respect for the witch. Her revenge was going to be public, and all the blame would be laid at Selena's feet.

"Where's Woggy?" Ceri asked, jogging up beside him.

"Last I saw he was in your hair. Here, let me look."

They stopped, and he dug through the thick, red hair. It was weird to see her without the blonde curls. She looked eerily like Amber in this costume. Woggy stuck his head out of the mass of hair and crawled onto his hand. "Here he is."

The pixie crawled onto Ceri's hand, immediately darting up her arm, trying to get back in her hair.

"Woggy, what is the matter with you," she said grabbing him. "I've never seen him this scared before."

Tommy looked around them. "Maybe he's scared of witches?"

"Oh, of course," she said, clutching the pixie close. He curled up in her palm, shivering. "I shouldn't have brought him here, but I worried about leaving him alone."

"He'll be okay. Just keep him with you and let him hide."

Amber walked over, followed by Gen, who was twirling her pitchfork like a baton.

"Should we go ahead and split up?" Amber asked. Despite the punk rock costume, she was still unmistakably herself. He was a little worried anyone that had met her would immediately recognize her.

"Yep, let's do it," Ceri said, adjusting her costume.

"Stay safe, okay?" Amber looked like she was barely resisting the urge to drag them all out of here. She was more mother hen than werewolf.

"We'll be fine. I won't let anything happen to Tommy, I promise," Ceri said, putting her hands on Amber's shoulders.

Amber nodded and grabbed Gen, walking toward the front of the big house. "You're going to hit someone with that thing."

"I haven't hit anyone yet!" Genevieve protested.

Ceri shook her head as they walked away. "She's going to have a nervous breakdown by the time we're done."

He laughed. "If she was going to have a nervous breakdown, she'd have already had it."

Ceri laughed at that and hooked her arm in his. They headed away from the crowd while doing their best to look nonchalant. His heart was beating a mile a minute but no one could tell underneath his costume.

It was hot and itchy, but the suffering was worth the offended looks on the faces of random witches. Some people didn't know how to take a joke.

They stopped at a hedge, and after a quick look around, jumped over it. Stooping down low, they ran behind the house. He gave Ceri a boost over a fence, then jumped over it himself. He didn't even have to use a hand. A *very* few things about being a werewolf were kind of awesome.

Three houses down was their target. It was quiet back there. The line of houses muffled the sounds of the crowd. Ceri held her finger to her lips to remind him not to speak and jogged ahead of him.

A few feet away from the property line, she stopped them. He looked around to make sure they were still alone as she knelt and pulled out a knotty wooden stick. She traced an intricate shape while chanting in a strange language. Magic tickled his nose, and he held back the need to sneeze.

The way she moved when she was casting was elegant. He'd seen a lot of witches do magic, but never like her. They were always so forceful and angry. She didn't try to force the magic; she just let it happen.

There was a light pop, and she stood back up, yanking him over the property line with her. "Sorry, we only had a few seconds," she whispered.

"It's fine. Let's get you inside. It's already a little later than we planned," he said, urging her toward the back door.

"This part is going to be a little harder. The wards on the backdoor are probably really intense," she whispered.

He nodded and stood beside her while she crouched in front

of the door. She ran her hands an inch above the surface from the bottom to the doorknob, then frowned.

"What is it?" he asked.

She cocked her head to the side and repeated the motion, checking it from different angles. Her frown deepened. "There's no wards. How could they possibly leave the back door unwarded? It's so…arrogant."

"I think you just answered your own question," Tommy said as he knelt in front of the door. "But it makes it way easier for us, so I'm not complaining."

He pulled out his small lockpick kit. It wasn't exactly professional grade, but it always got the job done. He used to break into the school so he could shower and sleep in one of the classrooms.

This lock was a little trickier, but after a moment of wriggling, he heard it click. With all his senses focused on detecting any movement inside, he turned the door handle slowly.

The door swung open silently, and Ceri stepped inside. They both held their breath, waiting for a shout of alarm, but there was nothing. He followed her in and shut the door carefully behind him.

Woggy stuck his head out of her hair and squeaked in alarm. Tommy pressed his finger to his lips and signed for the pixie to be quiet. Woggy looked around with wide eyes, then retreated back into Ceri's hair. He knew the pixie had understood him. Hopefully he would listen and stay quiet.

They were in some kind of dining room. The pictures on the walls were of old men and women with stoic faces and dark eyes that seemed to follow them as they moved across the room.

This house was creepy. When they'd moved into Thallan's guest house, the place had seemed warm and welcoming. Coming in here was like walking into a coffin. His skin prickled with goosebumps, and he stayed as close to Ceri as he could.

She'd told him the entrance to the spell room would be obvious. Because it was Halloween, there were also going to be coven members inside. That's where Amber and Genevieve came in. Ceri had given them each a handful of what looked like marbles. Apparently, they blew up. Sort of.

All it took to set one off was a loud noise, then they'd start popping in a chain reaction. They couldn't hurt anything, but they were loud, and they'd rattle everything around them with a shock wave.

As they walked through the house, the dark feeling he'd noticed when they walked in increased. His nose twitched at the overwhelming scents. There was something rotting here.

Most of the coven members were outside, but they were drawing closer to two witches. He tapped Ceri's arm and pointed at the door ahead of them. She nodded and led him out of view of the door. They crouched behind a bookcase, and Ceri pulled out her phone and shot a quick text to Amber.

He heard the warning whistle from Amber and clamped his hands over his ears. One loud boom rattled the windows, followed by another, and another.

Two witches ran out of the work room as the explosions continued. One was Selena. Her long black hair hung down her back, contrasting sharply with her bright green dress. The other witch was dressed in all black, so Selena must be the one presenting tonight.

He counted twelve of them then dropped his hands from his ears. Closing his eyes, he focused on the room behind them instead of the chaos outside. Once he was sure no one had stayed behind, he nodded.

Ceri ran inside. Full of misgivings, he pressed himself against the wall and listened intently for anyone other than Ceri. He really hoped she worked fast.

CHAPTER 29

*T*hey'd left the door standing wide open. *Idiots*, Ceri thought to herself. The coven must really think no one would dare try to break in. Or maybe they thought they were invincible.

The wards on the property line were strong. Most witches wouldn't be able to get past them without their full coven, which would make it obvious.

She stepped into their sacred space and smiled. If only her mother could see her now. She'd be *so proud*. Actually, she'd probably be pissed.

Woggy poked his head out of her hair and tugged on her ear like he wanted to drag her out of the room.

"Sorry, buddy, I'll be quick," she said, hurrying forward.

It was obvious what they were prepping. The ingredients were all laid out, and the spell book was open to the recipe they were using. It was a summoning spell for a flurry of wisps. If successful, they'd bring good luck to everyone who saw them. Supposedly.

Her eyes scanned everything that was laid out. She had to

think fast, but her mind had gone blank. Woggy climbed out of her hair and hopped off her shoulder onto the table.

She tried to grab him, but he darted under her hand and ran for a little pot of fine, white granules. She snatched him up just in time.

"That is not sugar, that's salt," she whispered disapprovingly. It looked exactly like sugar, but it was important to make sure you were using the right one. If you combined sugar with...she paused. "Oh my gosh, you're a genius."

She stuffed the pixie back in her hair and searched the room frantically. Over by the door was a spice cabinet. Sugar was used in spells often, as were other common spices.

She grabbed the jar of sugar and the little bowl of salt, searching for a place to dump the salt. There was a large furnace in the corner of the room. She yanked the door open and tossed the salt inside.

Replacing the bowl in its exact spot, she refilled it with sugar. Her hands shook as she poured, and a little sugar spilled next to the bowl. She grabbed Woggy out of her hair and held him above the spill like a vacuum. His tongue flicked out, cleaning up every grain.

"Good boy," she said, putting him back on her shoulder. He curled into her hair, smacking his lips in satisfaction.

She turned to leave but hesitated, her hand hovering over the spellbook. She could take it. Leave them crippled.

Shaking her head, she pulled her hand away. They'd come after her if she did that. There'd be no stopping them. Even without that, they'd be impossible to take on alone.

"Ceri!" Tommy hissed, appearing in the doorway. "Run!"

She ran back to the cabinet, shoved the jar inside, smacked the door shut, and then ran toward Tommy.

They sprinted out of the room and back around the corner. He clamped his hand over her mouth to muffle the sounds of her breathing, and they held perfectly still as Selena and the other witch hurried back into the spell room.

"I can't believe Erica didn't notice what was happening. They better find whoever caused those explosions," Selena said angrily.

Ceri shut her eyes and tried to slow her breathing. They hadn't caught Amber and Genevieve. Now they had to hope they could get our unnoticed as well.

Tommy pulled her to her feet and they crept toward the back door. Halfway there, he froze. Looking around frantically, he finally settled on a door next to them. He opened it and shoved her inside.

He pushed the door almost closed behind them and held his finger to his mouth to keep her quiet. She pressed her back against the wall and tried to breathe silently. Footsteps sounded in the hall a moment later.

"Where is Erica?" a woman asked harshly, pausing in front of the room.

Ceri looked at Tommy with wide eyes. If they came in this room, they were screwed. She looked around for a way out, but there weren't any windows or another door. They were trapped.

"I'm not sure, High Priestess, but I'll send her to you as soon as I find her," someone replied nervously.

"No, send her to the basement. If I see her now, she might not survive the encounter. We've been *humiliated*," the High Priestess said, taking a deep breath.

The door handle turned slightly, and Ceri tensed, her mind running through every defensive spell she knew. They'd have to blast their way out and hope they could run fast enough to get away.

"Madame," Selena said, interrupting the other two women's conversation. "We're about to begin."

The door handle turned back. "I'll join you then. We can't afford another mishap on a night like this."

Their footsteps led away, and Ceri slumped against Tommy in relief. He listened intently then nodded. They opened the door carefully and walked as quickly as they could toward the back door.

CHAPTER 30

GENEVIEVE

*G*enevieve took a few steps back as Selena climbed up onto the stage. Amber was on the other side of the yard, standing back in the crowd as well. They weren't sure exactly what Ceri had done to sabotage the coven's display, and she didn't want to be too close. Just in case. Ceri had promised she wasn't going to let any innocent bystanders get hurt, but accidents happened.

The witch lifted her hands, quieting the crowd. The conversations dropped off as everyone looked at her with a sense of anticipation. She'd gone all out with her outfit, wearing a bright green gown with an old-fashioned witch's hat perched on her head. Selena was the picture of elegance.

"On behalf of the Blackwood Coven, thank you for your interest tonight. In honor of this hallowed eve, we will display for you creativity, innovation, and power. The Blackwood Coven has long stood as a pillar of the community. We are ever ready to serve..."

Selena kept talking, but Genevieve tuned her out. This girl liked the sound of her own voice a little too much.

The girls in front of her were whispering about a spot where magic didn't work showing up right outside the city like it was a sign of the coming apocalypse. She leaned in, trying to hear the details. With all the upheaval, she hadn't exactly been paying attention to the news.

Trying to slip around the person in front of her to better eavesdrop, her tail hit someone in what felt like their nose. She turned to apologize and ended up face to face with a tall, hot guy dressed up as...well, she had no idea. He was just shirtless with pants that hung low on his hips.

"Hi," she whispered with a devilish wink.

He grinned at her and leaned in. "Hi."

"What are you tonight? Besides hot," she asked, letting the tip of her tail trace a line down his abs.

"Lust," he said, returning her wink. "One of the seven deadly sins. Fits perfectly with the devil, since you look pretty tempting yourself."

"Oh, you have no idea—"

A brilliant light flared behind them. She whipped around to face the stage. Selena was chanting, one hand held above a cauldron while she added ingredients with the other. Two more witches stood on either side of her, hands lifted. Their voices joined the chant.

"Tonight, we will summon an angel that will bless this night and this gathering." The crowd gasped as if on cue. Angels mingled with humans on occasion. They mostly hated any creature with magic, though no one knew why. To say that summoning an angel would be an impressive feat was a huge understatement. This would draw national attention.

Genevieve grinned. Since it was about to fail in a big way, it would get even more attention.

Selena traced a symbol into the air with deft strokes. She picked up a small bowl and poured the contents into the cauldron as she began to chant, "Voco Ishim—"

A loud pop cut her off. The cauldron began to spark and shake. Based on how tightly her jaw was clenched, it wasn't supposed to do that.

Genevieve took a step back and bumped into the hot guy. He assumed she was trying to grind on him and started dancing. She went with it while looking through the crowd for Amber.

Selena stuck her finger in the bowl she held and tasted the remnants. Her eyes went wide and she looked back at the coven leader.

The cauldron shook harder and then it...burped. Green fog erupted from the surface and drifted toward the crowd. Screams began as it engulfed the people closest. Genevieve gagged as her sensitive nose picked up on the smell.

The people at the front began trying to run. Selena shouted something over the cacophony, trying to calm them. The cauldron rattled once more, then exploded, sending green slime in every direction. Her perfect dress and sleek hair were coated in the foul substance.

"What the fuck," hot guy said, horrified.

"I thought this coven was supposed to be good," she said, shoving him backward. She forgot her strength and sent him flying into the person behind him. "Oops."

He glared at her. "What the hell are you?"

"Umm, I...lift weights," she said with a shrug before darting into the crowd, trying to find Amber. It was definitely time to go.

She glanced back over her shoulder in time to see the coven leader backhand Selena across the face hard enough to knock her on her ass. Ouch.

There was a loud crack, and the cauldron caught fire. The awful smell only grew worse, and the flames spread from the cauldron to the porch.

Amber grabbed her arm and yanked her in a different direction. "Ceri said they're running back to the truck."

Genevieve followed Amber, looking back one last time. The

whole coven was scrambling to put out the fire. A few of them stopped, gagging in the bushes due to the smell. Whatever Ceri had done worked even better than they'd planned. Selena looked like an idiot.

CHAPTER 31

TOMMY

They'd done it. He'd wanted to try, but actually pulling it off surprised the hell out of him. When the coven leader had almost walked into the room they were hiding in, his entire life had flashed before his eyes.

Genevieve stood on the couch reenacting the final display with dramatic flair. "I have been sabotaged! My perfect life is *ruined!*" she shrieked, flailing around before falling off the couch.

Amber was laughing with them. Actually laughing. He hadn't realized she knew how.

"Tommy! You were genius!" Ceri exclaimed, wrapping him in a hug.

He laughed and picked her up, twirling her around. "Me? You were the genius! You and Woggy made Selena look like a complete idiot! And in such a simple way."

Woggy was laying on a chair stuffed full with all the chicken he'd been able to eat. His little gray tummy was distended with food. He looked smug about it.

"It's going to look like an accident, too," Genevieve said, climbing back up on the couch. "The more Selena tries to claim sabotage, the more desperate she'll look."

Shaking his head with a laugh, he walked into the kitchen. He shut the timer off with three seconds left and opened the oven. The sweet smell of apple pie filled the kitchen. The filling was bubbling through the criss-cross of crust he'd laid over the top.

"Oh my god, is that apple pie?" Genevieve exclaimed from the living room. There was a crash and Amber's exasperated warning to be careful.

He pulled the pie out of the oven and set it on the stove. It was perfect.

Amber joined him in the kitchen and pulled out some plates and silverware. "You did great today," she said as she set them next to the pie on the counter.

"Thanks," he replied with a grin.

She shifted uncomfortably. "I'm glad you decided to stay. It couldn't have been an easy decision."

He scratched the back of his neck, feeling awkward. They hadn't ever talked about it, even though he knew that she knew. "I'm glad you didn't sell us out to Donovan."

Opening the drawer to his left he pulled out Amber's old pie server. It was silicone, and the handle had fallen off. Cooking definitely wasn't her priority.

"Maybe it would have been better to join his pack, though," she said, looking unexpectedly vulnerable. She crossed her arms and leaned against the counter.

"Donovan would never have helped Ceri. He probably would have had us as the pack slaves or some crap like that. You made the only choice you could." He began cutting the pie, remembering the look on his stepmother's face when she used to yell at him to wash the dishes or clean up her vomit. "You care, you know? That's all that matters."

Genevieve burst into the kitchen, and Amber moved away, letting her and Ceri crowd around him.

Genevieve held up a plate and looked at him with pleading eyes. "It smells so good."

He laughed and scooped a big piece onto her plate. "How much do you want, Ceri?"

"Same," she said with a smile, holding up her own plate.

Amber slipped out of the back door. He watched her go, torn between following her and staying with the rest of the pack. But he knew she wouldn't relax if he did. She put up a front none of them could crack. With a sigh, he turned back to the others, resigned to letting her stew in all her worries.

AMBER

*A*mber stood in the garden, head tilted back, eyes on the stars. The moon hung in her periphery. No matter where she looked, it was always there. Taunting her. It grew larger every day, dragging her like the tides toward the thing she feared most. Failure.

"Tomorrow is the full moon," Angel said, twisting into a smoky imitation of the moon.

"I don't want you bugging me during the Trials. It's too important, okay?" she said, putting her hands on her hips.

He changed forms again, appearing as her demonic twin this time. "I could help you instead."

"No."

"You're very bossy," he said with a pout.

"Stop looking like me, it's creepy," she said, turning away.

"I could make sure you pass the Trials. You made one deal to gain your sponsor, I'm surprised you won't consider another," he said swooping around to hover in front of her again.

She looked down at her hands. A small, bitter part of her wished she'd just run when she'd seen that wolf attacking people. This wasn't what she wanted, but it was her life now.

"Ohhhh," Angel said, drifting backward. "I get it."

"Get what?" she asked.

"You actually want to prove yourself," he said propping his head up on his chin.

She rolled her eyes. "So what if I do?"

"It's fine, I suppose," he said with a shrug. "If you can manage it."

"You're real encouraging," she muttered.

"I'm a realist."

She heard the footsteps first, followed by the cloying smell of cigarettes. Angel went quiet, then waved goodbye and vanished.

Thallan rounded the corner, pausing when he saw her.

She nodded in greeting. "The garden is nice at night."

"Yes, though I'm surprised to see you out here with the noise coming from the house," he said as he walked up behind her. "You don't seem like you are in as *festive* a mood as the others."

He plucked a rose from the bush, knocking a petal off with the rough motion. Holding it close to his nose, he took a deep breath, his face softening as he smelled it.

The tense line of her shoulders grew tighter. She wasn't in the mood to deal with him right now. "I guess I'm just a party pooper. Kinda like you. Maybe it's a side effect of the demon mark."

"More likely a side effect of your desperation. It's hard to be carefree when you have to be realistic about the future," he said, motioning toward the house. Laughter drifted from an open window but was carried away by the breeze.

She pressed her thumb into the mark. "Did the demon ever... talk to you?"

"When it gave me the mark, yes. Why do you ask?" Thallan narrowed his eyes and took a drag from his cigarette.

"It never visited you after that?"

He tilted his head, looking at her curiously. "No, never." Silence hung between them for a moment, then he said, "Don't let it talk you into another deal. It will try, and you will not come out on top in a negotiation with a demon."

She shook her head. "I know. He hasn't tried, not seriously at least."

"He?" Thallan asked, taking another drag on his cigarette. The red glow of the ember reflected in his eyes, giving him a menacing look.

"The demon, well, I call him Angel. It's kind of a joke, but whatever," she waved away the over-explanation.

Thallan's hand curled into a fist, crushing the rose. "*It* is not a man. Or an angel. *It* is a demon, and it hates you. It wants to harm you." He got in her face, teeth bared and the vein in his temple throbbing in rage.

She put her hand on his chest and pushed him back firmly. "I don't need to be lectured about what he is or isn't."

"Apparently you do," Thallan sneered. "Have you already let it seduce you? Did you know they crave children just as much as the angels? I'm sure your child would be quite the anomaly, a demon wolf."

"I have enough to worry about without you accusing me of screwing a demon. Get the hell away from me." She turned to walk away, but Thallan grabbed her elbow. His fingers bit into her skin hard enough to bruise.

"I am going to kill it one day. Never forget that."

She believed him. His eyes shone with madness, and hate. He dropped her arm and walked slowly away. The rose lay on the ground where he had stood, its petals bruised and bent.

She knelt and picked it up. A sweet, bright scent filled her nose. It reminded her of home and her mother's rosebushes. She turned and headed back toward the house, her mind full of past failures and the challenges that grew closer every day.

CHAPTER 32

*G*enevieve hissed as the piping hot coffee splashed out of her mug and stung her hand. They'd stayed up pretty late, and now she was running so late for work. Granted, she was running late most mornings, but since she intended to ask to leave early today, she figured she should at least *try* to show up on time.

Amber walked into the kitchen in her workout clothes. "Someone just drove up to the house."

"Just now?" She'd been in such a rush she hadn't even noticed.

There was a single hard knock on the door. Amber held a hand up, motioning for her to stay back. She ignored the command and followed instead. Neither she, nor the wolf, was willing to let Amber face the potential threat alone. Besides, it was no fun to hang back.

Amber checked the peephole then stepped back, frowning. "It's some werewolf in a suit."

"It could be a representative from the regional council," Genevieve said, eyes going wide. "They have to talk to you ahead of the Trials."

"She is correct," the man shouted through the door. "Also, I can hear you, since I *am* a werewolf."

A blush colored Amber's cheeks and she yanked the door open.

The representative nodded in greeting, clearly amused. He wore a suit, but it was clear that it wasn't his normal attire. It was freshly pressed, and Genevieve could smell the chemicals from the dry cleaner from where she stood. His dark brown hair was loosely tousled, and his eyes were so blue she wondered if he wore colored contact lenses.

"Sorry about that," Amber cleared her throat and stepped back to let him inside. "So, you're the rep?"

"Shane Weston," he said, extending his hand. "Can I assume you are Amber Hale?"

Amber nodded and shook his hand. "I am."

"And you are?" he asked, turning to her.

"Genevieve Bissett," she said, shaking his hand. This guy was smoking hot, and judging by the way he was looking at Amber, he had a thing for redheads.

"Your little pack has been hot gossip for the past couple of weeks," Shane said with a grin.

Amber looked surprised. "I didn't realize anyone knew we existed. Other than Lockhart, at least."

Shane chuckled. "You'll find that we're a very insular community, despite our separate packs. Gossip travels faster in the were community than at an all-girls high school."

"Greaaaat," Amber said, drawing out the word. Despite her tone, a smile played at her lips. It was almost...flirtatious. Now *that* was interesting.

"Perhaps sometime we can get together and I can fill you in on what everyone is saying about you. However," his demeanor changed to all business, "I am here to deliver a message from Alpha Clark Jameson, who will be presiding over the Trials on the next full moon. Two hours before sunset, myself and the betas of the other packs on the council will arrive to escort you to the Trials. Your pack, including your sponsor, must attend as well. If any one of them is not there, you will automatically fail."

Amber nodded her head in acknowledgment. "We'll be ready."

He hesitated for a moment then added, "Be careful to not let anything take you by surprise between now and then. Some of the gossip has been a little...heated."

"I hadn't realized how much werewolves resented bitten weres until I became one," Genevieve said, crossing her arms. This guy didn't seem like the bigoted type, but people could always disappoint you.

Shane managed to pull his eyes away from Amber to acknowledge her for a moment. "Not everyone shares that view, but I won't lie, most do."

"Is there a chance for me to pass the Trials, or will the powers that be not allow it?" Amber asked bluntly.

The smile returned to Shane's face. "You have the same chance as every other alpha that has gone through them. A born wolf doesn't have any advantage, other than an experienced sponsor perhaps."

"I don't suppose you can tell us what the Trials will entail?" Genevieve asked.

He shook his head. "I can't help or hinder you in any way. As Jameson's beta, I have to be completely neutral."

It sounded like he was telling the truth, but it was still total crap. Whoever made those rules wanted to maintain the status quo. It was ten times harder for a bitten wolf, despite Shane's claim that the Trials didn't give preference to anyone.

Amber pursed her lips and nodded. "Alright. Is there anything else you *can* tell us?"

"Trust yourself, and trust your pack. You'll need them." He patted Amber on the shoulder, his hand lingering a touch too long. *Definitely* flirting at this point.

Genevieve smiled to herself. Amber looked so awkward, like she wanted to flirt back but didn't know how.

"I guess we'll see you again soon," Amber said.

He nodded at the two of them. "Until then."

Amber shut the door behind him and Genevieve grinned at her. "He was *totally* into you."

"He can still hear you," Amber hissed, the blush returning to her cheeks. "And no he was not."

"Yes to both actually," Shane shouted from the driveway. They wouldn't have been able to hear him without the enhanced senses. Being a werewolf had *some* pros at least.

Amber stiffened, glaring at Genevieve.

She reached around Amber and pulled the door open. "I have to go to work."

"I'm going to murder you," Amber grumbled.

Shane's car started and he backed out of his spot, heading down the driveway.

"You have to wait until after the Trials," Genevieve said with a wink. "You should skip murdering me and just get his number."

She pulled the door shut before Amber could argue further and hurried to her car. Everything had been tragic and miserable since they were changed. It was nice to poke fun at Amber like they were still just *people*.

The warning Shane had given them made the feeling a little bittersweet. She didn't like the sound of being taken by surprise. Especially not with everything that had happened with the coven and with Donovan Lockhart.

CHAPTER 33

AMBER

*P*anting, Amber braced her hands on her knees and tried to catch her breath. She'd run flat out for two miles, but the wolf still didn't want to cooperate.

"How am I supposed to train if you keep hiding?" she asked the wolf out loud. There was no one around to hear and think she was crazy. Shockingly, the wolf did not reply. Sometimes the wolf seemed downright moody, which was odd for something that only existed in her head. It was annoying, too.

Huffing in annoyance, she jogged toward the house. If she couldn't shift, then all that was left to do was read.

Even though it was cool outside, stepping into the air conditioning was a relief. She opened the fridge and stood there, enjoying the cold air on her sweaty skin for a moment. Grabbing a bottle of water, she twisted off the cap and kicked the refrigerator door shut behind her.

Genevieve had left colorful notes sticking out of the books she was supposed to read. She eyed them as she quenched her thirst, not looking forward to an afternoon of study. Picking the thickest one up, she tested the weight in her hand. It must have been five pounds. With a sigh, she resigned herself to getting the worst one over with first. *Honoring the Wolf* sounded about as dry as it got.

A squeak from upstairs, barely loud enough to hear, made her pause. She held her breath as her senses rushed to high alert. A footstep. A heartbeat. There was someone, maybe two people, in the house.

Taking a slow step back, she glanced out of the kitchen window. The driveway was empty. Whoever was in the house had taken a different route.

Glass shattered as a canister was thrown through the living room window. Amber ran toward the back door, but a tall, muscled man wearing a balaclava that hid his features blocked her exit. She threw the book at him as hard as she could. It caught him square in the face as she rushed him and drove her shoulder into his diaphragm. The blow lifted him off his feet and they crashed through the door together.

The gas from the canister burned her nose and made her eyes water, but there was no time to hesitate. She slammed her elbow down on his face twice. Something cracked and he went still beneath her.

When in doubt, just pound their freaking face in, Dylan's voice echoed in her mind. She gritted her teeth, shoving away the memories. This wasn't the time.

Confusion filtered through the adrenaline as she looked around herself. They weren't outside. The living room was still behind her but...she was upstairs now. It smelled like Tommy's room. What the hell was going on?

"Where is she?" someone shouted downstairs.

"I hear her upstairs!" a gruff voice replied.

She shoved herself off the unconscious man and ran toward the door. The house was warded, but she'd never seen wards that could transport you around. She wasn't sure it was all that helpful, either.

A witch wearing a mask appeared at the top of the stairs. He lifted his hands and gestured as he began a chant. She turned and ran back to the room she'd come from when there was a loud thwack behind her.

Looking over her shoulder she saw the witch laying on the ground and the closet door slowly shutting itself.

"What the actual fuck," she muttered as she jumped into the room next to her. Everything blurred for a split second and she found herself back downstairs in the kitchen.

She dropped down behind the island, trying to catch her breath. Two of the attackers were headed away from her, but one of them was coming straight toward her. She sniffed the air and the scent of a werewolf filled her nose. It was familiar.

The steps grew closer. The other werewolf paused, inhaling deeply. "I can smell you," he whispered, as though he didn't want to draw the attention of his comrades. "Come on, Amber, don't you want to meet your maker?"

Her lip curled into a silent snarl. It was *him*. She could feel it. Something stretched between them, a strange bond that tugged at her. He had no power over her, but the connection was undeniable. She watched his reflection in the stainless steel refrigerator.

"You're an alpha now. I thought it'd be you after you jumped in front of the girl and tried to fight me off." He was full of nervous energy, bouncing on the balls of his feet as he picked at the seam of his pants. "Donovan knew I could pick the right three. He had no idea I could make such a strong wolf ,though. I *impressed* him."

A mix of joy, pride, and hate rushed through the connection. She wanted to recoil from his emotions, but she couldn't. She was trapped with them. Her lip curled back in a silent growl. The wolf was angry for different reasons, but they both wanted to rip him apart.

There was a scream upstairs, and she took advantage of it to dart out from behind the island and lunge at him. He didn't even try to block it or dodge the attack. Her fist hit his jaw.

Blood sprayed from his mouth as she knocked his tooth across the room. He turned his bloodied, yellow smile on her. "*So strong.*"

The kick came out of nowhere, catching her in the gut and driving all the air from her lungs. She growled at him and ran in swinging. This time he dodged, moving around each strike like she was moving in slow motion. He cackled as they danced around the room.

"Quit playing with her and grab her!" a woman shouted angrily from behind them. She tried to step into the room, but vanished as soon as her foot hit the floor.

The werewolf growled in irritation and lunged forward, wrapping her in a bear hug. She threw an elbow as best she could but he barely grunted. His arms tightened around her until she couldn't breathe.

Spots danced in her vision. There was no way she was going to die like this, though. She shifted into her wolf form in his arms and twisted her head around. Her long canines sunk into the side of his face before he shoved her away.

"You *bitch*," he growled, drool and blood dripping from his chin. Black fur rolled over his body, and he lunged at her. He hit her side, his teeth sinking into the thick muscles of her shoulder. She yelped and twisted away, snapping at his neck.

Anger and panic shot through the pack bonds. One of them was being attacked right now, and there was nothing she could do about it when she was struggling to stay alive herself.

Rage filled her and her wolf. He charged her again, and she ducked down then lunged upward, catching his throat in her jaws. Her teeth hit bone and cartilage. His flesh tore as he struggled, his claws digging into her legs and torso.

She wrenched her head from side to side, dragging him backward, and clamped down even tighter. Blood seeped into her mouth, coating her tongue. The warm liquid sent a thrill through the wolf, exultant that its enemy bled.

The other wolf's struggles slowed. His body grew weak as the supply of both oxygen and blood were cut off from his brain. She shook him viciously again. He had to be stopped.

Angel appeared in front of her and shouted, "Look out!"

She jumped away as a gunshot cracked through the air, striking the floor where she had been. It left a hole the size of a softball in the wood.

The witch held the gun with shaking hands. "Shift back, now!"

She shifted and stood naked before the witch, covered in the blood of the werewolf that had changed her. He was twitching on the floor, not quite dead.

Reaching behind her, the witch pulled out a pair of silver handcuffs. "Put these on," she said, tossing them at Amber. The handcuffs hit her leg, burning her skin and weakening her whole body for the instant it was touching her.

Someone stepped through the backdoor, but she couldn't see them. The witch shifted the gun toward them, then back to Amber. "Don't come any closer!"

"Don't worry, I don't need to," Thallan said, sounding bored. "Trespassers are not welcome. I'll give you one chance to leave."

The witch sneered at him. "We can take the girl and leave, or we can kill you and still do that."

"You will do neither." A smile spread across Thallan's face, and Amber was reminded of the demon's fiery-red grin.

"This isn't good," Angel said, startling her. "Thallan has a tendency to…overreact when he feels insulted."

She glared at the demon. Had he come to make jokes while she fought for her life? He wasn't even offering to help.

Thallan took a deep breath, then blew. Fire poured from his mouth like a dragon. Amber dove into the next room as bullets hit the wall behind her. She ended up upstairs again, in

Genevieve's room this time. The witch's screams echoed through the house.

The werewolf was down. The witch was as good as dead. But there were still at least two more intruders in the house.

"You need to work on your fighting skills," Angel said, a hint of worry in his voice. "That was almost tragic. You know I lose out on my favor if you die, right?"

"I really don't care," she said angrily. "And fuck off if all you're going to do is mock me. My pack is in danger."

He lifted his hands in surrender and mimed zipping his lips. It was still a dick move, but at least he wasn't talking anymore.

She shifted back and crept toward the door. Her pack was headed toward her. She could feel it. The wolf urged her forward. The fight wasn't over yet; they had to protect the pack.

CHAPTER 34

GENEVIEVE

*G*enevieve dropped the file folder she was holding, scattering papers at her feet. Something was wrong. Very, very badly wrong.

"Karen, I've gotta go! Family emergency!" she shouted as she raced toward the door.

The need to shift and howl pumped through her veins. She barely heard the door slamming shut behind her. Her heels flew off her feet as she ran through the parking lot.

Ten feet from her car, she slid to a halt on the asphalt. A growl escaped from her throat as the smell of another werewolf and nicotine drifted toward her with the shifting wind. A man she didn't recognize stepped out from behind her car.

He took one last puff of his cigarette and flicked it on the ground. He didn't smile, just watched her, his hands hanging loosely by his side.

"You look pretty menacing," she said, sliding one foot back as she prepared for his attack. "I don't suppose you're standing next to my car by mistake?"

"No mistake." He grinned, all teeth. "You look small. This is going to be easier than I thought."

Donovan and his pack had ruined everything. They'd turned them, then tried to control and threaten them at every turn. She hadn't expected them to try and kill her, but maybe she should have.

Genevieve laughed, and it sounded hysterical even to her ears. She was scared, but she was also mad as hell. "For the last three weeks I've had to hold back. You're about to be my anger management therapy."

He rolled his shoulders. "Big words for such a little girl."

She bared her teeth at him. "I'm a woman, not a little girl. Asshole."

He snorted in amusement. "You're a waste of a bite."

The shift rolled over him, and his hands hit the ground as paws. His wolf was as tall as she was, with burning yellow eyes and massive canines. She'd frozen in the last attack, but she wouldn't this time. This time she was going to *fight*.

He dug his claws into the ground, leaping toward her. The shift ripped through her as she jumped, hitting him midair. His teeth dug into her shoulder. She dug her claws into his belly and twisted, snapping at everything she could reach.

She may not know any technical fighting moves, but she knew fury. *Finally*, she didn't have to hold back the violence that had been churning in her since the moment she was changed.

The wolf inside her took over. Warm blood filled her mouth and she tore through the fur and flesh. She knew she was hurt too, but the pain never reached her. He'd come alone, and that had been a mistake. Everyone underestimated her.

Someone was screaming in the distance. The sound was drowned out by their vicious growls. She jerked away and snapped at his face. Her canines drug across his eye.

He howled in pain and stumbled. She took her opportunity and clamped her jaws around his throat. Her teeth sunk in until they hit bone.

Wrenching her head side to side, she shook him like a rag

doll. He fought back weakly, but he was half-dead already. She braced her feet on his body and ripped a chunk of flesh away.

Blood pooled around her feet as she panted. The wolf tilted back its head and howled in victory.

She could barely process what had happened. He'd tried to kill her. She knew she'd been justified, but the sticky warmth coating her paws made her want to vomit.

The jolt of alarm through the pack bond startled her out of her panicking. Amber was still in trouble. She backed away from the dead wolf, then turned and ran.

She didn't bother trying to shift back. There was only one thought in her mind. She had to protect her pack—and her alpha.

CERI

*C*eri slammed through the gate. A chunk of metal flew off and cracked the windshield of her car. Magic sparked at her fingertips. She could see what was happening in the house in her mind. Strange people. Their menace and the threat of strange spells being cast in the house tingled along her skin. They'd jumped in the car as soon as they'd both felt the threat, Tommy through his pack bond, and her through the blessing she had left on the house.

Tommy opened his door and jumped out, shifting as he ran toward the fighting. She could feel the wards rising up all around them. Thallan must be helping. The doors and windows of the mansion were clanking in alarm. Screams were coming from the guest house, but it wasn't Amber. She hoped.

She slammed on the brakes, and the car slid to a halt right in front of the house. Without bothering to shut off the car, she leapt out and ran inside. As she stepped over the threshold, the house took her upstairs, to Amber, just like she wanted.

Amber was stuck between two witches. Her foot was frozen to the floor, and her tail was singed. The witch closest to her was preparing a big spell.

Ceri may not have liked her mother's lessons, but she remembered them. Speaking the spell inside her mind, she snapped her fingers. A small flash of light as loud as a firecracker snapped right next to the face of the witch closest to her. He flinched and faltered in his casting.

Before he had a chance to face her, she thrust both palms out. The wave of energy hit him in the back, launching him toward Amber. Distract, attack, keep them down. She refused to use the spells that would truly harm him, but she could incapacitate him without those.

Amber lunged forward and clamped down on his hand. He screamed in pain, and Ceri turned her attention to the other witch.

"Somnum!" she shouted, gesturing sharply. The blue spell raced through the air and hit the wall instead of the witch as he dodged it.

From his crouched position, he thrust his palm toward her shouting, "Ardeo!"

The spell rebounded on him, engulfing him in green flames. He fell to the ground rolling and shrieked in pain.

She ran forward, leaping over Amber, and dropped to her knees in front of him. "Glacio!" She repeated it over and over as snow poured from her hands. It blanketed the witch, snuffing out the flames.

The spell he had cast burned so hot. He was an idiot to cast something like that in a warded house. The more intense the spell, the more likely it was to rebound.

"Ceri, are you okay?" Amber asked, putting her hand on her shoulder.

She ignored the question as she brushed the melting snow off her attacker. "Was that all of them?"

"Yeah, I–I think so," Amber said, her voice unsteady.

The man twitched, covered in burns. His eyes were glassy. She began a healing chant. Her hands shook as she gathered the magic. Sunlight wound around her fingers like golden threads. She coaxed them down toward the man.

"What is she doing?" Genevieve demanded angrily behind her.

"She's healing him," Amber said. There was a brief scuffle that shook her concentration slightly. "She can't save him, but you're going to let her try! It's the right thing to do."

She wasn't so sure that it was the right thing, but she had to try. She'd never been able to turn away from someone that was hurting. The magic seeped into the man's chest. His eyes widened and he exhaled as the pain faded, but Amber was right, she couldn't save him.

His breaths became gasps. She continued the spell anyway, chanting faster and faster. If all she could do was dim the pain, then she would do that until the end.

The gasps grew farther apart and his unfocused eyes widened. She could take the pain, but not the fear. His hand twitched, brushing against her knee as he fought to hold on. But the injuries were too great. Another breath never came. He was gone.

She fell back onto her butt and put her head between her knees. Amber crouched next to her and rubbed a hand on her back. "It's not your fault, Ceri."

Amber was right. It was these witch's fault for showing up here at all. It was this dead idiot's fault for casting that awful spell. She forced herself to look up. "Are you okay?"

Amber nodded, but there was blood streaked across her face. Her hair was singed, and anger was still burning in her eyes. "Genevieve is hurt a little but nothing that won't heal. Other than that, we're all fine."

"Gen is hurt?" She scrambled to her feet. No wonder she'd been angry. "I'll heal her. I had no idea."

Genevieve was limping toward Thallan, shouting something about *shitty wards* and *idiotic witches*.

"She'll be fine," Amber said, grabbing her before she could run off. "I don't think you could get her to sit still long enough to help her right now." She paused looking back over her shoulder. "Could you sit with Tommy, though? I think he's a bit...shaken."

"Where is he?"

"Out on the front porch."

"Okay, I'll go see him. Let me know if you need anything else," she said.

Amber nodded. "Thanks. And I mean that, thanks for showing up. You didn't have to."

"That's what friends do," she said, plastering a smile on her face.

Ceri hurried downstairs and found Tommy sitting on the front step of the house. Woggy stood on his knee, petting his hair, but Tommy wasn't paying any attention.

Halfway to him, she heard sirens. Her shoulders slumped in relief. They'd gotten here late, but at least the police would be here to clean things up.

CHAPTER 35

AMBER

*T*he flashing lights were beginning to give her a headache. Amber rubbed her fingers against her temples and sighed. The police had been here for over an hour. There'd been a hundred questions about what had happened. Who the attackers were, which she didn't know, and why they'd been targeted.

Worst of all, Peter, who she thought she'd killed, had disappeared. She was hoping the house had eaten him or something, but her gut told her he was still alive.

"Can I have a word?" Detective Sloan asked. He was a slender, unassuming man. His face didn't give away anything, and she wasn't sure if he thought she was lying or just didn't care.

She nodded and followed the officer away from the group. His shoulders grew tense, and his eyes kept darting around like someone might see them talking. He finally stopped once they were far enough away to prevent eavesdropping.

"Okay," he said, tapping his pen against his notepad. "Can you tell me again who you think is responsible for this attack?"

She dragged her hand down her face. This was the third time she'd explained this. "Donovan Lockhart somehow got a werewolf to attack myself, Genevieve, and Tommy. After that, he tried to coerce us to join his pack. I'm not sure why he wanted us. Ever since we turned him down, he's been trying to make our lives hell. I didn't expect him to try to *kill me*, but he did. I have no doubt he sent these people today."

"But you have no idea why he'd want you dead?"

"No. He wants something from me, but I don't know what," she said, crossing her arms.

"We'll look into it. However, we can't arrest anyone just because you're saying they don't like you," Sloan said.

She ground her teeth together. "That's not what I said. He's been threatening me."

The detective took a deep breath, then glanced around to make sure they were alone before continuing. "I'll be completely honest with you because I think you deserve it. Donovan Lockhart is respected and influential. My bosses won't let me talk to him as a suspect without rock solid evidence."

She curled her hand into a fist. "So that's it? You're just giving up?"

"It's not that simple—"

"Sure it is," she snapped. "You're either going to try to find evidence, or you're going to give up and walk away. Those are the only two options. It's pretty fucking black and white."

Genevieve's head popped up at the shouting and she walked toward them.

"This is my job on the line. I will do what I can, but I can't help anyone if I've been fired," he said, his face going red with anger.

"How many people has he done this to?" she demanded as Genevieve stopped beside her, glaring at the officer.

"I don't know," he said, his face going hard.

"Liar," Genevieve said, mirroring Amber's posture. "You're just scared."

"Look, I tried to help and be honest. If you can find any sort of hard evidence, here's my card," he handed it to Amber. "I *am* going to keep investigating. If I find a way to connect this back to Lockhart, I will. Going after him with a weak case will make me look incompetent, and it won't be enough to stop him. That's the truth, whether you want to believe it or not."

"Whatever helps you sleep at night," she said before turning and walking away.

Genevieve lingered for a moment before following her. "So they aren't going to do anything?"

"He's going to investigate, just like he said. And he isn't going to find any evidence, so yeah, they're aren't going to do a thing," she said from behind clenched teeth. The medics were carrying out a stretcher with a dead body.

Bile rose in the back of her throat. This wasn't how she'd wanted things to be. Tommy was barely seventeen; he shouldn't be fighting for his life. This was all wrong. She wanted to scream and rage against the injustice of it all, but it would be pointless.

Instead of protecting her pack, she was just dragging them into more danger. She had barely survived today. Tomorrow, she would probably fail the Trials. She shook her head. She couldn't even think about that. Failure was not an option.

CHAPTER 36

TOMMY

*H*e should have run that first day. It had been insane to stay. They were going to get killed if they didn't get shipped off to the freaking werewolf prison.

"Tommy," Ceri said, placing her hand gently on his shoulder. "Are you hurt?"

He shook his head and dug his fingers into his shirt a little tighter. She was the last person he wanted to talk to, because he knew if he left, he'd miss her most.

His whole body was starting to shake, and he felt weirdly cold. He always felt like this right before a panic attack. Every time it felt like he was dying. He hated feeling like that.

She sat down beside him and wrapped her arms around him. The scent of her citrusy perfume surrounded him, blocking out the oppressive smell of death. He relaxed just a fraction and leaned into the embrace.

"It's going to be okay," she whispered.

"You can't know that," he muttered. "Unless you're psychic."

She snorted. "Psychics are all fake. But I believe in Amber, and in you."

"I learned a long time ago that things don't always turn out okay," he said, finally lifting his head. Woggy climbed up Ceri's hair and patted his cheek. The pixie signed his name a few times and he couldn't help but smile.

"You were homeless, right?" Ceri asked.

He nodded. "Yeah. After my mom died, my dad started drinking. He married this woman. She was a total bitch. If they weren't drunk, they were high. We got in a fight one day, and he kicked me out."

"Where are you now?" she asked, laying her head on his shoulder.

"Getting attacked by mercenaries."

She gave him a sad smile. "That's what happened, but that's not where you are. You have people that care about you like you're family. Amber would do anything for you. You have a home, friends, and Woggy."

"For now," he said, tugging on a strand of her hair.

"Everything is temporary. Happiness doesn't last forever, but neither do the bad days. Soon, this will be over. Amber will be your alpha, and you'll get to move on. Don't forget that, okay?"

"How can you be so optimistic?" he asked. In the next twenty-four hours, he'd either have everything he'd ever wanted, or lose it all. Again.

She sat up and turned to face him. "It's just a choice. You miss your mom, but I wish mine would drop dead. She's the only person, other than Selena I guess, that I've ever hated. I was angry when I was your age, but one day I realized that every moment I spent being angry was a waste. I was letting her win. She wanted me to be ruthless, so instead I chose compassion. She wanted me to be ambitious, so instead I chose generosity. I can't live my life expecting every day to be awful, so I look for the positive and I cling to it like a life preserver."

There was a lot of positive, if he looked for it. He got to cook almost every night. He had Woggy, Ceri, and his pack. Even if he had to run after this, at least he'd had a good month. He'd forgotten what it felt like to be safe.

He rubbed his hands over his face. That was probably why this had shaken him up so much. Every morning he woke up terrified he'd lose this all. Today, that nightmare had been perilously close to coming true.

Amber and Genevieve walked over toward them. They both looked upset. He stood abruptly and walked over to Amber, wrapping her in a tight hug.

She stood shocked for a moment before returning the hug. She was trembling. It was easy to forget she didn't know any more about this than they did. He couldn't imagine being in her position. The pressure had to be unbearable.

After a moment he stepped back awkwardly, embarrassed by the impulsive action. "Sorry, you just...I'm just glad we're all okay."

She gave him an odd look but smiled. "Yeah, we're okay."

"We should order pizza tonight," Genevieve said forcing her lips to turn up to a smile. "And we got stuff for s'mores. We could have a bonfire!"

He grinned at her. That's exactly what they needed. A celebration, and a distraction. "I love s'mores."

Amber laughed and punched Genevieve on the shoulder. "All you people ever think about is food."

"The beast hungers," Genevieve said, growling dramatically.

Ceri bumped his elbow and winked at him. He smiled back. This sucked, but he could be optimistic for one more night.

CHAPTER 37

AMBER

*A*mber licked the sticky marshmallow off her fingers and laughed at Tommy, who was just setting marshmallows on fire instead of roasting them now.

She'd done this so often with her brothers. It still wasn't exactly cool this time of year in Texas, but that hadn't stopped them from spending all their time outside. Bonfires, sneaking beers, and mudding in their trucks had been the best part of high school.

Grabbing a broken piece of chocolate, she retreated back into the house. Tomorrow was the day of reckoning. She wasn't ready, but these sorts of thing never waited for you to be ready.

She walked back to her room and plopped down in one of the chairs they'd found in the attic. It was red brocade and looked a little like a throne. Genevieve had left it in her room as a joke: red for the alpha. She'd been meaning to move it out but hadn't ever gotten around to it. There was always something more important to do.

Sighing, she pulled out her phone. Her hand shook a little as she dialed Derek's number. So much had changed since she'd talked to him last. It felt like a lifetime ago. It rang twice, seeming overly loud in her ear.

"Yo, this is Derek's phone," her eldest brother said, answering the call.

She considered hanging up right away and not speaking, but she couldn't bring herself to. "Heyyy, Jackson."

There was a pause and a shuffling noise. "Amber?"

"The one and only," she said, trying to sound like her old self, but it came off a little sad. She'd completely forgotten it was Sunday. The weekly family dinner must have continued. That shouldn't have surprised her. A little thing like your son dying and your daughter leaving shouldn't mess with such an important tradition.

Jackson cleared his throat. "How are you these days?"

"Fine, nothing special going on," she said with a wince. Palming her face, she was glad she was sitting in a dark room alone where no one could see her facial expressions.

"Right."

She wanted to demand he put Derek on the phone, but that would be a little insulting. This might be her last chance to talk to her brother. She and Jackson had never been close. He'd been half grown by the time she and Dylan were even born. When she was in high school, she'd jokingly called him Uncle J.

"How have you been? Still seeing...Mary? Or whatever her name was," she asked finally, uncomfortable with the silence.

"Maria, and no, we broke up four years ago," he said, a little bitterness leaking into his voice. The *you would have known that if you had called* hung unspoken between them. She didn't need him to say it out loud to feel the reprimand. "Derek is finally out of the bathroom. Here he is, I'm sure you don't want to talk to me anyway."

Before she could protest, the phone was handed off.

"Amber?" Derek said, sounding surprised.

"Yeah," she said shortly, uncomfortably guilty after the short conversation with Jackson.

"What's wrong?"

"Who said anything was wrong?" she asked, leaning back in her chair.

"*You* called *me*. That hasn't happened in at least six years." A door shut in the background of the call and gravel crunched under his feet. He'd always preferred to take his calls out in the shop, away from the ruckus of the family.

"I just...wanted to see how you were. Catch up, or something," she said.

He sighed. "Well, I'm still working for dad. I've been thinking about opening my own shop, but I'd have to leave town to do that. The old man would throw a fit if he thought I was trying to compete with him."

"You? Get out of town? Never thought I'd see the day," she said with a laugh.

"You aren't the only one that wanted to get out. I've been thinking about leaving for a while, it's just never seemed like a good time. Now dad is having problems."

"He's got three other kids to take care of him. You should go, if you want to."

"It might have been easy for you to leave, but it's not that simple for me," he said. His tone was normal, but she felt the verbal jab like a kick to the chest.

"No part of that was easy, but thanks for the reminder," she snapped, angry that the old wound still hurt so much.

Derek sigh. "Sorry, I just...it sucks. I wish you and mom would reconcile."

"This is why I don't call," she said, pushing out of the chair. She couldn't sit still when she was this agitated. "It's always a guilt trip. I can't check in on any of you without you giving me hell. None of you will let me forget what happened."

"Amber, come on, don't be like that—"

"No, you *don't be like that.* Just…I love you, okay? Give my love to the whole family, even Mom. I'll talk to you later."

"Wait—"

She hung up the call, breaths coming fast as tears stung her eyes. She hated crying. Hated this weak, guilty, helpless feeling that came with remembering what had happened.

Dropping to the floor, she buried her face in her knees. The wolf howled inside her. It wanted the pack and comfort. She refused to go to them. They couldn't see her like this.

CHAPTER 38

GENEVIEVE

enevieve curled her hand into a fist to keep the shaking from being visible. The betas had shown up a few minutes ago. Thallan was watching the group, looking bored and smoking *in the house*. It was going to stink for days.

When Shane had greeted them this time there was no hint of flirtation, or even that he'd been to the house before. Tension was thick in the group of betas, which, as she'd read, was common when packs gathered. Everyone's instincts went a little haywire, and it was hard to hold back the need to compete for dominance.

"She is not a werewolf," a tall, lanky man with blond hair and a thick beard said, pointing at Ceri.

Genevieve tensed, ready to argue if needed. She had read *every* rule she could find. There was no reason they shouldn't be allowed to bring Ceri with them. Amber hadn't ever come out and said it, but it felt like she'd accepted the witch as part of the pack. Genevieve certainly had. Especially after what they'd done on Halloween. She'd go to bat for Ceri anytime, and she knew the witch would do the same.

"She's with us. With the pack," Amber said, stepping closer to the witch. "I'm not leaving her behind."

"It's Amber's choice," Shane said, waving away the other beta's objection. "Let's go."

They were ushered outside and piled into a van that Shane was driving. She crawled to the very back seat and squeezed into a corner. Shane stopped Thallan before he climbed in.

"No smoking in my car," he said, pointing at the smoldering cigarette in the elf's hand.

Thallan rolled his eyes and took a long drag before flicking it to the ground and snuffing it out with the toe of his leather shoe. He blew the smoke in Shane's face and climbed in.

A muscle in Shane's jaw jumped as he glared at the elf, but he didn't say anything. The blond werewolf joined them, sitting in the front seat, while the rest of the betas followed in a different car.

Amber sat in front of her, eyes fixed on a distant point. She was tense and it was making Genevieve anxious. She wanted to reassure her but she couldn't in front of these strangers.

These other wolves, even Shane, felt like a threat. Every instinct she had was screaming at her to fight and run. Instead, they were walking into even more danger. Willingly. Well...sort of willingly.

Shane drove them away from Portland. The woods grew deeper and darker as the sun slipped lower in the sky and the minutes ticked by. The only sound was the rumble of tires on asphalt.

She sighed in relief as he turned down a long driveway. Crammed with Tommy and Ceri in the back of the van was an uncomfortable spot.

"This property is owned by the regional council," Shane said, breaking the silence. "It's used for events like this one, or for celebrations."

"That's useful," Amber replied.

"How long has the council owned it?" Genevieve asked,

desperate to keep the conversation going. Silence wasn't really her thing. Especially tense, awkward silences.

"Since Portland was founded, but they've been using it since long before that," Shane said.

"This will only be the third time a bitten wolf has been tested here," Blondie said, glancing at them in the rearview mirror. She couldn't quite tell from his tone if he was happy about that or not. Shane had a good poker face, but this guy was completely unreadable.

The driveway forked off in two directions. Shane took the left path, and they arrived in a small clearing already packed with other vehicles. There must have been hundreds of people there. They parked near the front in a spot that must have been reserved for them.

Shane put the van in park and looked back. "Amber should answer any questions directed at your pack. Since you're bitten wolves, I'd like to remind your pack not to make eye contact with the other alphas. It could be taken as a challenge, and that's the last thing you need to deal with today."

Everyone nodded. She clasped her hands together anxiously. There was so much to remember. So many ways to screw up. Maybe they'd let her stay in the van.

They climbed out, and she stuck to Tommy and Ceri, taking comfort in their closeness. Before them was a wooden wall at least thirty feet high. The area felt a little like The Market, full of magic, and old.

They were escorted by the group of betas to the wide door in the center of the wall. Passing over the threshold, she suppressed a shiver as magical wards tingled over her skin.

She had to suppress another shiver when she saw the group of alphas gathered in front of them. The urge to challenge them was just as strong as the urge to roll over and show her belly. Behind them were dozens of packs. This must have attracted every werewolf in the area.

Ceri stiffened beside her. She followed her line of sight off to the side and found herself looking at the last person she expected to see there: Selena Blackwood. She'd managed to get off all the slime she'd been drenched in last time they saw her.

CHAPTER 39

AMBER

*S*hane gave Amber one last glance before leading the other betas to the side. She and her pack were left standing before the alphas, and that witch.

Selena only had eyes for Ceri. The witch's expression was cold and blank, but nothing could hide the rage in her eyes. Amber curled her hand into a fist and stepped in front of her pack, shielding them.

A grizzled, old alpha she assumed was Jameson stepped forward from the group. His gray hair was streaked with white, as was his thick beard. Three old scars stretched from his temple to his jaw where he must have been clawed years ago. Most injuries didn't cause scars on a werewolf; the cuts must have been deep.

"Amber Hale, before we begin the Trials, you have one last chance to consider the offer from Alpha Donovan Lockhart to admit you into his pack. If you accept, your alpha powers will be stripped from you and given to him, strengthening your new pack," he explained, his deep voice filling the space.

She ground her teeth together, refusing to acknowledge Donovan. "I decline."

A murmur went through the gathered crowd, but none of the alphas looked surprised.

Jameson accepted her statement with a nod. "So be it."

"What is she doing here?" she asked, pointing at Selena. The witch's presence was gnawing at her. This was bad enough with one person here who wanted her to fail.

The old alpha's brows furrowed. "A member of a local coven assists with the Trials. Is that a problem?"

She didn't like the sound of that, but there wasn't much she could do to object. The only reason Selena had to hate her was because of what happened on Halloween, which wasn't exactly something she wanted to explain.

"I guess we'll find out," she said finally.

Jameson pursed his lips, looking annoyed by her response. He sighed and turned his attention to the elf standing to her right. "Thallan Firedale, as the sponsor for Amber Hale, do you swear that she has maintained conduct becoming an alpha through the waning and the waxing of the moon?"

"I swear it," Thallan said drily.

Jameson motioned at Selena, who followed him as he walked toward the stone set in the center of the open area. He stopped in front of it and folded his hands in front of him, an air of ritual and formality settling over him. "Amber Hale, please come forward."

She took a steadying breath and joined them, standing on the opposite side of the stone. The top was discolored as if it had rusted. However, the old lingering scent of blood made it clear what had caused the discoloration.

"Once the Trials have begun, they cannot be stopped. Do you understand?" Jameson asked.

She looked up to his grizzled face and nodded. "I understand."

He pulled a small knife from his waistband. The handle was wooden, but the blade gleamed in the setting sun. "By the Moon, who gives us strength. By the Night, who gives us sight. By the

Wolf, who gives us life. Let the candidate's worthiness be measured." He held his hand over the stone and drew the blade across his palm without flinching. Smoke curled up from the wound. The blade must have been silver.

He curled his hand into a fist and squeezed. Blood dripped onto the stone, and magic rose around them. It was invisible, but she could feel it like a cool breeze. Goosebumps erupted on her arms.

He handed the knife to her. She took it, willing her hands not to shake. Before she could think too hard about what she had to do, she extended her hand over the stone and cut her palm. There was no turning back.

It hurt more than she expected, but she kept the hiss of pain from escaping. As her blood hit the stone, the magic in the air shifted. It seeped inside her, and the clouds parted above them. Moonlight fell on them, and she turned her eyes to the sky. The moon was full and bright.

Just like that first night it sang to her, but she felt its call even deeper than before. She wanted to change. Run. Hunt. But first, she had to pass the Trials.

CHAPTER 40

"The Trials test both your skills and your worthiness as a leader. You must display speed, cunning, strength, resolve, and control," Jameson said.

Amber nodded. They'd read that much, but that didn't actually explain *what* the trials were.

"The first trial is timed." Jameson stepped aside. "You will have four minutes to get through the obstacle course. You may use whatever form you prefer, shifting at any point throughout the course. We will watch from above, but no one is permitted to interfere or assist you," he said, casting a warning look at her pack. "Please strip down, then you can begin whenever you're ready."

She looked at the alpha, confused. "Strip down?"

Amusement flitted across his face before he schooled his features back to a neutral expression. "Nudity is a human concern. You'll become comfortable with it in time. If you prefer to shred your clothes during the shift, that is your choice. However, it might slow you down."

This was worse than those nightmares where you're naked in front of everyone you know...because it was real. A guy must have thought this up, because only a guy would insist you prove your worth by running naked through an obstacle course.

She yanked her shirt off angrily. No one reacted to the nudity except for Tommy, who turned his head away. He wasn't so embarrassed this time, just doing his best to be polite, which she appreciated.

Jameson took her crumpled bundle of clothes. She shivered in the cool night air. Not because she was cold, just out of sheer nervousness.

"The timer will begin as soon as you touch the wall," he said, pointing at the start of the course.

The first obstacle hid the rest. The wall was twenty feet tall. A rope hung down from the top, but she'd have to jump high enough to grab it without help. There wasn't a single handhold to grab and climb up.

Waiting any longer would just make the nerves worse. With one last glance at her pack, she took off at a run. Strength pumped through her as the wolf urged her on. She knew she shouldn't shift yet, but the wolf was eager to break free.

She jumped, weightless for a brief second before her hands wrapped around the thick rope. Her bare feet scraped against the wood as she hauled herself toward the top. She swung her right leg over first, then her left. From her perch, she took in the rest of the course. From here she had to jump across a small mud pit followed by a tunnel. It was hard to see what came after that.

Gritting her teeth, she braced her feet against the wall and launched herself forward. She flailed, trying to stay upright, then hit the ground. She landed on her feet. Barely.

The top of the tunnel came up chest high, but there was no way she could run through it without shifting. The change rolled over her as she ran toward the tunnel, completing just in time for her to duck inside.

It smelled like dirt and old moss. She'd expected a trap or a trick, but there was nothing special about this part of the obstacle course so far. It was a basic test. It proved she could shift, and that she was a werewolf, but that was it.

She darted into the tunnel entrance. The close quarters pressed in around her but her eyes quickly adjusted to the darkness. After a few turns, she reached the end. Slowing to a walk she stepped out cautiously.

The next obstacle was going to be a little trickier. She shifted back to her human form and looked up at the tall wooden posts that stood over the pit of spikes.

She'd already hesitated for too long. With a deep breath she ran for the first post, launching herself at it. She wrapped her arms around it and braced her feet against the rough wood. One step at a time she worked her way to the top.

The posts were spaced fairly close together. It was obvious the intention was for her to hop from one to the other. She could feel her pack. They were just behind her with the others, watching intently.

She jumped to the next post, wobbling slightly as she landed. Without pausing, she jumped to the next and the next, a wild thrill running through her. Maybe she could do this. Pass the Trials. Keep her pack.

The last pillar was a few feet away. She leaped for it, and for one elated moment, she was standing on it. Sudden pain lanced through her ankle, and it forcibly twisted. She pitched forward and fell.

Twisting in the air, she managed to grab the pillar before she hit the ground. Claws from her half-shifted hands dug into the hard wood as she held herself inches above the sharp spikes.

She dragged herself back up, cursing herself for her overconfidence. She'd been sure she'd landed that one. It had felt like something hit her ankle.

Ignoring the pain shooting through her leg, she jumped to the safety of the platform. In front of her was a doorway, and inside, it was pitch black.

She shifted, already feeling the wear of changing forms so many times in a row, and stepped over the threshold. The lack of light shouldn't have been a problem, but her eyes weren't adjusting to the darkness. She sniffed the air, and the unmistakeable scent of magic was present. This must be part of the test.

Letting her nose guide her, she took two cautious steps forward. With no idea how much time she had left, every second felt like an eternity. She picked up her pace and trotted forward. Underneath the other smells was the faint scent of Jameson, as if he'd walked this path earlier in the day.

That must be her clue. Nose to the ground, she moved even faster. Her tail hit something and she yelped in surprise but nothing happened. There must be walls around her, perhaps even a maze. The wolf grew impatient and urged her forward. It wasn't afraid. It had the scent and trusted it to lead them out of this darkness.

Giving in to those instincts, she let the wolf push them onward. The smell of magic grew stronger, almost overpowering Jameson's scent for a moment. She paused, one paw in the air, then sniffed carefully. Something popped and an awful smell filled the air.

In a panic, she fell backward, shifting to her human form. She covered her nose and mouth with her hands, wishing she had her shirt to breathe through. The smell dissipated almost immediately but the burning in her nose persisted.

She felt around on the ground for whatever had exploded but there was nothing. Reaching tentatively to the side she found a wall, and a foot above her, the ceiling. These tests had seemed simple but a trap made it more complicated. She wished she knew how much time she had left.

Shifting back, she sniffed the ground. The scent she'd been following might as well have been gone. She couldn't smell anything past the lingering burning in her nose.

With a huff, she rubbed it against her paw but that only made it hurt worse. Her bones ached from the back and forth of the shifts. And she was exhausted already.

"Amber, can you hear me?" Angel hissed in the darkness. "I can help you, if you want."

She shook her head vehemently, a motion that felt odd as a wolf, and glared in the demon's general direction. She'd been wondering when he'd show up.

"I could lead you out of here. You're running out of time," he said.

Ignoring him, she felt around for the wall, pressed her right side against it, and walked forward tentatively. No one could interfere so she had to get out on her own, no matter what. Making a deal with the demon wasn't an option.

The place felt like a maze. She ran faster as she started to panic. There couldn't be much time left. A flash of alarm startled her right before she ran smack into a wall.

"That looked like it hurt," Angel said. He was hovering close by, his warmth sinking into her fur.

Biting back a snarky response, she shook herself and tried to think through what had just happened. That hadn't been her emotion. It was from her pack. They must be able to see her still. She'd avoided using that bond because it felt intrusive but she hoped they'd forgive her for using it now.

A little more cautiously this time, she started walking again. As she moved she let the bond grow in her mind. There was worry, fear, and anger. She wasn't sure what that last one was about, but the others she expected.

She took off at a run again. When the alarm shot through her again, she slid to a halt and took a cautious step forward. Her nose bumped against the wall. She felt around until she had a clear path then took off at a run again. It wasn't as fast as following the scent, but it was all she had.

CHAPTER 41

CERI

*I*t was like Amber had gone blind suddenly. She wasn't even trying to follow the scent anymore. It didn't make any sense, unless…

"Are there boobytraps in there?" Ceri demanded, her fingers gripping the wooden railing tightly.

Jameson, who stood a few paces away from her, frowned and shook his head. "The first test is simple. She had to follow the scent but it looks like she lost it."

She had thought she sensed a flicker of magic when Amber had stumbled on the wooden posts. But she was sure of it now. Someone was sabotaging Amber's Trials.

It wasn't a question of who; it was obviously Donovan or Selena, most likely both working together. It was a question of *how*. Jameson had made it clear he wouldn't allow interference. She had a good feeling about the old alpha, so she believed him.

Amber's pack was watching the proceedings intently. She had taken off at a run and it was obvious she was about to smack into a wall again.

"*Stop*," Tommy whispered under his breath.

Amber slid to a stop, taking a cautious step forward.

Tommy looked up, shocked. "Did she hear me?"

Genevieve shook her head. "No, but I think she can sense our feelings."

"What?" Tommy looked alarmed.

"We'll talk about it later. Keep watching. Try to tell her where to go," Genevieve urged.

Tommy turned back to the course and focused all his attention there. With less than a minute left on the timer, it was looking less and less like she'd complete the first test in time.

Ceri stepped away from the group and looked over at Donovan. He stood with his betas, watching the proceedings and laughing at Amber's struggles. Selena, however, stood alone. She wasn't speaking to anyone and didn't seem particularly interested in the Trials. As Ceri stared at her, the witch lifted her head and met her gaze. Hate burned in her venomous green eyes.

Whether the sabotage had been her idea or not, she was the one doing it. Ceri had to get proof, or there would be no way of stopping her.

Thallan stepped up beside Ceri, startling her. "I see you've noticed as well."

She nodded. "Any suggestions on how to handle it?"

He pursed his lips thoughtfully. "No good ones."

The pack would help any way they could if she told them, but she was a little afraid Genevieve might do something stupid. Like try to eat Selena.

Her attention was pulled back to the obstacle course as Amber finally made it out. She raced up the last portion, a steep hill, but the buzzer rang loudly when she was only halfway up.

Amber didn't stop running despite her failure but it was too late. Genevieve cursed and turned away, her dainty features contorted in anger.

Donovan laughed loudly, pointing at her and saying something she couldn't quite hear to his companions. She heard the word bitten loud and clear, though.

One of the betas, the hot one that had defended her coming today, looked back at her. He seemed concerned rather than smug about Amber's failure. Maybe…he would help.

AMBER

*S*he shifted back, humiliation coursing through her. Donovan's jeers carried across the open space. Her hearing was unfortunately good enough to catch every word.

A door opened ahead of her and Shane stood in the space. He motioned for her to join him. She walked over silently, looking everywhere but him. Jameson was right. The nudity wasn't bothering her anymore. But the failure was.

"Chin up," Shane whispered as she fell in step beside him. "There's still four more chances."

"Was this the easiest trial?" she asked.

Shane hesitated, then nodded.

"Great."

They walked into some kind of arena. Her toes dug into hard-packed dirt as she followed Shane to the center of the space.

"Wait here," he said before jogging toward the side of the pit. He jumped up and grabbed the top of the wall, pulling himself up to join the others.

Jameson in the center of the group, her pack on his left. "In one minute, the doors below me will open. Wolves have no natural predators in the wild, but we do have one foe. A normal wolf would never be able to defeat this animal on their own, but we are not normal. We have been gifted with greater size and strength. As alpha, you must be able to defend your pack against even the most formidable threats. This trial demands you prove that you are capable of doing this."

She swallowed nervously. There was really only one thing that could walk out of those doors and she did not want to fight it. At all. "Do I have to kill it?"

Jameson nodded solemnly. "Yes. However, there is no time limit for this Trial. You will either prevail, or you will perish."

Well, shit. That wasn't exactly comforting. "Can I change now?"

"Yes, the doors will open in ten seconds," he said.

She shifted quickly, her heart pounding. When those witches had attacked, she'd only had time to react. Knowing what was coming filled her with fear. Having an audience didn't help much either. She really didn't want to be ripped apart in front of her pack.

Ceri leaned over the edge, making some kind of odd hand signal. She had no idea what to make of it but it felt like a warning. Since she knew she was about to have to fight something, that didn't make any sense. Was there something else going on?

The doors creaked open, pushing any thoughts of warnings out of her head. From the darkness came a huff and a rumbling growl.

She dug her paws into the dirt and crouched down, muscles tensed. One massive paw stepped into the fading light, then another. The bear's mouth hung open, saliva dripping onto the ground in long strings.

Thick brown fur covered the bulky animal. It padded out, watching her carefully. Once it was free of the confining room, it stood on its hind legs, and roared.

The challenge was clear. She lifted her head and howled, claiming the ring as her own.

The bear dropped down to four feet. Then it charged.

CHAPTER 42

CERI

*C*eri's fingers dug into the wooden railing as the bear charged Amber. She wanted to look away but was terrified to. This was awful, all of it. There had to be a better way to prove Amber was worthy than killing some poor animal.

The crowd erupted in cheers as they crashed into each other, drowning out the vicious growling. Tommy wrapped an arm around her shoulders and she realized tears were streaming down her face.

Wiping them away angrily, she squeezed him back. She should be trying to take care of him, not the other way around. He wasn't even an adult.

The bear swiped at Amber, catching her in the shoulder. She was tossed back twenty feet and hit the ground limply. Tommy's fingers convulsed on her shoulder, but she was barely paying attention.

When the bear had struck her, for a brief moment, there had been a curl of smoke. It wasn't something you'd see if you weren't looking for it. But it had been there. Just like the last test, this one was being sabotaged.

She looked up and caught Shane's gaze. He glanced at Donovan and a muscle in his jaw jumped.

"I'll be right back," she said, squeezing Tommy's hand. He nodded and stepped away, eyes glued to the fight.

She tapped Thallan as she passed him. He followed her through the crowd and down the wooden steps that led back to the ground. She ducked under the scaffolding that supported the stadium seating and waited.

The elf leaned against the wall and crossed his arms, clearly bored. A moment later, Shane joined them. Lifting her hand, she cast a simple muffling spell.

"She's being sabotaged and we both know it," she said angrily.

"I know, but I can't be the one that protests. It has to be Thallan," Shane said, pointing at the elf. "Especially as Jameson's beta, I have to remain neutral."

"How does he protest it?" she asked.

Shane took a deep breath, rubbing his hand along his stubbled jaw. "Bring your proof to Jameson. Declare the interference, accuse who you suspect, and be prepared to prove it."

"How the hell are we supposed to get proof?" She threw her hands in the air, exasperated.

"I want to help you, but I can't. Try to think outside the box, okay?" he said, taking a step back. "I shouldn't have even come down here. And I can't stay."

"Fine." She turned away and pinched the bridge of her nose between her thumb and forefinger.

"Perhaps we just protest and figure it out along the way?" Thallan suggested, unhelpfully.

"That won't work and you know it."

He shrugged. "You think there is something on the bear's claws, right? If you demand they be examined, they'll find evidence of interference."

She shook her head. "It's probably gone by now. If I was doing this, I would have put just enough so that the first few swipes got it in her bloodstream, but it would be undetectable after that."

GENEVIEVE

*G*enevieve looked behind her and realized Ceri was gone. So was Thallan. Shane walked past and gave her a strange look, almost guilty.

She grabbed Tommy and tugged his head down so she could whisper, "Do you know where Ceri is?"

He looked around, his eyebrows drawing together, then shook his head.

"Come on," she said, dragging him after her. Ceri was up to something, and there was no way she was going to leave them out of it.

She followed her nose. Thallan left a distinct trail that even a human could follow. It led through the crowd, then down the stairs.

There was a glimpse of white through the scaffolding that looked like Ceri's dress, but she couldn't hear them talking, or even their heartbeats.

She doubted Thallan and Ceri were just standing in there silently, so they were keeping anyone from hearing them intentionally.

"I think I see them," Tommy whispered.

"Me too."

They slipped under the scaffolding and walked over. Genevieve was turned away from Thallan like she was angry. The elf looked unconcerned, as always, but he was on his third or fourth cigarette. Even he didn't usually smoke that much.

Thallan looked up as they drew close but didn't say anything. Static zipped over her skin as she crossed some kind of invisible barrier.

She put her hands on her hips. "What the hell is going on?"

Ceri jumped and whipped around, her eyes bouncing between her and Tommy. "Umm, I just needed a minute…alone."

"Don't lie to us," Tommy said, sounding really hurt. He and Ceri had gotten pretty close over the last month.

"You either think Amber is being sabotaged or that she's about to die. Which is it?" she asked, wanting to get to the point.

Ceri swallowed uncomfortably. "Sabotage."

"Shane was down here, right? What did he say? Can we stop it?"

"Thallan has to protest it to Jameson, and then we have to prove that someone is interfering," Ceri said with a sigh. "We have a few minutes to figure something out, or Amber is going to die."

Genevieve crossed her arms, thinking. She'd been great in school debate competitions when she'd had to improvise but there had never been stakes this high before. "What if…we bluff."

Ceri looked up sharply. "Bluff?"

"Yeah, we know they're sabotaging her. Do you have any idea how?" she asked, trying to appear more confident than she felt.

"I know what I'd do," Ceri answered with a shrug.

"Then we go to Jameson, say what you think is happening, and point him toward something that would prove it. Is there anything that Selena or Donovan have done that would leave a trace?"

"When she was in the dark maze it looked like something blew up in her face. Could that have left a residue?" Tommy asked.

"It might have. It would be hard to detect, and it would be a very small amount," Ceri said.

"I could go look for it while you start the protest. If I find something, I'll bring it back."

Bluffing was risky but they didn't have many options. She might be able to pull it off just long enough for Tommy and Ceri to find something. "What should I tell them is in there?"

"Glass," Ceri said with a decisive nod. "If she left something, it would have had to be in glass. A very thin tube most likely, something that would shatter into pieces so small they're almost a powder."

"Do we even have time to find that?" Tommy asked.

"Probably not," Ceri admitted.

"Then we have to go with the silver. If Selena used it on the bear, then wouldn't she have some on her?" she asked.

"Yes, that stuff gets everywhere, like glitter," Ceri said, her tone going thoughtful.

"Are you thinking what I'm thinking?" she asked.

Ceri nodded. "Do you know how to do the protest?"

"Yes," she turned to Thallan. "Do I need to write this down, or can you remember it?"

"I think I'm capable of remembering it," he said, flicking his cigarette to the ground and snuffing it out with the toe of his shoe.

"Alright, then this is what you need to say," she said. Her heart was beating so fast she almost couldn't breathe. She hoped she remembered it correctly, or Amber was screwed. And it would be her fault.

CHAPTER 43

*T*hallan was walking too slowly. He had no sense of urgency at all, and it made Ceri want to strangle him. They had to squeeze through the crowd. Once they were back by the railing, she risked a glance down into the arena. Amber was stumbling around, barely dodging the bear's attacks.

"Alpha Clark Jameson," Thallan said, his voice booming over the noise of the crowd. "This sacred ritual has been tarnished by the actions of a coward. I name Donovan Lockhart as coward. I name Selena Blackwood as coward and mercenary."

Silence fell over the gathering. For a moment, the only sound was the huff of the bear.

"How dare—"

Jameson lifted his hand, cutting Donovan off. "In what manner have these Trials been sabotaged?"

"The first trial, through magic. A hex to twist the candidate's ankle, and a trap left to burn her nose. In this trial, through silver powder on the bear's claws."

Selena looked at Ceri directly. Her fingers twitched at her side like she wanted to throw a curse. She wouldn't be able to get away with it in a crowd like this, no matter how much the witch wanted to hurt her.

"Your protest is heard. Do you bring proof?" Jameson asked.

Ceri stepped forward. "Selena Blackwood will have silver on her body. Her hands, clothes, possibly her face. With a dust that fine, it's impossible to avoid getting it on you. If the maze were to be searched, you would find glass, but very little of it."

The old alpha waved the others back, parting the crowd. Selena stood a few feet away with her jaw clenched in anger. "How dare you accuse me of interfering in—"

"Occultatum fateor!" Ceri shouted, lifting her hand. The magic rushed between them, hitting Selena with a burst of light. Everywhere the silver had touched her glowed brightly. It was streaked across the hem of her dress and shimmering along the curve of her ear.

Jameson walked over to her and dragged his finger across one spot. Smoke drifted up from his finger. "Why is there silver on your clothes?"

"I work with silver often," Selena said, curling her hand into a fist. She held Jameson's gaze stubbornly.

"Please, stop the fight. Amber is being poisoned," Ceri begged. "You'll find silver residue on the bear's claws."

"This is a ridiculous ploy to save her friend," Donovan said, shoving forward to stand next to Selena. "A bitten wolf should never have been allowed to undergo the Trials in the first place."

Jameson pursed his lips. "If we stop this test, it must be counted as a failure."

"It's going to kill her if you don't stop the fight," she said, waving at the arena. "They've sabotaged her. You said we couldn't assist, but you also said no one could interfere."

"The sponsor must approve this action," Jameson said, looking at the elf.

Genevieve stepped up beside him, expression furious. "Do it. If she dies, it's a failure regardless."

236

"I approve, stop the fight," Thallan said, ignoring her.

Jameson nodded and waved at two of the alphas to follow him. They jumped down into the arena. Ceri couldn't wait for them to stop the bear, she had to get to Amber right now or the silver would keep weakening her.

AMBER

*S*omething was wrong. She shook her head but her vision swam. Her legs were weak. It wasn't from the pain, it was something else.

The bear charged in again. She darted under the first swing and bit its hind leg, wrenching it off balance. Frantically, she pulled on the pack bond. It was her only hope. Strength trickled through, and she had a brief burst of energy, but it was a losing battle.

She tried to lunge under the next swipe but her shoulder gave out and she hit the ground instead. It was numb now. Her good foot scraped against the dirt as she tried to force herself back to her feet.

The bear loomed over her, rising up to its hind feet. It roared and its paw came soaring toward her face. She couldn't move. This was not the way she thought she'd die, but maybe it was poetic justice that she die as a werewolf, just like Dylan.

Her eyes slipped shut, but she caught a glimpse of something hitting the side of the bear. Something large.

There was shouting. Someone shaking her. Pain. Bright light exploded in front of her. Ceri grabbed her and warmth rushed through her body, chasing away the bitter cold ache. She gasped for air and was finally able to take a full breath. The back of her hand scraped against a small rock and she realized she'd shifted back at some point.

"Keep still," Ceri warned.

"What? You can't—"

"There was silver on the bear's teeth or claws. Jameson stopped the test," Ceri said, pressing her hand against her chest. "Give me a moment and I'll have it purged from your body so it can heal."

"Am I going...to have to barf...again?" she asked as she panted. Whatever magic Ceri was using was *cold*. Her teeth clacked together as her body spasmed.

"Will she live?" Jameson asked, appearing near her head.

"Yes. I'm almost done, and then her body will take over the healing," Ceri said, shutting her eyes in concentration.

Amber's muscles twitched one last time, and then she felt her limbs fill with warmth. Pins and needles races down her arms as the feeling returned. Ceri removed her hands, and she pushed herself into a sitting position.

The wounds from the bear were stitching themselves back together, which was an odd feeling, to say the least. She watched one long cut close, pushing out debris as it went.

"Because this test had to be stopped, it must be counted as a failure," Jameson said, crouching beside her. "However, you can continue with the Trials, if you still wish to remain an alpha."

"So, even though someone interfered, they get rewarded, and I get punished?" she asked, anger clearing the shock.

Jameson's lips thinned. "They will be punished, but that will be separate from the Trials."

She sighed and let Ceri pull her to her feet. "I'll continue."

He nodded. "Take a moment with your friend while we prepare the next test. Then we will continue."

Ceri grabbed her arm and dragged her toward the room the bear had come out of. Once inside, she handed her a bottle of water.

"How'd you figure it out?" she asked before chugging half the bottle. It was cold and felt like heaven on her throat.

"It was mostly guesswork. How are you feeling?"

She shrugged. "Good enough. Just tired."

"Are Tommy and Gen okay?"

"Yes. Worried, but fine," Ceri said.

"I've failed two out of five of the tests. That means I have to pass the last three," she said, rubbing her hands over her face. They were still shaking, and she was so tired from the fight. "I can't do this."

Ceri grabbed her by the shoulders and shook her. "You can do it. You would have passed the first two if they hadn't sabotaged you. Even Donovan believes you can do this."

That comment brought a smirk to her face. "Well, when you put it like that."

CHAPTER 44

AMBER

The crowd was still gathered above the arena, but this time, Jameson and the other alphas were down there with her.

"I have personally inspected the weights. They have not been tampered with in any way," he said, pointing to the large boulder sitting in the dirt. There were three. The smallest one came up to her knee, while the largest would reach her hip. "You must lift them and carry them across that line. If you drop one, you fail the test and the Trials." About twenty feet away, a red line had been sprayed onto the dirt.

The outside of the boulders were mottled black and dirty as though they were coated in something. As she approached them, she realized where she had seen something like that before; her grandmother's old silver. Tentatively, she touched one. Burning pain seared her fingertips as her body weakened. The entire thing was shot through with silver. There was no way to pick the boulder up without touching it. Handling silver like this wouldn't poison her like it did when it had gotten in her bloodstream, but as long as she was in contact with it, she would be severely weakened.

She had failed the first two tests. That meant that she had to pass the last three or it was all over. In the previous test, while almost getting murdered by the bear, she'd felt something change in the bond. It was more than just sensing her pack's emotions—they had given her strength.

Taking a calming breath, she tried to think instead of react. This test had to be passable. The strength of an alpha lay with the pack. If she could use the bond to overcome the pain and the weakness the silver inflicted...that had to be it. It was the only way.

Please, help me, she begged the wolf internally. It looked out of her eyes, surveying the alphas watching. Donovan was grinning. He wanted nothing more than to see her to fail.

Walking toward the largest boulder, she crouched down and wrapped her arms around it. This was only going to get harder, so she wanted to get the largest one over with first. The wolf growled in her mind and the pack bond grew inside, stretching taut. Strength that wasn't her own poured into her muscles. It couldn't stop the pain, but she could deal with that.

With a pained grunt, she forced herself to her feet. Claws extended form her fingertips, digging into the hard stone to keep it from slipping out of her hands. The pain was almost overwhelming. She could barely breathe. She took one wobbly step forward and almost toppled over.

The crowd gasped and began shouting. Half jeers, and half encouragement. She shut it all out and focused on the pack bond. She couldn't hear what her pack was saying but she could feel their strength. Tommy, the homeless kid with a heart of gold. Genevieve, an intelligent woman that hid her talents because she was afraid to fail. And Ceri, the white witch.

Her eyes snapped open. She wasn't sure when Ceri had become a part of the pack like that. There hadn't been a bite to bind her to them, but she could feel Ceri just like the others.

She took another step forward, then another, and another.

The red line drew closer and she was filled with elation and determination from her pack. It mixed with her own, giving her a new kind of strength. She could do this.

The cheers increased as she drew close to the line, drowning out the boos completely. She picked up her pace. Her legs were shaking and it felt like she had no flesh left on her arms, but she didn't stop. Sweat rolled down her forehead and slipped into her eye. It stung and her vision blurred but she could still see that red line. Angel was floating behind it. He was shouting encouragement too, almost like he cared if she made it.

Grinding her teeth together, she took the final three steps to cross the line. She dropped the stone at her feet and turned back to the other alphas. Donovan's face was beet-red with fury, but Jameson was smiling.

Straightening her shoulders, she walked back to the next boulder. Success felt damn good.

CHAPTER 45

"*K*ick this test's ass!" Genevieve shouted, leaning out from the crowd.

Amber winked at her with a smile as she followed Jameson into the squat building. The rest of the alphas, and Thallan, filed in behind them. The cottage consisted of a single room with roughly hewn floors and old wooden chairs set in a semicircle. It was dark and quiet, a stark contrast to the loud arena.

"Your physical body and your pack bond have been tested," Jameson said, folding his arms in front of him. "However, an alpha must also be in control of his mind. The fourth trial tests your mind." He opened the lid of an ornate wooden box and lifted out a smoking pipe. A rich, warm scent drifted toward her.

"Am I meant to say no to drugs?" she asked, raising her eyebrow.

A few of the alphas chuckled, and she even got a smirk from Jameson. "Aconite, or wolfsbane, is a poison that used to be used to kill wolves and werewolves alike in darker times. However, while searching for an antidote for the poison, the first Alpha discovered something. When combined with myrrh and dogwood under a full moon, it changes. Instead of killing you, it opens your mind to the wolf within. It allows you to face your inner demons."

She swallowed uncomfortably at the word demon. Hopefully Angel wouldn't be waiting for her in her mind. "Let me guess. If I fail to defeat my *inner demons*," she used air quotes to emphasize the phrase, "I'll die?"

Jameson shrugged. "Not immediately. The ones that fail simply do not wake up."

"Will I be timed?"

He shook his head. "Not really. If you haven't woken by dawn, we'll assume you have failed, but most people pass or fail within less than a minute. Though, it will seem longer to you."

She nodded and shifted on her bare feet. The movement reminded her she was standing naked in a room full of strangers, but she shoved the embarrassment down. No one seemed to care; they were all focused on the Trials just like she was. "Okay, let's do this."

Jameson pulled an oddly shaped lighter from his pocket and handed her the pipe. "Three puffs as I light it."

She eyed the mouthpiece, hoping they washed it between trials, then put it in her mouth. It felt awkward, and she was sure she wasn't holding it right. Jameson clicked the lighter and passed the flame in a tight circle over the bowl of tightly packed herbs.

"Inhale," he reminded her.

She sucked in and her mouth filled with smoke, making her eyes water. She blew it out of the corner of her mouth and tamped down on the urge to cough. Whatever was in the smoke was making her tongue go numb.

Dutifully, she puffed twice more. Her entire body tingled. A loud ringing in her ears drowned out all sound. Gray seeped in at the edges of her vision. She pulled the pipe from her mouth and tried to hand it to Jameson but her body was numb and she was...she was...

CHAPTER 46

AMBER

"*A*mber!" *Dylan shouted, wrapping her in a tight hug. "Tonight is the night. I can already feel the moon calling to me."*

She rolled her eyes and slapped him on the arm. "No, you can't. Quit being so dramatic."

He grinned, his whole face lighting up. "I'm going to find a way to get you in the pack too, I promise."

"I'm not worried about it, okay? If they didn't want me, there must be a reason. Maybe I wouldn't be able to handle the change." She wrapped him in another hug. "I still think you should tell mom and dad. They're going to freak when they find out."

"That's exactly why I'm not telling them until it's done. They take bad news better once they can't do anything about it. Ask forgiveness, not permission. You know how it goes."

She snorted and buried her face in his neck. "That only works for you because you're their favorite."

"No, I'm not!" he protested, pushing her back.

Dark. Cold. Something growled behind her. She turned and found herself looking into the face of a large, ruddy wolf. Its eyes glowed red.

"Weak." It spoke without moving its mouth, but she knew the words came from it nonetheless. With soundless steps, it prowled around her. "Angry."

"Who are you?" Her body trembled but she couldn't move. "Why are you showing me those memories?"

"You let your brother die," it said.

"No!" Her voice echoed around them, repeating over and over until it made her head ache. "I didn't know it would kill him. I didn't know."

The alpha held Dylan down, one paw on his back, then struck. His teeth sunk in deep. Dylan screamed. He wasn't supposed to scream. It wasn't supposed to hurt.

The werewolf jumped away, muscles tense. His tail drooped and he backed up, putting distance between himself and her brother. Then he lifted his head in a mournful howl. The pack's howls joined in.

Dylan screamed again, clawing at the bite wildly. She rushed from her place behind the pack and shoved her way through the circle. Dropping to her knees beside him, she tried to grab his arms, but his flailing limbs hit her. His eyes rolled back in his head and his body seized.

"Dylan!" She turned to the alpha. "What did you do? Help him! You have to help him!"

The alpha shook his head and turned away.

Crack. Dylan's arm snapped, wrenched to the side as his body tried to change but couldn't. Blood poured from the wound. From his eyes. From his mouth. Her hands hovered uselessly over his convulsing body.

More bones cracked and snapped as they were brutally twisted by magic gone wrong. His skin peeled away in random spots, replaced by mottled fur that grew straight out of the muscle.

"Am—ber—" he choked out, blood bubbling out of his lips. "Hel—p —hurts—"

"Someone help him!" she screamed, but the werewolves were all backing away...leaving him to die.

She wrapped her hands around her head, a guttural yell coming from her sore throat. It barely felt like she was the one screaming. The wolf huffed behind her.

Enraged, she turned and swung at it, barely registering that she could now move. "Stop showing me this!"

"You let him die, why shouldn't I show you your greatest failure?" the wolf taunted.

"I didn't let him die! I tried to save him. I would have done anything!"

The wolf's body slimmed, shifting back into a human form. Dylan's. Bloody, broken, and lifeless. His eyes opened slowly.

"Mom loved me best, and you let me take the bite even though you knew I might die. Why didn't you stop me?" he asked, lifting his broken and twisted arm toward her.

She took a step back and felt warmth seep through her shirt. "Get away from me."

"Don't freak out. It's just in your head," Angel whispered. Any other time she would have jerked away, but she was so relieved to not be *alone* with this horrible apparition that she leaned in closer instead.

"How do I make it stop?" she asked, voice thick with tears.

"Is what it's saying true?" Angel asked.

She shook her head. "No, I didn't know. I would have stopped him."

"Then convince it you're innocent," the demon suggested, drifting to her side and taking his warmth with him. "I can't help you in here, not even for a demon's mark."

"You blame yourself!" Dylan's ghoulish doppelganger screeched. "The guilt gnaws at you every day like cancer, spreading through your mind." It shifted back into the wolf, red eyes boring into her. "Why should I join my soul to such a pathetic creature? Even *you* don't think you deserve to be an alpha."

She took a step back. "You're...my wolf?"

The creature cocked its head and stepped closer. "Did you not recognize me?"

"No," she said as she lifted her hand toward it. She hadn't realized it was a completely separate creature. "I don't understand. I thought you were just...instincts. Maybe something more, but not like this."

"That is how we begin, but as you grow, I grow. You will not be able to see or hear me like this again for many years. If you even survive," the wolf said, circling her.

"Is the aconite killing me?" she asked.

The wolf huffed. "No, but I might."

She tensed, readying herself for an attack. "Why?"

It ignored her question and turned to the demon instead. "Why did you let the demon inside you?"

She glanced at Angel who was circling the wolf curiously now. "I had to in order to find a sponsor for these Trials."

The wolf watched the demon for a moment, then swiped at it. Angel shrieked and disappeared with a pop.

"What did you do to him?" she asked, alarmed.

"Just sent him away for a while. This is not for him." The wolf went back to circling her. "Why do you want to pass the Trials?"

"I have to protect Tommy and Genevieve. They're depending on me, and if I let them down, they'll be stuck in the System," she said, edging away from the wolf. It was too close; she wouldn't be able to move out of the way if it attacked.

"Would you defend them against anything?"

She furrowed her brows. "Of course I would."

"Even him?" the wolf asked, stepping aside to reveal an apparition of her brother. This time it was how she liked to remember him, young and smiling.

"Dylan is dead," she said, shaking her head.

"Yet everything you do is still centered around him. Your choice in career, your hatred of me, and your avoidance of your family. They were your pack once, but you abandoned them. Will you abandon this pack as soon as you make a mistake?" The wolf bared its teeth at her with its hackles raised.

"No!" she shouted, infuriated by the old memories and the accusation.

"Then choose. Your past, or your future?"

"What does that even mean?" She threw her hands in the air angrily.

The wolf vanished and Dylan's expression grew dark. He looked up at her with glowing red eyes. "I should have been the alpha and we both know it. So, if you want it, you have to defeat me and take it."

She bared her teeth at her twin, and for an instant, intensely hated every choice that had led her to this moment. Werewolves and their obsession with proving yourself, as if it mattered if she measured up to some stupid ideal. Donovan and his lust for power. And herself, for ever thinking she could do this.

Dylan lunged at her. She knew how he fought, and the wolf must have known, too. Or have been able to see it in her memories. She dodged the first punch and struck back. They threw elbows and kicks, and she bit him, even though they were fighting as humans.

She'd been running and shifting all day. Her body was exhausted, and so was her mind. Dylan caught her with an uppercut and she stumbled backward, spitting blood.

"Come on, little sister! You used to be tougher," he said with a sneer.

She growled and lunged at him, ducking down low at the last moment. Catching him around the waist, she lifted him from his feet and slammed him down. He wheezed as all the air was driven from his lungs.

He grabbed her hair and yanked her head to the side, but she dug her fingers into his face. He dropped his fistful of hair and tried to elbow her. She caught it and forced her way on top of him. Her elbow slipped through his defenses and cracked against his temple.

The strike dazed him, giving her the barest opening. She struck again, and again, bloodying his face. A vision of him dying, with blood bubbling from his lips, made her hesitate. He reared up and head-butted her.

Enraged, she punched him again as blood dripped from her nose and over her lips. He fell back and she pounded her fist into his face, his neck, anywhere she could reach. His struggles slowed until he lay underneath her, barely moving.

She stopped, horrified, and stared down at him.

His eyes opened, the red glow of the wolf shining through. "Finish it. Kill him."

"No," she sobbed, shoving off of him. "I won't kill my own brother. This isn't right. Why are you doing this?"

"Don't you want this? More than anything?" the wolf demanded, crawling toward her still wearing Dylan's face.

She shook her head. "I didn't want this at all. This was forced on me, and I'll do everything I can to be a good alpha, but no, I didn't want this."

The illusion fell away and the wolf sat before her. "You are strange."

She laughed, sounding hysterical even to her own ears. "You just had me fight my own dead brother, and you're calling me strange?"

The wolf huffed and she got the impression it muttered something unflattering under its breath. "Your pack submitted to you that day in the woods. To us."

She nodded. "Yes, I felt it. They chose me to be their alpha. That's why I can't abandon them."

"But you did not choose me," the wolf said. For a moment, she thought it sounded sad.

"No, I didn't," she said, honestly.

It rose to its feet. "Will you choose me now?"

She looked up, meeting its eyes in surprise. "Choose you?"

"Most werewolves do not know this, but while we're in this place I could leave you, turn you back to a human if I wanted. The first alpha didn't find an antidote to wolfsbane, he found a cure. You didn't want to be a werewolf, much less an alpha. I can give that choice back to you. Do you want to go back to being human and living your life however you choose, or will you choose to be the alpha?"

She froze, looking at the wolf in shock. A choice. It had been so long since she truly felt like she had one. "Why would you give me a choice?"

"Perhaps because it is the right thing to do," the wolf replied.

She looked down at bloodied knuckles and tried to think it through. But she realized there was nothing to consider, not now. She cared about Genevieve, Tommy, and Ceri. It wasn't just the wolf's instincts or the pack bond. She wanted to make sure they were safe.

Maybe a psychologist would say it was guilt from her brother's death motivating her, or the way her mother kicked her out. But those were the things that made her who she was today. The reasons didn't matter anymore.

She looked back up. "I want to be their alpha."

The wolf charged at her, hitting her like a battering ram. For a moment, she couldn't breathe, then everything shifted and power rushed through her body.

With a gasp, she awoke on the floor. The exposed beams of the cottage hung over her. Her body was trembling and she was panting as though she'd just run a marathon. Jameson was standing over her along with two other alphas. They looked extremely concerned.

"That was fucking strange," she said hoarsely. Grimacing, she sat up and rubbed her aching throat.

"We thought you were dying," Jameson said, handing her a

bottle of water. "I've never seen anyone convulse like that and live."

She laughed. "I think I almost did die. The wolf...it..."

He nodded solemnly in understanding. "You are a vessel for two souls now. It changes you." He extended his hand, which she took, and pulled her to her feet. "It's time for the final trial."

She met his gaze, not terrified for the first time. "I'm ready."

CHAPTER 47

"We will return to the altar for the final test."

Jameson led her outside. She saw Genevieve first, then Tommy, who slumped in relief upon spotting her. The pack bond was richer now, and she felt their worry and elation like her own emotions.

The crowd parted, then fell in behind them as they walked through a large, wide archway that led back to the beginning. Moonlight still shone on the altar like a spotlight.

They stopped a few feet away, and Jameson waited for the crowd to spread out around them. A few younger werewolves climbed up on the wall that had been the first obstacle in order to get a better view.

The tension within the crowd was palpable. Some of them wanted her to fail, some were just curious, but a few shouted encouragement. It was a relief to see that not every werewolf was a bigoted asshole.

The presiding alphas gathered behind Jameson, who turned to face her.

"As a werewolf, the rest of your life will be a struggle to balance your humanity with the soul of the wolf that now lives inside you," Jameson said, tapping on his chest over his heart. "You must be stronger than the wolf. You must stay in control. For this final test, you will take a potion that will force you to shift. In order to pass, you must keep from fully shifting for at least five—"

Donovan shoved his way forward, anger clear on his face. "I challenge her."

"I'd advise against doing this out of anger. You can't forget the unnecessary risk you are taking," Jameson said, folding his hands in front of him. "If you fail, your spot on this council will become hers."

Donovan sneered at the warning. "I'm not at risk of being beaten by a *bitten* wolf."

Genevieve stiffened at the insult, her lip curling up into a snarl, but she held herself still. Tommy moved a little closer and wrapped his arm around her. Even in the midst of all this, he thought about the people around him. He noticed everything.

"So be it. Your challenge is accepted. Please step down into the arena." Clearing his throat, he continued. "In normal circumstances, the test requires you to maintain control for five minutes. However, since you have been challenged, you must instead outlast Alpha Lockhart."

Amber kept her eyes on the stage as Donovan hopped down and walked over to stand beside her. His heart was beating as hard as hers. Every step of the way he had tried to make her fail. She was glad he was challenging her openly now. The strength of the wolf and her pack was pumping through her. He didn't stand a chance.

Jameson waved Selena forward. She approached, holding a large bowl. Leaning down, he inhaled deeply, then looked up at the witch. "If I find out that you have meddled with this potion in any way, you will answer to me. Your coven won't be able to protect you."

Selena's fingers tightened on the bowl, a slight tremor of fear running through her at the threat. "The potion is as it should be."

He took the bowl from her. "I will administer it to them myself."

Jameson hopped down as well and walked over to them holding two small cups. He handed one to each of us. "Dip the cup in here and drink the potion. It will force you to change. The challenge, laid out by Alpha Lockhart, is that you must resist the change longer than he does. We are werewolves, but we are human first. You must maintain control over yourself, and your wolf, for the rest of your life. If you want to lead others, you must prove today that you have that control."

She nodded, accepting the cup he handed her. Her pack was standing near the stage. Their presence was comforting, but it did add to the pressure.

Jameson lifted the bowl toward them. Inside was a strange, silvery liquid that smelled like grass after fresh rain. She and Donovan dipped their cups into the bowl in unison. Watching out of the corner of her eye to make sure he drained it completely, they both drank.

It was cool and almost sweet at first. As it slipped down her throat, it grew hotter and hotter, until it felt as if she'd drunk liquid fire.

Silently, Jameson directed them to sit across from each other next to the altar. She dropped to the ground, crossing her legs and planting her hands on her knees. Donovan's eyes never left her.

"Remember, both of you will shift eventually," Jameson said.

Someone from the crowd shouted, "For the bitten!"

Cheers and boos fought for supremacy as some shouted encouragement to Donovan and some to her. She could barely make out what they were saying over the ringing in her ears.

The need to shift shot through her muscles. She ground her

teeth together and fought against the urge. Nothing could make her give in.

Donovan sat across from her, his face red from the effort to control himself. Her muscles ached like they were cramping. Her leg twitched. The claws pressed against the skin of her fingertips. She curled her hands into a fist and sat up straighter, keeping her gaze locked on her foe.

He hated her. She didn't know why, but he truly hated her. She'd gotten involved in all this from bad luck. If it hadn't been her sitting here it might have been someone else. Or perhaps they would have fallen for his scheme. He might have gotten away with it. She'd make damn sure he never got a chance to do this to anyone else ever again.

"You will fail," he hissed at her, spittle flying from his lips.

"You don't really believe that," she shot back. "You were so afraid I'd succeed you tried to sabotage me."

He bared his teeth at her like a wild animal. "You should never have been allowed to participate in this ritual!"

"You should never have sent that omega to attack three innocent people. You brought this on yourself," she said, trying to calm down a little. The anger only pushed her closer to a shift. That was probably his plan for starting the argument in the first place.

He jerked and fell to the side, chest heaving as he gasped for air. His fingers curled inward and he shook, fighting so hard against the shift that his teeth clacked together.

The pain was growing worse. It spread out from her stomach like she might explode. Her head ached. Every muscle in her body seemed to have contracted. She dug her fingers into her legs to stay upright.

All around her, she could feel the pack bond. It could not stop this, but it gave her the strength to keep fighting. They believed in her. They needed her. And she had chosen them.

"You have no place in this world," he growled, a muscle in his jaw twitching.

"Yet, here I am," she said, leaning toward him.

Donovan screamed, his voice echoing through the arena. The crowd went silent. He arched back, and his clothes were ripped to shreds as he shifted.

The large black wolf turned his hateful eyes to her and lunged for her throat. Time seemed to slow as she gave in to the shift that she had been holding back for so long. She crashed into Donovan, and they tumbled to the ground.

His teeth dug into her chest, but she clamped her jaws around the back of his neck and jerked his head to the side. The challenge hadn't been enough. She knew it wouldn't be. She wanted to finish this now.

Strong hands grabbed her by the ruff of her neck and yanked her away. Jameson kept dragging her backward as three other alphas wrestled Donovan to the ground. He yelped as silver chains were tossed over his body to weaken him and hold him down. He howled, full of rage and pain.

Jameson slowly loosened his grip on her. "Shift back, if you can."

Her body shook with the effort, but slowly, she changed back. Panting, she turned on Jameson. "Why did you stop me?" she demanded with a growl.

"Donovan Lockhart has broken the sacred bonds of the Trial through interference and attempted murder," Jameson said, turning toward the crowd. His voice boomed throughout the space, silencing all the chatter. "His council spot is forfeit to you, and he will now answer for his actions according to the old laws."

Still shifted, Donovan growled and thrashed in his bonds. His pack was fighting in the crowd, but they were quickly subdued.

"Get them out of here," Jameson said. "It is time for a celebration as a new alpha joins our ranks. We are moon-blessed tonight, and we will *run*." The crowd erupted into cheers.

She was struck suddenly from the side and found herself in the middle of an enthusiastic group hug. Ceri was crying, Genevieve was shouting something, and Tommy was just hanging on for dear life.

"I'm okay, I'm okay," she repeated, trying to soothe the worry that was pounding against her mind through the bond.

Howls erupted all around them and the energy in the air changed. Everyone, even the ones that had wanted her to fail, were celebrating. People began stripping off their clothes and shifting. Wolves rushed past them, racing toward the forest.

Jameson walked toward them, eyes glowing bright red. "Run with us, and tomorrow we will talk about everything that has changed."

CHAPTER 48

CERI

Ceri stepped back from the group. She was so relieved Amber had survived and passed the Trials that she could barely breathe.

"This should be better than that first night," Amber said, nudging Genevieve with her elbow.

She laughed and pulled her shirt off over her head. Tommy blushed and turned away, stripping off in a more sedate manner.

Amber looked at her and held out her hand. "Will you join us?"

"I can't shift, and I'm not in the pack," she said, confused.

"You are, actually. I could feel it in the third trial. The bond isn't as strong as the others but I think it could be, even without turning you. Come with us tonight."

Her hand went to her chest, remembering the strange feeling she'd had throughout the Trials. She'd chalked it up to nerves and how much she wanted Amber to succeed. This whole part of the pack thing was something she'd have to talk to Amber about later, but like Jameson said, tonight was for running and tomorrow was for answers.

"I won't be able to keep up," she objected, not wanting to hold them back from enjoying themselves.

"I'll run with you," Tommy said, looking at her over his shoulder. "Please, come with us."

Even she could feel the excitement in the air. Shaking her head and smiling, she gathered her curls into a high ponytail. There was no reason *not* to go with them. "Alright. Let's do this."

Amber smiled at her and began to shift. Ceri bounced on her toes, excitement pumping through her. The energy around them was amazing. She'd never been around werewolves on a full moon. It was truly magical. She lifted her face to the moon and let the magic and the wonder sink into her.

Once all three of them were shifted they gathered around her and nudged her toward the woods. Amber ran ahead of the group, stretching her legs. She ran right behind with the others flanking her.

Amber lifted her head and howled. Her pack's voices joined the chorus. The sound awoke something in her, and she joined them. Any other time she'd be embarrassed to tilt her head back and howl like a wolf, but it felt right.

Genevieve raced up beside Amber, then started inching ahead of her. Amber seemed to take it as a challenge and they pulled away from her and Tommy. He chose to stay with her instead.

A gray wolf joined their race, and she smiled to herself. She guessed it was Shane, and based on the way he was chasing after Amber, Genevieve was right about him.

Tommy picked up his pace a little and she pushed herself to keep up. Her feet flew over the ground faster than she'd thought possible. She should have been tired already, but she knew she wouldn't tire for hours. Just like the pack bond had given Amber strength, it was giving her the same now.

CHAPTER 49

AMBER

*A*mber accepted the bottle of water Shane handed her gratefully. The run had been amazing, but she was thirsty, hungry, and exhausted now. He pulled out a slip of paper and scribbled something on it, then handed her that too.

"Here's my phone number. I hope you'll call soon," he said with a smile that was boy-next-door, apple pie, and *trouble* all rolled into one.

She took the card and fought to keep the smile off her face. "Just to chat?"

He tucked his thumbs in his belt loops. "I was thinking more like a date."

"A date?" she asked, raising her brows. "Is that...allowed?"

He chuckled. "This isn't the dark ages. We date who we want." He stepped in closer, his eyes hot on hers. "And I'm not intimidated by powerful women. I can handle you being an alpha."

She lost the struggle to keep the smile off her face and burst out laughing. "Sorry, I just...you were so serious," she said, gasping for air.

His face dropped for a moment, then he joined her laughing. "Damn, you are hard to flirt with," he said, still smiling.

She wiped the tears from her eyes. "My brothers scared off all the boys when I was growing up, so I never got much practice."

"How many brothers do you have?" he asked, looking alarmed.

"Four—I mean three. Just three, now," she said awkwardly.

"I'll see you around, Amber," he said, taking two steps backward like he couldn't tear his eyes from her before turning on his heel and walking away.

Someone whistled behind her and she turned around to find her entire pack had watched the exchange. Genevieve was laughing hysterically.

"It was not *that* funny," she said, rolling her eyes as she walked toward them.

"It so was," Genevieve said between gasps for air. She wiped her eyes and attempted to get control of herself.

"Joking aside, there is something I need to talk to y'all about," she said, smoothing her hair away from her face.

"What is it?" Tommy asked, immediately sensing how serious this was.

"During the fourth test, I spoke with…the wolf. My wolf," she said, tucking her hands in her pockets. Part of her didn't want to give them this option, it terrified her. But she had to. "I had to smoke this stuff…the point is that if you wanted, you could too, and it would be possible to cure you, in a sense. You could go back to being human."

Genevieve looked up sharply. "Are you serious?"

She nodded. "You have to know that you have a choice."

"That's crazy. How does no one know about that?" She threw her hands in the air and began pacing. "Do all werewolves know?"

"Just a few alphas, I think. The wolves know but they can't always talk to us."

Tommy, who had been silent thus far, looked up with tears in his eyes. "That means that you chose to stay a werewolf. Even though your brother...and even though you didn't want this."

"I chose the two of you. If being a werewolf is what I need to protect you, then so be it," she said firmly.

He crossed his arms. "I don't want to go back to being human. I want to be in your pack."

Genevieve kept pacing with her hands on her hips. "If I decided to go back to being human, it wouldn't be because I don't care."

Amber grabbed her, and made her stop walking. "You're right. It's your choice, I'd understand if you wanted to be human again, okay?"

"I should want to be human again," Genevieve said, her lower lip trembling. "But I don't, and I don't understand why."

"You don't have to decide today," Tommy said. He then looked at Amber. "Wait, she doesn't right?"

"Of course not. I know how it's done, so it doesn't matter if you decide tonight or in twenty years. You're not trapped in this pack, and you aren't trapped as a werewolf. I promise," she said.

Genevieve's whole body relaxed. "Then I don't want it right now. I want to stay in this pack."

CHAPTER 50

"What are you getting all dressed up for?"

Genevieve turned and smiled at Amber, who was standing in her doorway. She twirled, her dress spinning around her. "You like it?"

Her alpha smirked at her. "You look like a fairy princess. It suits you."

"Steven wanted to go over the Trials since he couldn't attend, so he's taking me out to dinner," she said, turning back to the mirror and wiping at the corner of her mouth. Her lipstick was slightly uneven and it was driving her crazy, but it was the kind that lasted for twenty-four hours even if you went through an actual hurricane. There was no budging it now. She sighed, she'd just wanted to look...perfect.

"A date?" Amber asked, cocking her head to the side.

She stiffened and whipped around. "No, of course not. That's old news, we're just friends now."

"Whatever you say," Amber said, turning away with a laugh.

"Gen has a date?" Tommy parroted from his bedroom. "With Steven?"

"No! It's just DINNER!" she shouted back.

The doorbell rang, and for a half second, everyone froze. Then they ran for the front door. Amber was already halfway down the stairs, but she jumped off the balcony, landing past the couch. Genevieve sprinted for the door, throwing an elbow to keep Amber from passing her. When she tried to stop, her heel slipped on the new hall rug, and she slammed against the door.

Shoving off with a huff, she adjust her hair and plastered on a smile, then yanked the door open. "Steven, let's—"

He was standing on their porch holding...flowers. A lot of them. A whole freaking bouquet of a dozen different kinds of pink flowers.

He shifted on his feet and swallowed nervously. "You look really nice. And I, uh...got these. For you, of course. Not myself. That'd be weird."

She snatched the flowers out of his hand and stomped back down the hallway. After a moment he followed.

Amber was doubled over with silent laughter in the living room. When she heard Steven coming, she dropped down behind the couch. She could smell Tommy hiding back there, too. They were both nosy *brats*.

Realizing Steven was standing there looking like a kicked puppy, she sighed. "Thank you. They're nice."

He brightened. "For a second, I thought you were going to murder me with them."

She turned away to hide her grin and heard a snort from across the room. Steven turned around. "Is your pack—"

"Can you trim the ends for me while I find a vase?" she said frantically.

"Oh, sure," he said, hurrying over.

She handed him the scissors and positioned him in front of the sink. As soon as he wasn't looking, Tommy's head popped up. She gestured at him sharply, trying to get them both to *go away*, but he just grinned at her evilly. And to think she had ever believed he was a nice person.

"So, uh, the Trials. They went well?" he asked.

"Yep," she said, looking through a cabinet for a vase. She wasn't sure there even was one in the house, but she had to put the flowers in something, or Steven would get that look on his face. That look was the worst.

"Yesterday you said you were choosing to stay a werewolf? Why? I thought you hated it," he said, pausing in his snipping and turning to look at her.

She swallowed, uncomfortably aware the others were listening. She hadn't even told Amber yet, figured her alpha would just figure it out when she never asked for the cure. "Well, I like it."

"That's it? You *like it?*"

"Yeah," she said, turning away again. That wasn't the whole truth. The rest was…awkward to say aloud, but Amber deserved to know why. She cleared her throat. "Because I feel like I belong. I never felt that before. I don't have a sob story like them. I just— you know. I push people away. I don't want to push them away."

She spotted a big vase at the back of the cabinet under a dusty old waffle-maker. Reaching back, she grabbed it and pulled it out.

When she stood, Steven was giving her an odd look, like he hadn't expected her to share that much. "I'm glad you feel like you belong."

"Yeah, me too," she agreed with a smile.

CHAPTER 51

CERI

*C*eri woke up in a cold sweat. She touched her fingers to her cheek and found them wet with tears. Rubbing her face with the palm of her hands, she tried to remember what the dream had been about. The details were already slipping out of her mind, but she remembered fear, fire, and a cool touch, like water in the desert.

She swung her legs over the edge of her bed and hopped down. These strange dreams had started the night she'd moved in. Sometimes they were scary, like tonight, but other times they just felt...important. Like someone was trying to tell her something.

Woggy was laying on her dresser in his favorite tuna can, which she had lined with felt, snoring. She watched him sleep for a second, then padded quietly out of the bedroom. It was always hard to get back to sleep after these dreams, and since it was five a.m., there was no point in even trying this time. Coffee would have to suffice.

Grabbing her book off the end table next to the couch, she headed toward the kitchen. The coffee pot was set to brew the coffee automatically at seven a.m., so she just hit the start button and got it started early.

Leaning back against the counter, she cracked open the book and scanned for the spot she'd left off. A sound from the door pulled her attention away from the novel. Using her finger as a bookmark, she shut it and crept around the island.

The front door opened slowly, and Genevieve walked inside, freezing when she saw her.

Ceri smiled and winked at her. "Did you have a good date?" she whispered.

Genevieve blushed furiously, but straightened and nodded. "I remember why I dated him for so long now."

She cocked her head to the side. "Ohhhh, is he...talented?"

"And imaginative," Genevieve confirmed with a nod. She sniffed once. "Is that coffee?"

She nodded. "Yeah, I didn't sleep much either. I'm going to need it."

"Perfect," Gen said, hurrying forward and dumping her stuff on the couch. "There's no point in going to sleep now. Coffee will have to sustain me."

They watched the coffee drip into the pot slowly. She yawned, then brushed her unruly curls away from her face. Most of them had come out of the braid she slept in. It never liked staying bound so she mostly let it do whatever it wanted.

"I know why I'm up so late...early, whatever. What's your excuse?" Gen asked, leaning against the counter and yawning.

"Just bad dreams," she said with a shrug.

Gen's brows pinched together, catching the undercurrent of her response. "Magical bad dreams? Or just normal nightmares?"

She shifted on her feet uncomfortably. She'd been avoiding asking herself that very question. "I don't know."

"But you're worried they are?"

"Yeah, it...sometimes curses are insidious. It could be something my mother is doing, but it doesn't feel like that. It could be nothing, but my gut is telling me that this is something...weird."

The coffee pot clicked over, and Gen poured them each a cup. "Is there anything you can do to stop them?"

Ceri accepted her cup and took a deep breath of the hot, rich drink. "No. It might be dumb, but I'm curious. If it's not malevolent, then I want to figure out what they mean."

Tommy walked down the stairs, bleary-eyed. His hair was sticking up in every direction. "What's wrong? Why is everyone awake?"

"Nothing's wrong," she said with a smile. "Gen just happened to wake up and we decided to get coffee."

Genevieve blushed and mouth *thank you*.

Tommy just grunted and flopped on the couch, falling back asleep almost instantly.

"He's like a puppy," Genevieve said looking at him fondly.

Amber's bedroom door opened and she trudged down the hall as well. "Is that coffee?"

Ceri nodded and poured her a cup. "Here, you look like you need it too."

Amber accepted the coffee, but got the milk out of the fridge and poured in so much you could barely tell it was still coffee. Then she added three spoonfuls of sugar.

"You could just eat the sugar straight," she teased.

Amber gave her a half-hearted glare then took a long sip, her eyes closing in satisfaction. "I prefer my sugar coffee-flavored, thank you very much."

She laughed and leaned back against the counter, taking in the group. In less than a month, four completely different people had been brought together by one man's power grab. They still weren't sure why Donovan had been so desperate to gain more power, but he was being punished, so maybe motive didn't matter.

Amber met her gaze and smiled. Some of the tension went

out of her shoulders. Whatever these dreams meant, she didn't have to be afraid. Her pack wouldn't let her down.

~

TOMMY

*T*ommy did a fast walk to the dining room. The pot holder was too thin, and he'd taken this dish right out of the oven. Instead of using the big, formal dining room, they liked to eat in the smaller one. It had a round table just big enough for them to each have a seat and elbow room.

"Sunday family dinners should be a new tradition," Amber said as he set it on the table, waving his fingers around to cool them off.

"Just as long as someone else does the dishes." He'd left a huge mess behind in the kitchen, and there was no way he was cleaning it up alone.

"That seems fair," Amber said with a grin.

"Genevieve, food!" he shouted over his shoulder. Amber wouldn't let them eat until everyone was there, and he was starving.

"Sorry!" Genevieve shouted. She ran through the doorway and plopped down in her chair. "I just got off the phone with my new employer."

"New employer?" Amber asked, surprised.

"Yeah, I…I'm actually a lawyer. I passed the bar over a year ago. I just hadn't wanted to actually work as a lawyer because if you screw up, well, that's someone's whole life." She started picking at her napkin, tearing off tiny pieces. "But I really want to do it. I think I could help people."

"That's awesome," he said, beaming at her. Gen was wicked

smart, but she normally played it down. She would kick ass in the courtroom.

"What will you be doing now?" Ceri asked, digging into the closest dish. Woggy hopped off her shoulder and pounced on the spoon. She dragged him off and set his serving on the small plate next to her to distract him.

"I'm starting out as part of a legal team that deals with inter-species disputes. Every race has their own rules, and trying to balance those with actual laws can get messy. I really liked this firm because they make it a point to take on more than the minimum mandated pro bono cases per year," Genevieve explained as she buttered one of the fresh rolls he'd made.

"Have you thought any more about getting your GED, Tommy?" Ceri asked.

He nodded. "Yeah, I want to get it before the beginning of the year so I can start applying to colleges for the fall."

Amber visibly tensed, but took a deep breath and deliberately unwound her shoulders. "What colleges are you thinking about applying to?"

"Yale," he said with a grin, just to watch her freak out. She didn't disappoint. Her head snapped up, and that fake calm she tried to project shattered.

"That's on the other side—" she snapped her mouth shut when his expression finally registered. "You're just screwing with me, aren't you?"

He laughed and shook his head at her. "There's a college in Portland I'm applying too, but my first choice is in Seattle."

"Seattle is close! Barely a three hour drive away," Ceri said, beaming at him. There was a thunk under the table, and Amber flinched, then nodded.

"Yeah, that's great, super close," she said through gritted teeth.

He leaned over and fed Woggy a vegetable. The pixie got the whole bite in his mouth, then glared at him and spit it out. He signed *no*, which was his new favorite word.

"Oh, did you hear that they found another spot where magic isn't working in Portland?" Ceri asked, changing the subject. "There's one out near Tillamook, too. They think it might have been there for months before someone noticed."

"Are they sure the spots haven't always been there?" Amber asked.

"I thought that at first too, but they're popping up in places where people *know* magic used to work. It's super weird," Ceri said with a shrug.

Tommy shoved a forkful of food in his mouth, but worry gnawed in his gut. He was always a little worried in the back of his head that one day he'd lose this newfound peace. The no-magic spots could turn out to be nothing, but they gave him a sense of foreboding.

"Well, I'm sure every major coven is trying to figure it out and fix it. Not to mention the elves. This could be a natural thing," Amber said, reassuringly.

He wondered what would happen if a werewolf stumbled into one of those. The pack bond was magic, and the thing that allowed them to change forms was as well. Would it come back as soon as you moved out of the spot? Or was it permanent?

"How's your job search going?" Gen asked Amber.

She shrugged. "Not great, to be honest. But I'll figure something out after my trip."

Every time the trip came up, Amber got tense and quiet. He knew he bottled stuff up, but she took it to a whole different level.

"What's your family like?" he asked, pushing some food around on his plate. Maybe he shouldn't have asked. But he knew everyone was curious, and maybe if she wasn't trying so hard to avoid the topic, it wouldn't bother her so much.

Amber looked a little surprised by the question. She cleared her throat and shifted in her seat. "Well, I grew up with four brothers. I had a twin, Dylan. We were the youngest, so we were kind of spoiled compared to the others I guess. My dad owns a diesel mechanic shop, and we all grew up helping out there. Went to a small high school, small town, that whole stereotypical Texas thing."

"Had a twin?" he asked quietly. Ceri and Genevieve were listening intently, not saying a word, like if someone spoke too soon it'd shatter the moment.

She took a deep breath and nodded. "Yeah. Right after we graduated, we both applied to a local werewolf pack. He got accepted, I didn't." She set down her fork and stared hard at her plate. "It's rare. One in a million, but some people can't handle the bite. It kills them."

Genevieve's eyes went wide. "That's who you were talking about the night of the full moon when you said you knew someone that hadn't survived the change."

Amber nodded. "I guess I didn't handle being changed into a werewolf after all that very well. Thanks for sticking with me, even though I'm a little crazy."

That explained a lot. Everything, really. He wished she'd just told them earlier, but it looked like it was still hard for her to talk about.

"Sorry," he said.

She shrugged. "It's okay. Y'all needed to know."

"Did you like working with your father?" Ceri asked, changing the subject. Amber's shoulders relaxed slightly.

"Yeah, it was a pretty good way to grow up," she said with a smile. "Me and Dylan used to take our dog and go hunt squirrels. We tried to cook one once, and it was awful."

"What kind of dog did you have?" he asked.

Amber shrugged. "A mutt we got for free in the supermarket parking lot. My parents didn't believe in paying for pets."

"I never had a pet," he said. His mom had said she'd get him one before she got sick. But after that, well…lots of promises got broken.

"We should get a dog!" Genevieve announced with a grin. "Maybe a cat *and* a dog. I like cats better."

Amber looked horrified. "What? No!"

"There's a rescue shelter in town that's waiving adoption fees right now," Ceri said, jumping on board just like he knew she would.

He grinned at Amber. "You know you've already lost, right?"

She groaned and put her head in her hands, but he could tell she was hiding a grin. "Y'all are going to be the death of me."

"Pshh, you love it," Genevieve said, smiling with a mouthful of food.

"I *guess*," Amber said, dropping her hands and looking at the pack fondly. She stood and picked up her beer, lifting it in a toast. "To our pack, our future, and happiness."

He lifted his glass and let himself feel optimistic for the first time in years.

CHAPTER 52

"*A*re you sure? I can always wait until next month, or—"

"Oh my god," Genevieve exclaimed, cutting her off. "Go. Get out. We're going to be *fine*. It's a week. We are adults, and we will not starve to death, I promise."

Amber sighed and let Genevieve shove her out of the front door. Ceri was already in the truck, waiting to take her to airport.

"Have fun!" Tommy shouted from the couch. He was more concerned with his tv show than with her leaving. It was *almost* insulting, but she was just glad he had gotten so comfortable. The days of worrying about him leaving were long gone.

Ceri honked and rolled down the passenger side window. "Come on, we're going to be late!"

"Fine," she said, throwing her hands in the air. She jogged to the truck and tossed her backpack on the floorboard before climbing inside. Looking at her friend, she sighed. "This is a terrible idea. What if something happens while I'm gone?"

Ceri leaned over and put her hands on both sides of her head. "Then we will handle it, and you will come back early."

"Ugh, fine."

Laughing at her, Ceri dropped her hands and put the truck in reverse. "Now, Tommy might come pick you up from the airport—"

"Tommy?" she asked, alarmed. "He doesn't even have his driver's license yet!"

"He's getting one while you're gone," Ceri beamed. "Genevieve has been teaching him, and he's going to take his test tomorrow."

She slid down in her seat and let her head fall back. "Y'all waited for me to leave to plan this, didn't you?"

"Absolutely. You were freaking him out with your *lessons*," Ceri said, raising an eyebrow at her.

"There's nothing wrong with learning evasive maneuvers," she muttered.

"He should probably learn how to parallel park first, though."

She sighed and rubbed her hand over her face. Sure, she was committed to being their alpha since the Trials, but that didn't mean that she didn't have days where she doubted herself all over again. It made the wolf moody.

"So, you've been a little...on edge the past week. You're worried about seeing your family again, right?" Ceri asked hesitantly.

"My brothers are all mad at me, my mom hates me, and my dad, he just...ignores me. I don't know why I'm even doing this."

"It's been a long time. It's not crazy to think you might be able to repair those relationships. Maybe your mom has been scared to call after so long," Ceri suggested.

She shrugged. "I just hope the rest of them have forgiven me."

Ceri reached over and grabbed her shoulder as she drove. "There's nothing to forgive. Your brother made his choice, and he died, tragically, because of that choice. All the arguments that you could have stopped him are crap."

"I just want to stop being angry about it," she said with a sigh.

"Let me know if you figure out how to," Ceri said with a

laugh, lightening the mood. They'd bumped into her mother a few days ago, and…it had not gone well, to say the least.

"You promise to call me if *anything* happens, right? Even if someone stubs a toe?" she asked, still feeling antsy.

"Absolutely not," Ceri said firmly. "I will call you if something bad happens, or if something good happens. But I am not going to call you over something silly. Stop fretting. You're going to drive yourself batty."

She sighed. "Fine. I don't like it, but you're right."

"Such sweet words from my dear alpha," Ceri said with a laugh.

She stuck her tongue out at Ceri and crossed her arms. "No one shows me any respect around here."

Ceri busted out laughing, and Amber couldn't help but join her. It eased some of the ache in her chest.

⁓

*T*he rental car agency had given her some elf-spelled electric, eco-friendly car. She wasn't sure it would hold together long enough to make it down the gravel road that led to the house. Her brothers were going to have a field day mocking her car and asking if she was a hippie now. If they spoke to her at all.

She rolled down the windows and let the brisk air flow through the car, whipping her hair around her face. Now that she was a werewolf, she could smell so much more. Pine trees, cow manure, and a hint of exhaust from a truck that must have passed this way recently.

She'd missed Texas but less than she expected. It felt like home, but the country was prettier than she'd ever imagined. People were still polite in other states and still willing to lend a hand if you needed it. The weather was way better. Even now, her shirt was starting to stick to her skin from the humidity.

After a curve in the road, she saw the beat up old mailbox with HALE in black, boxy letters on the side. Her stomach did a weird flip that she did not appreciate. She took a deep breath and turned down the driveway. A couple of dogs ran around from the back of the house, barking to announce the intruder. She didn't recognize them, which meant Rusty and Princess had passed while she was gone.

She parked next to her dad's truck and climbed out. The dogs slid to a halt a few feet from her, tails drooping as they recognized the predator that now lived in her.

"Hey, guys, I'm friendly," she said, trying to sound nice. The white dog yelped and ran for it. After a moment, the other dog followed suit.

Hoping that wasn't setting the tone for the next reunion, she straightened and looked at the house she'd grown up in. Two story brick house with a wrap-a-round porch that had hosted many a summer barbecue. Her dad had cooked in an old metal barrel, cut in half lengthwise and converted into a charcoal grill.

She couldn't see her room from there. The window had overlooked the backyard and the pond, where she and her brothers had spent most of their time playing. The sun was setting behind the house, casting the whole thing in a warm glow.

With a deep breath, she shook off the nostalgia and walked up to the porch. The wooden steps creaked under her feet, and the noise startled her so badly she almost bolted. She rubbed her hand down her face and tried to slow her heartbeat. Even during the Trials she hadn't been this nervous. She wanted to throw up or run away. Maybe both.

With a shaking hand, she knocked twice on the old red door. She heard footsteps, a heartbeat drawing closer.

The door opened and Derek stood in the doorway. His eyes went wide.

"What the hell are you trying to do, air condition Texas? In or out!" her mother shouted from behind him.

He stepped back, opening the door wider. Her mom was sitting on the couch in her favorite pair of stained jean shorts. She must have been out in the garden earlier.

"Hey, mom."

Her mother looked up, face going pale as her hands fell into her lap. Her mouth worked for a moment, no words coming out, then Derek dragged Amber inside. He wrapped her up in a hug and squeezed so tight she thought he might break a rib. She hung on tightly, trying to crush the disappointment she felt at her mother's reaction. At least one person was happy to see her. That was enough. It had to be.

Even a thousand miles away, she felt the pack bond next to her heart. It beat strong and steady. Even if this went badly, she still had them. They might be misfits that didn't fit in anywhere else, but they had chosen her, and she had chosen them.

She buried her face in her brother's shoulder. "I missed you."

"Missed you too, little sister."

MAKE A DIFFERENCE

Reviews are very important, and sometimes hard for an independently published author to get. A big publisher has a massive advertising budget and can send out hundreds of review copies.

Leaving an honest review helps me tremendously. It shows other readers why they should give me a try. It also shows Amazon that readers are enjoying the book.

If you've enjoyed reading this book, I would appreciate, very much, if you took the time to leave a review. Whether you write one sentence, or three paragraphs, it's equally helpful.

Thank you :)

P.S. Who's your favorite character? Let me know in the Facebook group.

https://www.facebook.com/groups/TheFoxehole/

Follow Me

Thank you so much for buying my book. I really hope you have enjoyed the story as much as I did writing it. Being an author is not an easy task, so your support means a lot to me. I do my best to make sure books come out error free. However, if you found any errors, please feel free to reach out to me so I can correct them!

If you loved this book, the best way to find out about new releases and updates is to join my Facebook group, The Foxehole. Amazon does a very poor job about notifying readers of new book releases. Joining the group can be an alternative to newsletters if you feel your inbox is getting a little crowded. Facebook and Goodreads, are linked below :)

Facebook Group:
https://www.facebook.com/groups/TheFoxehole/
Goodreads:
http://goodreads.com/Stephanie_Foxe
BookBub:
https://www.bookbub.com/authors/stephanie-foxe

MORE BY STEPHANIE FOXE

The Witch's Bite Series is a complete series that follows Olivia Carter –

We all have our secrets. Mine involves a felony record, illegal potions, and magi–well...the last one could get me killed.

I've been living in a small town working for the vampires for the last six months. All I want is to save up enough to open an apothecary, so I don't have to heal the neckers anymore.

Of course, nothing in my life can be *that* simple.

Two detectives show up at my door asking questions about a dead girl and trying to pin the murder on my employer. Next thing I know, I'm dodging fireballs in parking lots.

The police and the witches want me to roll over on the vampires. The only problem is, I'm almost certain they didn't kill the girl. Although, my best friend and favorite vampire has been missing and won't answer my calls.

Time is running out for me to save my paycheck... and do the right thing or whatever.

∼

Stephanie Foxe also writes with her husband as Alex Steele. In The Chaos Mages Series you will meet Logan Blackwell and Lexi Swift as they solve crimes in a world full of magic and myths, much like in Misfit Pack.

Vampires don't rob banks. Werewolves don't bust into jewelry stores. And Detective Logan Blackwell doesn't work with a partner.

Too bad all three of those things happened in one day. Supernaturals are getting possessed, wreaking havoc, then turning up dead. Blackwell has been tasked with finding out who is responsible and stopping them before they kill again.

After a series of unfortunate incidents that include blowing up part of the Met, Blackwell's boss is fed up. He sticks Blackwell with a partner who has issues that only complicate his life.

Assassination attempts threaten both their lives, but no one will tell him who is trying to kill Detective Lexi Swift, or why. He's already lost one partner, and he's not willing to see another die. It's a good thing she's tough and wields magic almost as chaotic as his.

Old enemies, new threats, and more destruction than his boss can handle are bad enough, but sometimes our inner demons are the most dangerous. When they find the person responsible, Blackwell will face a fight he never expected, and one he may not win.

But most importantly, will the pink ever get out of his hair? He should never have taken that bet...

www.StephanieFoxe.com
www.AlexSteele.net

facebook.com/StephanieFoxeAuthor
goodreads.com/Stephanie_Foxe

www.ingramcontent.com/pod-product-compliance
Lightning Source LLC
Chambersburg PA
CBHW052024240626
47153CB00006B/1946